LIKE UNCLE, LIKE NEPHEW

Heather had had painfully sharp experiences with both the attractiveness and the imperiousness of Sir Leslie Kinwell, who had forced her to yield first to his scandalous desires and then to his even more shocking plans for her.

She thought that his charming, handsome nephew Philip was made of different stuff—a friend to be trusted, a companion with whom she could feel safe.

But now Philip's arms were around her, his lips were pressing down on hers—and Heather felt herself weakening in the embrace of a man bent on making her abandon her vows to the very man who had made her abandon her innocence. . . .

An
Improper Companion

An Improper Companion

by
April Kihlstrom

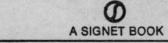

A SIGNET BOOK

NEW AMERICAN LIBRARY

SIGNET TRADEMARK REG. U.S. PAT. OFF. AND FOREIGN COUNTRIES
REGISTERED TRADEMARK—MARCA REGISTRADA
HECHO EN CHICAGO, U.S.A.

SIGNET, SIGNET CLASSIC, MENTOR, ONYX, PLUME, MERIDIAN
and NAL BOOKS are published by NAL PENGUIN INC.,
1633 Broadway, New York, New York 10019

First Printing, February, 1983

4 5 6 7 8 9 10 11 12

PRINTED IN THE UNITED STATES OF AMERICA

Chapter 1

In retrospect, I know that I was an incredibly green girl. But at the time, I believed no fate could be worse than to remain at the school. I suppose I saw myself as another Evelina. Had I been less trusting, all might yet have been well. But I was only eighteen. Precisely eighteen. For it was on my eighteenth birthday that Mrs. Gilwen summoned me to have tea with her—an unusual privilege. I felt strange sitting in the elegant drawing room in my best dress. Mrs. Gilwen must have guessed this for she tried to put me at ease. "Well, Heather, I am told you are an excellent student," she said.

"I enjoy books," I answered cautiously, for Mrs. Gilwen was rarely lavish with praise.

"You enjoy the school?"

"Yes," I lied.

"Good. Then would you like to become a teacher here?"

"A t-teacher?"

"Don't repeat what I say," she said sharply. Then she smiled, "Of course you are overwhelmed, dear. But come, I should like an answer."

"No," I managed finally. "Thank you, but no I would not like to be a teacher here."

It was true. I hated the school. I could not remember a time when I had not been in school and I wanted to get away. Then I realised Mrs. Gilwen was speaking again. "I am afraid you have little choice."

"Why?" I demanded. "Did my parents leave me nothing?"

"Nothing."

"Well, then," I said resolutely, "I shall find a position. As a governess. Or companion. Or something."

Mrs. Gilwen was angry now. "I'm afraid not," she said.

"I hoped I should never have to tell you this, but it is the only way you will believe me. You have been told your parents are dead. This is not quite true. Your mother was no one. She took your father's fancy for a while. He tired of her before you were born, but he was a fair man. When your mother died in childbirth, he took responsibility for you. He placed you in the proper schools and agreed to pay your expenses until you were eighteen. He did this on two conditions. One was that you never be told his name and the other was that he never have to see you."

"And my name?" I demanded.

"Your mother's," Mrs. Gilwen replied grimly. "You are, in short, a love-child. So you see, we really could not write you references. And without references . . ." She shrugged. Then her voice became kindly, "Your father has been a generous man. But today you are eighteen and the funds have stopped. I could have you turned out, you know. But your understanding is excellent and I do not despair of turning you into quite a creditable teacher. Of course, for the first year or two you would not be paid. But I am sure when you have thought it over, you will agree to my proposition. You may have the rest of the day and tomorrow as well to decide."

It was clearly a dismissal. Somehow I curtsied and found my way to my bed in the dormitory. "Generous!" she had called my father! Well, I didn't think so. He'd sent enough for two dresses a year and four of each of those articles most girls had twelve of! I couldn't remember a time when my dresses had fit properly or I wasn't having to patch underthings. And when other girls bought ribbons or pastries I had to admit I had no money. If there was anything I needed it was necessary to go to Mrs. Brenner and ask if there were house funds for it. It was also house money that paid for any treats during the vacations when I was the only girl who had nowhere to go. And when, occasionally, another girl invited me to visit her over the holidays, invariably her mother would take note of my clothes, and thus rarely was I asked twice to the same home. Some of the teachers pitied me, but they earned little enough themselves. And this school! As with the others before it, the school catered to girls of the *ton.* We were taught genteel accomplishments and given a little knowledge. I knew from things the teachers said that it was a school for girls whose families were not very plump in the pocket. Yet compared to me, my classmates were well-to-do and most could expect a Season. Of necessity, my poverty and lack of parents had set me apart, and I had learned long ago to surround myself with books and pretend not to care. But books could not fill the void of loneliness that now seemed vaster than ever. Before today, I could dream that, like Evelina or Mrs. Radcliffe's Adeline, someone might somehow appear and take me home. In my more realistic moments, I would dream of a responsible position in a good home. I would be a beloved governess or trusted companion. And yes, I had read *Pamela* and confess that I dreamed of a handsome young gentleman who would fall in love with me. But never had I envisioned myself a drudge in a school such as this, with the girls roasting me for a shabbiness I could not help. Now I had no dreams. Better had my father sent me to learn a trade than educate me as a young lady and wash his hands of me when I turned eighteen! I had loved the parents I never knew. Now I hated the father who refused to accept me. And I was bitter for the sake of my mother. Somehow I blamed him for her death.

I was crying when Mrs. Brenner entered the room. She walked calmly toward me and sat on the edge of the bed. It was a measure of her kindness and wisdom that she did not ask what the trouble was, but waited patiently for me to speak. At last I wiped my eyes and forced myself to be calm. "Mrs. Gilwen has offered me the position of unpaid teacher," I said, proud that my voice did not tremble.

"I know," she answered quietly.

"I intend to decline the honour," I continued.

"What will you do, my child?" she asked. "You have no relatives and she has said she will not write you a reference."

There was no need to ask who "she" was. Hopefully, I said, "Perhaps *you* could write the reference?"

She shook her head sadly. "It would mean nothing. Hers is the only reference that would be heeded and its absence would outweigh the good of mine. I know you have no wish to stay, but it would be best for a time. Perhaps later she would alter her opinion."

I turned away. Mrs. Brenner meant well, I knew, but she could not understand how I felt. She believed my silence meant acquiescence for she added, "It will not be so terrible, my child."

I did not answer, and after a little while she left.

Dinner was the usual dismal affair of potatoes, bread, and little meat. I was not altogether a solitary creature and my silence did not go unremarked. "What's afoot?" my neighbour asked. "You were not in history today."

I forced myself to smile. Not for the world would I have anyone know of my humiliation. "No, Melinda," I replied, carefully, "I've just had a bit of a surprise."

"Oh, please tell me," she said at once.

I shook my head solemnly and bent toward her. In a whisper I said, "It's a secret. But you shall know within the week."

Delighted by my confidence, Melinda smiled. "I'll not speak a word of it. But promise that I shall be the first you tell?"

Solemnly I assured her. I was not resolved what I would do, but instinctively, I felt the need not to draw attention to myself. Somehow I survived the evening, though I remember none of it. I felt years older than the other girls, and the artless prattle I had delighted in only the day before now seemed shallow and pointless. But I must have answered appropriately for no one else challenged me at dinner.

I lay awake long after the dark had closed in upon our dormitory, resolved I would not stay at the school. By morning, I must be prepared to leave. But it must be done carefully, or someone would thrust a spoke in my plans. There were no tears now; I had no time for pointless sorrow. Finally, I slept soundly.

Perhaps too soundly, for Melinda had to shake me awake. "Hurry," she said, "or you shall be late!"

Instantly, I was alert. This would be useful. "Melinda, dear," I said. feigning weakness, "I don't feel well."

As I expected, she was distressed. "Poor dear! I shall tell Mrs. Brenner at once."

With these words, she turned and fled. The other girls were dressed and leaving already. A few called over their shoulders, "Hurry, Heather!" or "sleepyhead." When the last was gone, I vouchsafed myself a smile. Quickly I rose and dressed. I was brushing my hair when Mrs. Brenner entered.

"Heather, what is this I hear? You are ill?" she said suspiciously.

I set down my brush and turned to her. "I'm sorry, I did not mean to say I was ill, exactly." I forced some tears to my eyes. "Mrs. Brenner, I just can't bear to act as always today."

"There, there, child," she said gently. "I understand. You need time by yourself. You need not attend lessons today, nor meals if you choose not to."

"Thank you," I said, truly grateful.

"But tomorrow you must be yourself again," she warned, trying to speak sternly.

I nodded and she touched my cheek. Then, abruptly, she turned and swept out of the room. I would miss the rustle of her petticoats. As I waited to be certain that everyone would be at table, I surveyed my few possessions: a brush and comb given me by a kind teacher, a locket left by my mother, a light pelisse, hat, gloves, one dress, a few undergarments, and a small bag to carry them all. It was not much for a woman eighteen years of age. I might also have had a stack of letters from schoolgirl friends save that a permanent lack of privacy caused me to burn letters after I had read them. And in any case, they would not have been so many.

It was a warm spring day. This was fortunate for I had no heavy cloak. In winter, I simply never went out. Or if I had to, I borrowed one. My hat and gloves, moreover, were worn and shabby. I hesitated. Melinda had often loaned me gloves or hats and urged me to keep them. In my pride I had heretofore refused. But now I could not afford such pride so I hesitated no longer but put on her gloves and bonnet. Then I was ready and it was time to leave. I would surely not be missed before dinner for the girls would assume I was in the sickroom and Mrs. Brenner would assume I was here.

Carrying my bag, I walked quickly down the hall and out the door. It seems strange that I felt no fear, no premonition of what was to be. Outside the door, I chose a direction at random, anxious only to get away from the building. My plans were vague. I knew I must seek a domestic agency but had no notion where to begin. I determined to keep walking until I found such an agency or someone to guide me to one. I had lived in London all my life, but knew it no better than a

5

country cousin might. It seemed now a dreary place: gray and dirty, full of screaming urchins and rattling carriages.

I was beginning to feel tired and discouraged when I bumped into a young woman returning from market. I apologised, and because she seemed disposed to be friendly, I added, "Do you know where I might find a domestic agency?"

She eyed me a moment. "Aye, there be one nearby. Turn right at the corner and walk four corners more. But I'm not sure . . . That is, they are not very particular. . . . P'rhaps you'd best be going to Mrs. Baker's office, much more respectable. But you can't be thinking of walking the way. You'll be needing a chair."

"Thank you," I said coolly, "the nearby one will do."

She eyed me again and shrugged. "Good luck, dearie."

I was not at all sure I wanted a more respectable bureau. Surely they would demand references. And in any case, I had no funds and felt I could not walk much farther. I had always been sensitive to heat and I regretted the lack of breakfast already. I found the place easily, though it was some two streets farther than she had said. Once there, I halted outside, for the first time truly afraid. A long bench lined one wall and several women were seated there. At the far end of the room, a young woman sat at a desk with a ledger before her. "Name?" she asked crisply as she saw me advance.

"Heather Wade. Age twenty-two. I would like a position as a governess or companion," I replied.

She regarded me for a moment, then said, "Please be seated. Mr. Thornsby will speak to you directly."

I nodded meekly, but she seemed to have forgotten my existence. At the time, it did not seem odd to me that the domestic bureau should be under the direction of a man. Men seemed to control everything else, why not this? As I waited, a portrait of Mr. Thornsby began to form in my head. He would be slender with spectacles and somewhat timid. And, I hoped, kind. It was well past midday when my turn came. The assistant's smile seemed mocking, and the room of an interminable length. But finally it was traversed and I entered the inner sanctum escorted by the assistant who repeated the information I had given her. "Thank you, Mrs. Kay," Mr. Thornsby said in a gentle voice. "Please be seated, Miss Wade."

I sat gingerly. "References?" he was asking.

"I do not . . . that is . . . this would be my first position," I stammered.

"I see. Family?" he asked.

"I . . . have no family," I said and, to my shame, felt tears spilling down my cheek. I rose. "I am sorry, sir. I realise I am wasting your time."

His voice stopped me. "Sit down. I am quite accustomed to women's tears. When you are ready, then you shall tell me your story."

It was several minutes before I could speak. I studied the room to calm myself. It was small, filled by Mr. Thornsby's desk and the three chairs. His desk was frightfully cluttered as I had expected it to be. But Mr. Thornsby was a surprise. He was young and wore no spectacles. I could spy no signs of timidity, rather he seemed accustomed to making decisions and would expect others to accept them. He spoke first. "My dear, I must inform you that we have no openings for a governess. Here, we have very few at any time." He grimaced. "Most women distrust a man to recommend someone to care for their children. And as you have no references . . . However, perhaps a companion . . . Please, tell me how you come to be here."

I began slowly. "My parents are dead. I have never known them. Instead I have spent my life in schools. The last such one was Mrs. Gilwen's School for Young Ladies. I have just left it. Mrs. Gilwen informed me that there are no longer funds to provide for me."

"Why did she not write you a reference?" he asked.

"We had a disagreement," I said in a small voice.

"Quite. And have you no relatives?"

"I know of none, sir."

"I see. And you wish to be a companion? Yes, well, are you aware of the responsibilities of a companion?" he asked kindly.

"I believe so, sir. I would be expected to fetch things, read aloud, perhaps write letters, and perform similar tasks," I replied.

"Yes, well, our requests for companions are for often somewhat different duties," he began.

"Please, sir," I said so naively, "whatever the duties, I am certain I can learn them. I must find a position. Today. I-I have no money."

7

He sighed. "Very well. I shall see what openings we have." He pored over his ledger. "I am sorry, my dear, there seems to be . . . Wait, Sir Leslie Kinwell. Stand up please!"

I stood. Mr. Thornsby circled me, eyeing me carefully. "Have you other clothes?" he demanded.

I shook my head. "Very well, we will try you," he said. Then, in explanation, "Sir Leslie is somewhat eccentric. He has requested 'someone unusual, this time' to use his precise words. He will explain your duties to you himself. Sir Leslie is a generous man. He has provided funds for your journey and for a few suitable garments, if necessary. In this case, I believe it is necessary. This afternoon we will see a dressmaker."

"Thank you, sir," I managed to say, astounded by my good fortune. I had not expected to find a position so easily, nor with such an open-handed employer. "Wages?" I asked.

"You will settle that with Sir Leslie," he answered. "Wages will be suitable to your qualifications and how well you please your employer."

I did not, even then, consider the position or the interview strange. Nor did I realise how feeble my story must have sounded. I can only say I was too desperate to comprehend fully all that took place. For had I guessed what would be asked of me, I should have fled back to Mrs. Gilwen.

Mr. Thornsby stood. "I think it best we begin at once. Come along and bring your bag." He took my arm, guiding me toward the door. "Mrs. Kay," he announced, "no further appointments for the day."

"But sir," I stammered.

He seemed amused. "Don't worry, my dear. Sir Leslie Kinwell is a very important client. I will be reimbursed handsomely for my time."

We were outside by then and Mr. Thornsby hailed a carriage. He did not seem inclined to speak further and I was content to dwell on my new position. How old was Sir Leslie? Was I to be companion to his mother, or perhaps his wife? She must be a difficult woman or Sir Leslie would not have to seek a new companion for her so often. And he had requested someone unusual. Well, I was determined to satisfy my employer.

"Mademoiselle Suzette's," Mr. Thornsby explained, as he handed me out of the hack a short while later. The establish-

8

ment had a modest facade but even I had heard of its reputation. It was neither the most expensive nor the most exclusive such establishment in London. But it was favoured by many ladies of the *ton* who did not wish to pay exorbitant prices yet wished to be well dressed. My puzzlement grew. It was hardly the sort of establishment for a companion. Mr. Thornsby seemed aware of my astonishment for he said with a grimace, "Not the sort of place *I* would have chosen. However, Sir Leslie has an account here and Mademoiselle Suzette understands what he considers appropriate for any member of his staff. I have said he is eccentric. He feels it simplifies matters if he need only worry about bills from one London *modiste*."

I nodded. Perhaps Sir Leslie was so plump in the pocket that convenience should always outweigh cost. If this were true and I was satisfactory, I could expect generous wages. Though truly I had no conception of what would be generous and what would be merely customary. As we entered the establishment, a forbidding woman dressed in grey approached. "I believe you have the wrong—" she began.

Mr. Thornsby interrupted her. "Please tell Mademoiselle Suzette that Mr. Thornsby wishes to see her on a matter for Sir Leslie Kinwell."

The woman's eyes swept over me with disdain. "I will put you in a fitting room until Mademoiselle has time to see you. This way," she said.

We followed, I timidly, Mr. Thornsby with calm self-assurance. This assurance was justified for we waited not above five minutes before Mademoiselle Suzette entered the room. "Monsieur Thornsby. What have you for me today?" she asked imperiously.

He took my hand and brought me forward. "Miss Heather Wade. She is to be the new companion Sir Leslie requested."

Mademoiselle regarded me but briefly. "You are hoaxing me!"

"Sir Leslie requested 'someone unusual, this time.' Also, he is growing impatient and I have no one else to send," he replied smoothly. "And Miss Wade is greatly in need of a position. She has no money and no family or friends to help her. She has assured me she will try to provide satisfaction."

"I see," Mademoiselle said sharply. "And where will she stay until she leaves for this position? She has no money but she cannot stay with you!"

"I had hoped she might stay here," he replied, "with your seamstresses. Tonight. She leaves tomorrow for Sir Leslie's estate."

"Now I truly know you are mad!" she said. "What do you expect me to do for her in one day?"

"She only needs a few things," he said meekly. "Three dresses: one day, one evening, and one other. And whatever nether garments you think suitable."

"*Tiens!* You ask much!"

"But you will do it?" he asked.

"Yes, yes. For Sir Leslie. I must to take dresses promised other ladies, but yes I will do it."

"And she can sleep here?" he persisted.

"Yes, yes. Now leave us. You know where my office is. Wait there. I wish to speak further with you on this matter," she commanded. As he withdrew she turned to me. "Remove your dress, child. I must to see how large you are so I can to find the correct dresses."

She helped with the buttons and soon I stood in my shift. She had just placed a tape around my waist when, for the second time that day, I disgraced myself. I fainted. In the distance I heard Mademoiselle exclaim, *"Mon Dieu!"*

I came around to find Mademoiselle and a young woman bending over me. "Are you ill?" Mademoiselle demanded anxiously.

"I'm sorry," I said flushing, "not ill, only I have not eaten since last night."

"Not eaten?" she echoed. Then to the young woman she said, "Stay with her. *Mon Dieu*, Monsieur Thornsby is a fool. You will have tea immediately. *Bêtes!*"

She swept out of the room and my companion giggled. "She will ring a peal over poor Mr. Thornsby. Is he your father or guardian?"

I shook my head. "No. He has a domestic agency. He is sending me to Sir Leslie Kinwell to be a companion."

"Sir Leslie?" she seemed impressed. "Top-of-the-trees, he is. I saw him once. He came here with a young woman."

"His wife?" I asked.

She looked at me oddly. After a moment, she replied, "No, he—"

"*Tais-toi*, Ellen!" a voice snapped. Startled, we turned to see Mademoiselle Suzette standing in the doorway. "I have

10

ordered a tea, Miss Wade. After you have eaten, we begin. We have not enough of time, even so. Ellen, come with me, you are needed elsewhere.''

As they left I felt a wave of remorse. I had forgotten one of Mrs. Gilwen's rules: never encourage tradesmen or servants to gossip. Mademoiselle was quite right to be angry with me. But I could not forget what Ellen had said. Sir Leslie was a nonpareil. Well, what of it? I asked myself. That will not concern you. If he has an account here, surely he is married or has grown daughters. He would not stand the nonsense simply to dress servants. I was still daydreaming when Ellen entered with a tray. ''Can't stay,'' she said, setting it on the small table, ''enjoy!''

Then she was gone—nervously, it seemed. I surveyed the tea tray. The pot was filled with a tea comparable to that served in Mrs. Gilwen's school. On a plate were several small pastries and buns. I was not quite sure it was all meant for me and at first I was timid in serving myself. No one entered to join me, however, and gradually I grew more bold. As though she had been waiting outside until the moment, Mademoiselle Suzette entered just as I ate the last crumb. ''You have eaten it all?'' she asked. ''*Bon*. Now, we begin. Again with the size. You have a small waist, *bon*. The hips, they are not so small. The bosom, a little small, but do not worry, *mon enfant*, Mademoiselle Suzette knows how to dress this.''

I wondered at Mademoiselle's concern with my figure. Earnestly, I hoped that Sir Leslie was not the sort of loose-screw who requested attractive servants so that he might flirt with them. Still worse if he had a young son who was so ramshackle. I was comforted by Mrs. Gilwen's assertion that a young lady who was careful need never fear improper advances.

''Sit,'' Mademoiselle commanded and then she left.

She returned a few minutes later with Ellen, who carried several dresses of various colours and fabrics. Ellen held each in turn against me as Mademoiselle watched. Occasionally she would murmur something such as, ''*Tiens!* Not such a colour with her hair,'' or ''*Mon Dieu*, with this one she looks ill.''

At last the process was completed and all the dresses were scattered on the chaise. ''We begin with the green!'' Made-

11

moiselle announced. To me she explained, "It is perhaps a little heavy for summer, but the castle is always cold."

So, I thought, Sir Leslie has a castle. I was eager to know more but dared not ask. As Mademoiselle had promised, the green dress suited me well. It concealed the unevenness of my figure and I was amazed to know I could look so pretty. "Her hair!" Mademoiselle commanded.

Ellen took my chestnut hair out of its severe knot and brushed it, curling the ends slightly with her fingers. Then she pinned my hair so that a curl rested against my neck, a green ribbon threaded through it. The effect in the glass seemed to me enchanting. *"Bon,"* Mademoiselle sighed. "So. The day dress, it is decided. Set it to the side, Ellen. Now we begin with evening. The blue silk, Ellen."

When Ellen had arranged the dress and stepped back, I felt naked. My shoulders were bare as well as most of my bosom. And in the glass I saw that I looked like a child dressed in her mother's gown. Mademoiselle shook her head regretfully. "I cannot to make you older than you are. Ellen, the dress for Lady Welton's daughter."

Happily, I exchanged the silk for a more modest gown of gauze and satin. This time the choice was a success. My only concern was that Sir Leslie might consider me too daring or presumptuous in wearing such a lovely dress. I said this to Mademoiselle and she smiled, "I know Sir Leslie well. He will approve. *Bon,* this also is decided."

"Lady Welton's daughter?" I asked tentatively.

Mademoiselle grimaced. *"Mon Dieu,* that child. Nothing will improve her. Another dress will do as well. Better this one for you."

The third was chosen with little discussion. There was but one ready that might be worn by me as an afternoon dress. I was fortunate that it was a gentle shade of primrose and not unkind to my features. Mademoiselle Suzette was as relieved as I when the choices had been made. *"Enfin!"* she sighed. "We must to make little changes here and there and so with this one. But all will be ready. The rest is no difficulty. We must to have a trunk but this Monsieur Thornsby brings already. *Tiens!* Sit, child."

This last remark was addressed to me and I was happy to obey. There are few occupations (for a gentlewoman) more tiring than the fitting of dresses. The selection of three gowns, with the subsequent pinning and marking, had absorbed more than three hours. I was grateful that Mademoiselle Suzette felt there would be no need for a session for fitting undergarments. I was alone, once more, in the little room. Ellen had left with Mademoiselle; one to alter my new dresses, the other to supervise her busy establishment. The extent of Mademoiselle Suzette's attention to me marked the importance she attached to Sir Leslie's patronage. I did not mind being left alone. I only hoped someone would remember me later when dinner was served to the seamstresses.

I should have realised, of course, that Mademoiselle Suzette was far too efficient to forget any task and that no doubt was how she viewed me. She sent Ellen to summon me to the evening meal she presided over. There were six of us, that evening: Mademoiselle, Ellen, myself, the woman who had greeted Mr. Thornsby in such a top-lofty manner (I thought of her as Dragon), and two young women slightly older than Ellen. The meal was eaten in a silence broken only by Dragon and Mademoiselle Suzette. To my surprise, there was no cutting up stiff over mistakes made during the day, though I had gathered from Ellen that several had occurred. My respect for Mademoiselle Suzette increased, for it seemed she gave few sharp setdowns. Dragon, however, I found quite odious. The feeling seemed mutual. Often, as I glanced at the head of the table that night, I discovered Dragon regarding me with unconcealed disapproval. I could not understand her enmity. Did she feel I was encroaching? And could this alone account for her dislike? It never occurred to me that she knew or cared about my new position and that this was the basis for her disapproval. After dinner, Mademoiselle asked me to stay behind. When the others had gone back to their work, she asked if I could sew. I replied that I could. Well? Again I said yes. She seemed pleased. "*Bon*. There is much to do and if you could help with hems . . ."

I smiled and answered truthfully, "It would please me to have a task."

She hesitated. "Child, are you certain you wish to be this companion? I could perhaps find work for you here."

It was meant kindly, but pride made me stand straight and calmly reply, "It is what I wish."

She sighed. "I felt you would speak so. But, if later . . . come here and I will help you."

I thanked her stiffly and followed her to the workroom where she gave me the primrose dress to hem. I hoped that Mademoiselle understood. It was not that I disliked sewing; indeed, often when I wished to relax at school I turned to my needle. Nor did I feel it would be beneath me to be a seamstress. Had I been unable to find other work, I would have joined the profession cheerfully. Rather, it was a need to prove myself. What value in finding a position only to throw it over for another before the first is even begun? Mr. Thornsby would have rightly felt me to be a gadfly. And yet I will not say that as I worked among the laughing seamstresses, I felt no call to linger here. I liked the women I had met at Mademoiselle Suzette's establishment. Of Sir Leslie I knew nothing save that he lived in a castle and had need of a companion for some woman of his family. Yes, I felt an urge to stay, but I will not deceive myself: it was no premonition. I felt far removed from the schoolroom as I fell asleep that night.

Chapter 2

We were at the posting house, Mr. Thornsby and I, with the trunk which now contained my new clothes and the bag I had brought with me from the school. It was a sunny morning with a slight breeze that sang through the city. Even dour tradesmen seemed to smile more than was their wont. I felt competent and sure of myself and was conscious that now I had a sense of purpose. Mr. Thornsby, however, did not share the mood of the city. He seemed, to my surprise, sharp-set. As we waited he repeated his instructions for the eighth time. "You are to give the letter of introduction to Sir Leslie's housekeeper and she will be sure he receives it. You have the letter? Are you certain? Let me see. Good. Now then, you will arrive too late for an interview with Sir Leslie this evening, but you are expected. Tomorrow, no doubt, Sir Leslie will explain all your duties to you. I trust you will try to provide satisfaction. I wish I could be sure . . . but you will remember that you wanted this position badly, regardless of how unusual it might be?"

I assured Mr. Thornsby that he should hear no complaints from me and none from Sir Leslie if it were in my power to prevent it. The next moment the mail coach arrived, and Mr. Thornsby had no opportunity to plague me further with instructions or questions. The last vision I have of the courtyard is Mr. Thornsby's anxious face. I wondered if he were so fatherly with all the young women who passed through his agency.

My only regret, that morning, was that travel was by mail and not chaise and four. (I had had little experience with either save rare occasions when a school friend had taken me home with her for a visit to the country. But the jolting of carriages I recalled could have been no worse than this.) I was soon feeling too uncomfortable to interest myself with the scenery. Particularly as one of the women in the coach was finding it impossible to soothe her infant. I do not know how many miles we travelled, but it was well past nightfall when my stop was announced. With a sense of relief, I stepped onto the ground. The evening was pleasantly cool and my earlier mood returned. I felt almost gay as I asked the hostler how I might reach Sir Leslie Kinwell's castle. His reply surprised me. "Why the divil do ye want to go there?" he demanded.

Though startled, I retained my composure. "I am to be a companion at the castle."

His eyes swept over me, the disbelief evident. "Ye don't look like a companion."

Pride rescued me. Frostily I said, "That's as may be. Nevertheless, there are those who do not question my qualifications."

He eyed me almost sadly, or so it seemed. "Well, lass, if ye're determined, I'll take ye up there meself. Where's yer cloak? 'Twill be a chilly ride."

This last remark came as the innkeeper put my trunk in his wagon. I flushed and was grateful for the night that masked my colour. "I-I have none," I stammered "and it's not so cold, I think."

He shook his head but said nothing more about it. As we rode he returned to the question of my position. "How did Sir Leslie convince ye to come to his castle?"

"Oh, I've not seen Sir Leslie," I explained. "Mr. Thornsby sent me."

"Mr. Thornsby?"

"He has a domestic agency in London," I said.

The hostler was quiet for a moment. "Domestic agency, ye say," he murmured. "As with maids and governesses?"

"Yes, of course, and companions."

"Lass," he blurted, "I'm thinking ye do not realise exactly the sort of work ye'll be expected to do."

Haughtily I interrupted him. "Mr. Thornsby explained it was a somewhat unusual position. That does not disturb me. And Mr. Thornsby seemed certain that Sir Leslie would be satisfied."

I had reduced the gentle old man to silence. And in silence

we travelled the remainder of the short journey. I regretted this for there were many questions I would have asked had he been less disapproving. But I was determined to give him no further opportunity to cast me down. The castle was dark when we approached, and I could not truly judge its size that first night. My first thought was that Sir Leslie might be elsewhere and the castle shut. I must have spoken aloud for my companion growled, "Ye'll not be so lucky." He turned to me, "Lass, if ye find the job not to yer liking, come to me, Mike, at the Three Ducks and my wife and I will help ye."

I thanked him, but could not help feeling impatient with all the people who doubted I would be happy in my new position. I waited as he brought my trunk to the door. How good a bed would feel!

The door opened suddenly and a sharp voice demanded, "Well, what do ye want?"

Mike answered for me, "I've brought Miss—"

"Heather Wade," I said.

"She's to be the new *companion*," he continued. "A *Mr. Thornsby* sent her, Mrs. Morgan."

Apparently Mrs. Morgan knew Mike well, for she answered curtly, "That will do, thank ye. Good-bye."

Grumbling, he turned and walked away. I called after him, "Thank you, Mike, for bringing me."

I could not hear his reply and I turned to greet Mrs. Morgan. "Good evening," I said, "I've a letter from Mr. Thornsby."

She took the letter and placed it in her pocket. "Come in, Miss Wade. John!" she yelled. Then to me, "He'll bring yer things. There's a chamber ready, of course, though Mr. Thornsby might have warned me earlier. Well, come, come. I suppose ye'll be wanting tea?"

I signified I would. Mrs. Morgan seemed to wish to intimidate me and I would not have it. So, with a mutual sense of dislike, we proceeded to my chamber with John close behind. My first impression of the room was that someone had made a mistake, that this room could not possibly be meant for me. The chamber was large with a fireplace and sitting room at one end, the bedroom at the other. Several carpets were placed about and the bedcurtains were velvet. I turned and faced Mrs. Morgan. "Thank you. Tea will be very welcome."

Without a word, she withdrew. John still carried my trunk. "Set it down there, please," I said, pointing to the floor beside one of the wardrobes.

As soon as he had left, I carefully surveyed my chamber again. Well, I told myself, Sir Leslie must be very wealthy if a mere companion is assigned a room such as this. Or perhaps the position is so difficult he feels the companion must be cosseted.

In one corner, behind a screen, was a stand with pitcher and basin and other necessities. Near the bed was a dressing table with a large mirror, and along one wall there was a small bookcase. This surprised and pleased me. I enjoyed novels and would not scorn these. And surely Sir Leslie had a library I might have access to if my duties left time for reading. I was thus musing when a young woman appeared with tea and a light supper. She stared at me, forgetting to set the tray on the table. "Come in," I said, "and do set that down. What is your name?"

"Margaret, ma'am," she half curtsied.

I was surprised at this deference, for I knew companions are considered scarcely above servants themselves. To hide my confusion I spoke quickly, "Yes, well I am Miss Heather Wade."

"Yes, ma'am." She bobbed. "Is that all?"

"Yes, Margaret. Thank you."

She fairly fled the room, hurrying to the servants' hall to tattle about me, no doubt. Well, a lady always ignores gossip, Mrs. Gilwen had taught us. As I sipped the welcome tea I began to relax. I was finally here! And Mrs. Morgan would not overset me. But I was tired and admit I was relieved I need not face Sir Leslie before morning. By the time Margaret returned to clear away the dishes, I was ready to sleep. When she left the room, I opened my trunk and carefully hung the dresses. I continued to unpack, though tired, for I knew it must be done. When I pulled forth my new night-dress, however, I could not contain my dismay. It was of such fine lawn as to be transparent! I should feel naked wearing it, I thought. No doubt Mademoiselle Suzette had given me the only one available. I laid it on the bed. It was pretty, I admitted to myself, if only it were not so sheer. But a pauper has no choice, and I could not say I had been dealt with unkindly.

Though tired, I also put away the garments I had worn that day. I did not wish the servants to gossip that I was careless with my things. As I moved about the room, blowing out candles, I wondered at the extravagance of a household that would use so many to light one room. Mr. Thornsby had called Sir Leslie eccentric, but why did his wife not restrain his wastefulness? Were they so beforehand with the world that they need never count cost? Or was Lady Kinwell an invalid, too weak to watch over her household or restrain Sir Leslie's impulsiveness? It would explain much. Perhaps it was Lady Kinwell, then, to whom I would be a companion. I cannot remember my other thoughts for I fell asleep soon after. But I was conscious of the comfort and size of the bed.

I woke sometime later. Someone was in my room. Frightened, I tried to call out "Who is it?" but the words were scarcely a whisper. I became aware that the candle beside my bed had been lit and now flickered, doing little to dispel the dark. I clutched at the bedsheets, listening to the sound of heavy breathing nearby. I was conscious of my hair loose about my shoulders, for I had been too weary to plait it. And above all, I was aware of the inadequacy of my nightdress as a cover. Then I saw him—a vague shadow beside the curtains on the far side of my bed. I must have gasped, for he moved forward quickly and pulled the sheets from me. I could not see him clearly and only had time to note that he was tall with dark hair. For in the next moment he lay in the bed beside me, unclothed. And I fought. First to push him away, then to escape from the bed myself. He laughed and I could smell strong fumes on his breath. I fought, truly I did, as well as I was able. But I could not stop him. And in the next few moments my dress was above my waist and he was upon me. More I will not say, save that soon, with a sharp, stabbing pain, I mercifully lost consciousness.

When I woke again, later, I was alone in the bed. The candle had almost spent itself. The bedclothes were in disarray and a small pool of blood stained the sheet. I began to weep and could not stop myself nor the shudders that swept over me. Soon, like a child, I had cried myself to sleep, though in my shock I wished it were something more permanent.

I woke for the third time. It was morning. The room, which

had so pleased me the night before, now frightened me. I must speak to Sir Leslie, I thought. He must find the man who did this to me and send him away. I must have a lock on my door!

I dressed feverishly, though remembering to wear the new morning dress. My hair I savagely pulled off my face and forced it into a knot at the top of my head. I would be certain not to entice any man. John. It must have been John. He knew I was here. No, that was foolish. Every servant must have known and had a description of me as soon as Margaret had returned to the servants' hall after bringing me tea. I began to pace. I had to see Sir Leslie at once. But I confess I was afraid to wander the castle halls alone. Then I remembered the servant's bell. I strode quickly to it and tugged on the tassled rope. A few minutes later, Margaret knocked at my door. "Come in," I called nervously.

She entered and curtsied, staring at me. "Yes, ma'am?"

"I wish to speak with Sir Leslie. Immediately," I snapped.

"Yes, ma'am." She bobbed again. "Please come with me."

It was too late to change my mind and I followed her. Several times, she glanced over her shoulder at me. I wondered what disturbed her. Was Sir Leslie an ogre? To my surprise, Margaret led me to the dining hall. He sat alone, Sir Leslie, at a long table, with a servant behind his chair to supply his plate. His dark head came up as I entered and he stared at me for a long time out of dark questioning eyes. Finally, nervously I spoke, "Sir Leslie?" He nodded and I gained courage, "I would like to register a complaint, Sir Leslie. Last night—"

He interrupted me, "Who the devil are you?"

"The new companion, sir. Mr. Thornsby sent me."

His next few words astounded me. "Let down your hair."

"I would rather not, sir," I replied, struggling to retain my composure.

"Let down your hair," he repeated.

Nervously, I complied. He stared at me, almost hungrily it seemed. "Mr. Thornsby gave me a letter of introduction," I said. "Sir Leslie, I must tell you. Something terrible happened to me last night. I—" I hesitated. He continued to stare and I thrust forward my chin, determined not to be a watering-pot. "I was ravished, sir!"

"Ravished!" he exclaimed. Then sarcastically, "I suppose next you will tell me you are a virgin."

"I was, sir, until last night," I replied, the tears harder to hold back. "The blood on my sheets will prove that. And I fought, sir. Truly I did."

Still he stared at me. "Mr. Thornsby sent you? Jeffries, the letter. It must be on the sideboard," Sir Leslie snapped.

The servant bowed, carefully averting his eyes from me. He found the letter and returned to his place. Sir Leslie tore open the cover and read it rapidly, glancing at me from time to time. When he had finished, he swore vehemently. "Jeffries, I shall need my phaeton. I must go to London at once. Have it ready in the hour."

"Very good, sir." Jeffries bowed and retired.

Hastily, I said, "Sir, about last night. You must do something."

He turned to me and spoke deliberately. "You need not worry, Miss"—he glanced at the letter—"Wade. You will be perfectly safe. I was the man who ravished you and I will not be here."

My head reeled, and had less been at stake I might have fainted. Instead, I carefully pulled my hair back into its topknot as I said coldly, "I wish to return to London at once, sir."

He laughed harshly. "But not with me, surely?"

"No, not with you," I agreed. "Nevertheless, I wish to return to London."

The sneer left Sir Leslie's face and he spoke gently. "That is impossible for the moment. With or without me. I am afraid you must wait here until my return. Don't worry, you will be perfectly safe. Neither I nor anyone else will touch you. But you must stay until I return in a sennight or less."

I could not speak, but Sir Leslie must have guessed how I felt, for he added. "I intend to speak to Mr. Thornsby. You may be sure he will send no more virgins to be *companions* anywhere. At least, no *unwilling* virgins."

The question in his voice was clear. I spoke somehow. "Sir Leslie, I did tell Mr. Thornsby I needed a position, and that I would accept any post as a companion, even if unusual. But had I known—" My voice broke, "How could I know? It was a domestic agency!"

Sir Leslie stared at me impassively as he rang for a servant.

A short time later I heard him say, "Escort Miss Wade to her chamber."

Then, numb, I was following someone back to my room. The appalling truth of my position was becoming clear to me. I would escape. I must escape. Oh, my God, what would I do? Suppose I were with child? Did one always become pregnant? I was as ignorant as any young woman of my class on certain facts of life, though curiously knowledgeable on others.

Then I was back in my room. It was not, however, empty. Margaret stood by the sitting-room table where she had placed a tray. By the bed stood Mrs. Morgan, staring at the sheets. She turned as I entered. "Yer a virgin!" she said accusingly.

With trembling knees I walked to a chair and sat. "Not anymore," I said lightly, blinking back tears.

"But why, child?" she demanded.

I could contain myself no longer and began to cry, my face in my hands. In the distance, I heard Mrs. Morgan dismiss Margaret. A cup of tea was forced into my hands. I shook my head in denial, but Mrs. Morgan persisted until I sipped the tea. A few sips were all I could manage before thrusting the cup away. Mrs. Morgan waited patiently. After a while, I began to talk, unable to order or halt my words. "Sir Leslie . . . he . . . last night . . . Oh, God! I did not . . . understand . . . Mr. Thornsby said *unusual* . . . I had to find a position . . . no one *told* me . . . everyone said I was too young or wrong for the position, but no one *told* me. . . ."

Mrs. Morgan spoke gently, "Yer family . . .?"

"I have no family," I retorted bitterly . . . "My parents are dead. I was in a school! They offered me a teaching position without pay. I felt anything would be better. But, oh God! I must get away. Mrs. Morgan, you must help me!"

I was on the verge of hysteria and Mrs. Morgan sensed this. "Stop shouting," she commanded. Then with a sigh, "Why don't ye simply ask Sir Leslie to send ye back to London?"

"I did. He refused."

"My lord!" she exclaimed. "Is he mad? Ye cannot escape then, for he'll have ye watched. But I promise ye, child, he'll not touch ye again. I don't understand, but I swear ye'll be safe."

"But I cannot remain here!" I cried.

"Child, I've promised I'll protect ye. Perhaps Sir Leslie means to provide for ye and wants ye to stay here until he can," she said.

"I don't want his help," I retorted. "I'll not have it!"

"Now child, do not be a pea-goose. What would ye do? Where would ye go?" she asked reasonably. "And suppose ye are with child because of this? Ye'll need his help. For the sake of the child."

At the thought of a child, I began to weep anew. After a time, Mrs. Morgan left and I wept harder still. But I could not cry forever, and at last I dried my eyes and cheeks. I could not eat, but the tea calmed me a little. I began to pace about the room. Time passed, I suppose, for Margaret brought me another tray with tea and food. I wanted to refuse it, but my body betrayed me and demanded nourishment. I felt shame that I could wish to eat so soon after . . . after . . .

I'd not have believed it, but I felt better for having eaten; well enough to wish to escape my room and see the castle, now that Sir Leslie had left it. From my chamber I had seen him drive away, or I'd not have dared to believe he were truly gone. Perhaps it will seem strange that I could interest myself in such a thing as a castle at such a time. But it was a means of fixing my thoughts on other than what had happened. And I would feel less trapped if I knew my way about. When Margaret returned to remove the tray, Mrs. Morgan entered with her. "Child, are ye feeling any better?" she asked.

I forced myself to nod. "Yes, Mrs. Morgan. I thought—do you think I might look about the castle?"

She smiled in reply. "That's better. I was worried. A look about the castle will do ye good. Ye can come along with me; ye'll see most of it then."

I assented readily and felt a sense of relief as I heard Mrs. Morgan say to Margaret, "The sheets must be changed at once. And bolt the door to Sir Leslie's chamber."

I turned swiftly. "Door? To Sir Leslie's chamber?"

"Aye," she said sadly. "There in the corner. But 'twill be bolted and ye need not fear his intruding. Ye'll also have a bolt on this door by nightfall. Ye'll be safe, child."

I stared for a moment at the curtain that hid his door. Of course there would be such a door. A way for Sir Leslie to visit his "companion." Why had it never occurred to me the word might mean such a thing? There was much I did not know. Had he a wife? Who else lived here? How old was he? Ah, that one I could answer. Sir Leslie counted less than thirty summers, I would wager.

I followed Mrs. Morgan. The chamber next to mine was Sir Leslie's, of course. He had no wife, Mrs. Morgan explained. He was a rake, but not the sort of man to shame a wife publicly. I see, I thought to myself, Sir Leslie has a sense of propriety. All his affairs would be discreet once he married. Such consolation to a wife! Though perhaps she would be grateful his attention were directed elsewhere.

There were other chambers in the hall, but all were closed, now. They had once been used by Sir Leslie's family, and at the far end of the hall was the nursery. But now his parents were dead and his sisters married and elsewhere. The floor above held the guest rooms, and Mrs. Morgan explained that in the old days, with Sir Leslie's father, the castle had often been full. These chambers were still aired regularly, for guests who might arrive. I timidly asked if I might move to one of these rooms. Mrs. Morgan hesitated. "Ye *could*, but I'd be grateful if ye waited until Sir Leslie returned. 'Tis an extra set of stairs for the servants to carry water and trays and all. And until he returns, there's really no need, is there?"

Though I now hated my chamber, I was reluctant to cause trouble. I also sensed that in Mrs. Morgan's eyes, my status was uncertain and perhaps could not claim a guest room. Thus, I agreed to remain where I was until Sir Leslie should return.

The servants' quarters were at the lowest level of the castle: half belowground. I did not see these, since Mrs. Morgan hinted me away. She wished to give no additional cause for gossip or speculation. Instead, she showed me about the ground floor of the castle. There were several sitting rooms, the largest one long and drafty (as was most of the castle). The furnishings of these rooms varied, reflecting the times over which they had been accumulated. There was also a game room for the men, and near this a large library. This room overshadowed all the others for me, even the huge ballroom with its crystal chandeliers. The library was crowded with books: some on open shelves, some in glass cases, some simply on tables. The room was ideal for reading, with its many large, comfortable chairs. Beside each chair stood a small table to hold fruit or tea or other oddments as one read. A large fireplace would keep the room cosy in winter, for the many bookshelves would prevent any draft. But dominating the room was a desk littered with books and papers. Clearly this belonged to Sir Leslie. I shuddered and wondered if I could be comfortable in a room so ruled by his effects. But I determined to try, for if I could not even face this room, how should I face Sir Leslie? And face him I must, for there had to be a reckoning. Accordingly, I asked Mrs. Morgan if I might spend the rest of the day here.

"Of course," she replied, "Sir Leslie's given orders yer to be allowed wherever ye wish about the castle and grounds so long as we're certain yer not trying to run away."

It was more than I had expected of Sir Leslie, yet I was angry that he had given orders to have me watched. Perhaps he hopes, I thought bitterly, I shall become so afraid and unhappy that I shall kill myself and the problem cease to exist for him. Well, he should not find me so craven. I chose a book and, tucking my feet under me, curled up in a chair.

Thus began my imprisonment at Sir Leslie's castle, for that was how I thought of it. I was treated kindly, but nevertheless, I was a prisoner. If I went for a walk, someone must accompany me. And at night my bedchamber door was bolted shut. True, it was I who bolted the door, yet this did not make me less a prisoner. For as long as I felt the need to bolt my doors, I could not call myself free. I spent much of my time in the library and walking about the estate. There was a garden which, had Sir Leslie cared about such things, might have brightened the castle in spring and summer. There were fields, and some distance from the castle, a copse of trees beside a stream. But the nearest of dwellings were well away from the castle and it seemed the servants had orders to keep me out of sight of strangers. As the days passed I grew calmer and firmer in my resolve to face Sir Leslie as soon as he might return. And yet, when, on the ninth day, I saw his phaeton approaching, I fled to my chamber and bolted the doors. It was a hen-witted notion, of course, since he must inevitably find me there. Too late I realised my error.

Chapter 3

From my chamber, I heard Sir Leslie's muffled voice shouting orders. Then silence. I waited, my heart pounding, for a summons I dreaded yet was not certain would come. After some time, there was a knock at my door. "Yes," I called, "who is it?"

"Margaret, ma'am. Sir Leslie wishes to speak with you in the library."

"All—all right. Tell Sir Leslie I shall be down in a moment," I replied, not at all sure I would be.

"Begging your pardon, ma'am. Sir Leslie said I was to bring you," she answered, as nervous as I.

So, the matter was not to be evaded any longer. Taking a deep breath, I unbolted the door to the hallway. "I'm ready," I said.

"Your hair, ma'am?" Margaret suggested.

I stepped back to look at the mirror. She was quite right, my hair was disarrayed. I retightened the knot at the top of my head and pinned the few stray strands of hair. Then I was as ready as I could be and we began the long walk to the library. Margaret opened the library doors and held them for me. Once I was inside, however, they closed behind me and I was alone with Sir Leslie. I advanced with as much dignity as I could muster to his desk. He stared at me for some time before he said, "Please sit down, Miss Wade."

"I would rather stand," I replied.

Carefully, he examined me from head to foot. "Miss Wade, I wish to discuss with you the event that has occurred and certain steps I have taken. I cannot do so if you remain standing."

I sat. Such was the force of his voice. He continued to

regard me warily. "Are you well?" he asked. "Have you any complaints about your treatment *while I was away?*"

"As well as I can be in the circumstances," I said coldly. "The only complaint I have is that I have been kept a prisoner here."

He smiled. "So you would have run away? To where? To whom?"

Stung, I retorted, "I might at least have had the choice!"

The smile left his face. "I am afraid you could not. I wronged you, this I freely admit. And now I've a responsibility for you. Had I allowed you to run away, you might have been in worse trouble. Incidentally, I have spoken to Mr. Thornsby. Such an incident will not occur again through his agency."

"Marvelous!" I muttered.

"What did you say?" Sir Leslie asked.

"Nothing," I replied sullenly. "Please continue. You were explaining that you feel a responsibility for me."

Angrily he retorted, "I have expended a great deal of effort on your behalf this week, Miss Wade. And I have arrived at the only possible solution. But before I tell it to you, you might consider the fact that this is not entirely my fault. Had you bothered to demand a clear explanation of the duties of the post you were to occupy, all this might have been avoided!"

"And if you were not so debauched as to have women sent up for your private amusement—"

"Enough!" Sir Leslie's voice cut through mine as sharply as a sword. Then, with an obvious effort to control himself, he continued, "I have brought a trunk of clothes for you from Mademoiselle Suzette. She is sending others. I have also arranged for a personal maid for you. She will arrive later today."

As he paused for breath I spoke quickly, "That was very kind of you, but not necessary as I shall be leaving the castle as soon as I have packed my things."

Sir Leslie stared at me with a curiously bleak expression. "I am afraid not, Miss Wade. In about an hour, you will be married to me."

I stared at him incredulously. "But you—there's been no time to post the banns."

"I procured a special license in London."

27

Angrily I jumped to my feet. "Well, it don't signify, for I shan't marry you!"

Now he stood, over a head taller than me. "You will, for you have no choice."

"But why? You can't possibly wish to marry me!" I protested.

"I've no choice either. You have no one to look after you. You cannot find another position: no one would hire you knowing you've been here. And even could you conceal that fact, it would be impossible for you to find a respectable position without references. But none of these matter so much as the fact that I am not in the habit of ravishing young women. And above all, not respectable young women. I've no choice. I must marry you."

"Ah, but I'm not respectable," I said eagerly. "I am . . . my parents were not married. So you see, you need not marry me."

Sir Leslie spoke slowly and deliberately. "I have spoken with Mrs. Gilwen and I am fully aware of all particulars of your background. I also have your . . . *guardian's* permission to marry you. I intend to do so, and I usually have my way."

For a moment I was too stunned to speak. But there was too much at stake and I could not let matters rest so. I managed to choke out, "You cannot imagine, surely, that I would ever accept you as my husband! Or—or welcome you to my bed! I'll run away first. I think I would even kill myself first!"

I was breathing heavily and feeling on the verge of hysteria. Sir Leslie replied contemptuously, "Spare me the Cheltenham tragedies, Miss Wade! I am marrying you to give you my name and protect your reputation. That is all I intend. I might have wished for heirs, but that is irrelevant now. I do not intend to force my attentions on you. We will, of course, have separate rooms. If you wish, your maid may even sleep in your room as an added protection. Though that would no doubt give rise to gossip. You will have an ample allowance, and if it should prove insufficient I will increase it. Should you take a fancy to some man, I will not interfere provided you conduct the affair discreetly. I have already taken steps to ensure that none of the servants gossip outside this castle and I think we shall be all right. Is that clear?"

I stared at him. "Perfectly clear. A marriage in appearance only. You must have windmills in your head! I refuse. Of what benefit is it to save my reputation if I am riveted to you?"

He flushed. "You will have every freedom except marriage to someone else. And after . . . after . . . you are not marriageable anyway. You will have security and be well placed in the *ton*. I will not inflict myself on you more than is absolutely necessary. After a year or two, we may contrive to rarely find ourselves in the same place together. I have a house in London that will be at your disposal."

"I see. That's all very well but what are you going to do the next time this happens? You won't be able to marry the poor girl."

"Damn you, shut up!" he shouted. I backed away as he came toward me. "There will not be a next time. If I have any affairs, they will be discreetly conducted with women whom I choose personally and who are quite willing. I assure you that not everyone finds me abhorrent."

"Not everyone knows you as well as I do," I said sweetly.

He stood still. "You don't know me at all. No, don't say it. You—"

I do not know what he was about to add, for at that moment someone knocked. "Yes, who is it?" Sir Leslie called, without taking his eyes from my face.

"The vicar, Sir Leslie," Mrs. Morgan called.

"Show him in," Sir Leslie replied.

As the doors opened I ran to Mrs. Morgan. "Will you explain to Sir Leslie that I cannot marry him?" I said.

"Now child," she said soothingly, "ye must marry him. 'Tis a good marriage. Why, else ye could not marry at all, and less marry as well."

I was stunned by her defection. The vicar was already standing by the desk and now Mrs. Morgan and another servant (Sir Leslie's valet, I later learned) shepherded me to Sir Leslie's side. The vicar regarded me kindly as he began the marriage service. I held quiet until it came to be time for my response. "I will not," I said calmly and clearly.

I felt Sir Leslie about to speak, but the vicar forestalled him. "Child," he said gently, "is it true that you're not a virgin; that Sir Leslie ravished you?"

I nodded. He gave me a pitying smile. "The bride assents," he said and continued with the service.

Shocked, I could not protest. I did not hear the rest of the words of the service and scarcely felt the ring being placed on my finger. Then I was signing something. It did not matter. There was nothing I could do. I should never be free. Then I was alone in the library with the vicar. "My dear Heather," he said, "You must accept this marriage. You are very, very lucky. Sir Leslie is an honourable man. I know you have had a shock and this is not the best way to begin a marriage. But others have started worse and been happy. Accept Sir Leslie and your marriage. In time, too, children will help to ease matters. In the joys of motherhood you will find—"

"Motherhood? Children?" I repeated. Then angrily, I said, "No! No children. Sir Leslie promised. I won't! I won't!"

"Calm yourself, child," he said hastily. "Of course there is no need to consider such things now. But in time—"

"Go away," I said through clenched teeth.

"Go away? But—"

"Please?" I said. "Please? I need to be alone."

Worried, he rang for a servant. Sir Leslie appeared at the doorway. I heard him say, "Take her to her room."

A hand guided my elbow as, dazed, I returned to my chamber. Inside, I threw myself on the bed and wept. Of all the fantasies I had ever had of my marriage, none approached the actual event. I had always assumed I would marry for love or at the very least, a man for whom I felt the proper regard. But this! I was truly trapped now. Sir Leslie was young and I could not even hope my marriage would be ended by his early death. I felt that fate had been unfair to me. I could only console myself that my tormentor, Sir Leslie, was no happier than I.

I had ceased to cry and lay face upward on the bed when someone knocked. "Go away!" I called.

"Ma'am, it's your new abigail," Margaret's voice replied.

"I don't wish an abigail!" I retorted.

The voice that spoke next surprised me. "It's Ellen, Miss Wade. I mean, Lady Kinwell."

I jumped to my feet and hurried to unbolt the door. Mademoiselle Suzette had promised to aid me, and Ellen I looked upon as a friend. As I opened the door I noticed Margaret regarding me strangely. No doubt she believed me slightly mad. Well, perhaps I was. But could anyone wonder at this? I shut and bolted the door behind Ellen. "How? Why?" I asked. "Sit down."

"Well," Ellen began dramatically, "Sir Leslie came into Mademoiselle's establishment and demanded to speak with her *at once*. She said to deny her, but he went from one fitting room to another until he found her. Then, well! They went to her office and you could hear his voice *all over* the place, cutting up stiff over *something*. Then Mademoiselle called *me* into her office. Sir Leslie was that angry! I thought he would shout at me. But he was very polite. 'Did you speak with Miss Wade when she was fitted here?' he asked.

"Well! I confess I had forgotten your name. 'The *companion* for Sir Leslie,' Mademoiselle said.

"Well, then of course I knew who he meant. 'Well, sir,' I replied, 'a little, though of course I know well enough not to tattle.'

"He glanced at Mademoiselle, but spoke to me. 'Did Miss Wade speak about her position? Did she seem eager to begin her work?'

" 'I wouldn't know, sir,' I said, 'I didn't wish to gossip. Only . . .'

" 'Only what?' he cried angrily.

" 'Well, sir, she seemed desperate for any position and fainted once because she had not eaten since the night before. And she had almost no possessions and slept with the seamstresses that night. But she was well bred, sir, one could see that.'

"Well! My answer only made him angrier. Mademoiselle dismissed me after warning me to keep my tongue between my teeth. Then Sir Leslie left. Well, of course I wondered what had happened. I tried to ask Mademoiselle, but she said to be quiet, to forget you. Well! Imagine my surprise when Sir Leslie came back to see Mademoiselle yesterday and asked to speak with me again. 'Ellen,' he said, 'do you know how to dress hair?'

" 'Yes, sir,' I said.

" 'How would you like to be my wife's abigail?' he asked me. 'You would be well paid and you already know her. Miss Wade is to marry me tomorrow.'

"Well! I was that surprised! Me, an abigail? Of course I accepted. And you, Lady Kinwell! So then he said I would have to leave at once. As soon as I said I could, he turned to Mademoiselle and said, 'I shall take with me the clothes you have ready. The rest you will send as soon as possible.'

"Well! Mademoiselle had said there was a rush order, but I never guessed it was for you. Then *he* left and *she* gave me a message for *you*. She said she believes all will be well now, but to tell you that if you are dreadfully unhappy, to go and talk with her when Sir Leslie brings you to London. It was her notion Sir Leslie should take me as your abigail. Said you'd like someone your own age. And warned me to help you. Well of course I will! But tell me. Are you truly Lady Kinwell? How did it happen?"

I did not answer for a moment, for I needed time to absorb all that Ellen had told me. And I needed time to determine how to answer her. I was not eager to speak of the shameful thing that had happened. At last I compromised between truth and untruth. . . . "Yes, Ellen, I am truly Sir Leslie's wife. We were married this afternoon. I . . . he felt he had compromised me and he insisted upon our marriage. He went to London to procure a special license."

"Lor'!" she cooed. "And have you a *tendre* for him? Is it monstrous exciting to be Lady Kinwell?"

Distaste swept over me. Yet what had happened could not be undone and I must not gossip with the servants else my position would be even more unbearable. "There are no words to tell what I feel," I answered truthfully. "I am tired, Ellen. Will you please ring for tea?"

She nodded. "Of course, my lady." Then she hesitated, "You will not be taking tea with Sir Leslie?"

I closed my eyes. Of course it must all begin sometime. But I was not yet ready to face him. "No, Ellen. There are . . . certain matters he must see to this afternoon."

"Very well, my lady." She nodded and rang for Margaret.

I stared out the window as she gave the necessary orders. The whole world seemed mad. I was leg-shackled to a man I hated and forced to pretend I did not. I was not so goosish as to believe I could do other than pretend our marriage was a normal one. Any other behaviour could only damage my reputation. If this farce could be successfully acted, then in time I might expect more freedom. And acceptance in the *ton*. I knew that I was not the only young woman to be forced into an unwelcome marriage. Yet this did not lessen my resentment or hatred for Sir Leslie. Publicly I might be a dutiful wife, but in private he should know precisely how I felt. And each night I would be sure the door between our chambers was firmly bolted! Ellen interrupted my thoughts. "My lady, the tea is here. Shall I put away the clothes from Mademoiselle?"

"Yes, Ellen," I replied, moving to the table. "And lay out a dress for this evening."

"Yes, my lady."

She was thus occupied when Mrs. Morgan entered my chamber. "My lady," she began tentatively, "Sir Leslie asks if a late dinner hour will disturb ye?"

I forced myself to reply calmly, "That will be perfectly acceptable, Mrs. Morgan. Please have hot water for a bath sent up an hour and a half beforehand. Oh, and Mrs. Morgan, perhaps it would be best if you show me about the castle again tomorrow. I must begin to familiarise myself with my new responsibilities, such as the management of the household."

"Yes, my lady," she said coldly. "I am glad to see ye are not still unreconciled!"

As she left I sighed. No doubt she thought me encroaching. Yet, for all my background, I was now Lady Kinwell. If I was to play the role, I must do so fully. Though she would not like it, Mrs. Morgan must learn to treat me as befitted my new station. I smiled. I suspected Sir Leslie would be surprised to learn I intended to join him for dinner. Well, let him be surprised. I was no Bath miss to spend the rest of my life hiding in my chamber.

I dressed with care that evening, in the gauze gown with a shawl about my shoulders, and Ellen dressed my hair in a style that made me appear older than my years. My reflection in the mirror gave me confidence, and with a deep breath, I descended to the drawing room. Sir Leslie's back was to the doorway. He stood alone, holding a glass of some amber fluid. His head was bent and I realised he was weary and tense. Was he as afraid of this meeting as I? Boldly, I stepped into the room. "Good evening, Leslie."

He turned quickly. "Good evening . . . Heather," he managed.

I stood quite still as his eyes swept over me, coming to rest on my face. He stared into my eyes and, instinctively, drew himself taller. "Would you like some sherry?" he asked coolly. When I shook my head, he sipped from his glass. "Mr. Watly, the vicar, has kindly consented to join us for dinner. He was quite worried about you."

"That I was," said a voice behind me. "My dear, how are you?"

I turned and extended my hand to the vicar. Suppressing the distaste I felt for him, I said lightly, "How kind of you. But surely, sir, you are aware that most brides are somewhat hysterical on their wedding day?"

"My dear Heather," he said, pressing my hand, "I cannot tell you how delighted I am that you have taken such a mature attitude. I realise this was all very sudden and did not commence auspiciously; however, I am sure all will be well."

I merely smiled and gently withdrew my hand. Sir Leslie moved to stand beside me and I noted with a malicious pleasure the tremour in his voice as he asked, "Would you care for some sherry, sir?"

"No, no, my boy. I take a little wine with dinner, but my doctor forbids alcohol in any other form. Though I regret it, you may be sure."

"Then may I suggest we go into dinner?" my husband said.

Before Sir Leslie could offer me his arm, I took Mr. Watly's and gently prodded him toward the dining hall. He seemed surprised but flattered, and I counted him a tactless fool who had no understanding of people. At the head of the long table, Sir Leslie was seated with me on his left and the vicar on his right. "I am always happy to eat with Sir Leslie," Watly confided to me, "as he always sets an excellent table."

I smiled sweetly. "Yes, Sir Leslie never stints on his worldly pleasures."

Sir Leslie glared, but Watly smiled indulgently. "Yes, my dear, your husband is quite open-handed. And now that he is safely married, I am sure his. . . er . . . indiscretions will cease."

"Oh, yes," I replied, "Leslie has assured me he will be most discreet in the future."

Watly stared at me uncertainly and did not reply. I might have said more, but the warning in Sir Leslie's eyes was clear. And for my own sake, I had to choose my words with care. I lapsed into silence as the first course was served. With the second, I determined to end the uneasy quiet. "Tell me, sir," I said, "is yours a large parish?"

Watly waved a hand airily. "Oh, no larger than I would want, and not, by far, the smallest in England. Well, but you shall see for yourself this Sunday. You will be there, in the family pew, will you not?"

I was about to reply negatively when Sir Leslie forestalled me. "Of course we shall. Perhaps you might then give a special blessing over our marriage," he said smoothly.

"Oh, quite. Quite," Watly replied. "An excellent notion. You will hold the customary reception?"

"Yes," Sir Leslie replied, to my amazement, "Sunday afternoon tables will be set out on the lawn, and food and drink will be served."

"Excellent. I shall announce it from the pulpit."

So, it would come so soon. My first public appearance. Difficult it might be, I told myself, but far easier than would be my entrance into the *ton*. I took a bit of wine to fortify myself. I must be careful, I warned myself, I was not accustomed to the substance. Yet its warmth was welcome and I began to relax. "My education? Most recently I was at Mrs. Gilwen's School for Young Ladies," I answered.

"Ah, yes," Watly said. "An excellent establishment. And Mrs. Gilwen is an excellent woman. My daughter was there several years ago. I was completely satisfied."

"I should have been surprised if you felt otherwise," I said.

Sir Leslie's eyebrows rose, but he said nothing. Watly continued, "Of course, for sons the question is rather different."

"Quite," I murmured, stifling the sarcasm.

"No doubt Sir Leslie will wish to send your sons to the university, as he was." He waved a finger at me, "You'll find it a difficult time. Young men need to cut up a bit and that's when they usually do so. Mothers always worry, but the boys come out right in the end. Consider Sir Leslie."

Too late, Watly realised his gaffe. And I could not stop myself from saying, "I would rather not."

We three stared at one another in an awful silence. Then Watly spoke hastily. "Well, well, no need to think about such things now. Time enough when . . ."

"When and *if* there are children," Sir Leslie finished for him. At Watly's startled gaze, he added, "It is not unknown for a man and wife to have no children. I prefer not to make plans for children I am not certain I shall have. After all, so far as I know, I've no side-slips about the countryside."

Watly's knife clattered as it fell. "Sir Leslie!" he exclaimed. "Really! In the presence of your bride!"

Sir Leslie spoke bitterly, "In view of recent events, I seriously doubt that aught I could say would surprise my wife."

"Well, but still . . ." he expostulated nervously, "surely common decency . . . Perhaps this marriage was a mistake after all. . . ."

"It seems a little late to think of that," I said. "Unless there is a way, perhaps, that it might be annulled?"

"No!" Sir Leslie answered angrily. "The reasons for the marriage have not changed. You seem to have forgotten your position, Heather. An annulment would complete the process of your ruin. And may I point out that you could not request an annulment on the grounds of nonconsummation?"

I stared down at my plate just as I was sure Watly did. I felt cold and miserable. Watly's voice did not improve matters as he said, "Quite, quite, Sir Leslie. I had forgotten. Nonetheless, I do think you might make an effort to avoid certain . . . er . . . matters that would disturb your wife." His voice calmed as he commenced a speech he had surely given often. "Matrimony is not a state to be entered into lightly. It is like a seed one plants in the ground. Without careful nurturing it withers and dies. Yet even the weakest seed, if one expends sufficient effort, can grow into a sturdy plant that in time blossoms and bears fruit. When there is love, the process is somewhat easier. But no seed is without potential. All that is required is a determination on both sides to bring the seed to fruition: a successful marriage. It is not a process that follows a schedule. Sometimes success is achieved at once. In other cases it requires years or even decades. I knew a man and woman who—"

"Hated each other for years. Then, after several children, at the age of fifty, discovered contentment with each other," I supplied wearily.

Watly gazed at me in surprise. "You know Lord and Lady William?"

I choked back laughter and stifled that which escaped me with a napkin. Sir Leslie had also covered his mouth with a napkin and appeared to be coughing. My voice was a trifle unsteady as I answered, "No, sir. But I guessed such cases were not unknown."

Watly beamed. "So you see, my children, your position is not entirely hopeless. Others have overcome greater obstacles."

We nodded gravely, both afraid to answer. Soon after, I eased back my chair. "Well, gentlemen, I shall leave you to your port," I said.

They stood as I left the room. I hurried to the drawing room where, behind closed doors, I loosed my laughter. Did Mr. Watly truly exist? Surely he was the creation of some satirist. Or perhaps God simply had a sense of humour. I was still smiling when Sir Leslie joined me. "Mr. Watly has left," he said gravely, "I paid your respects to him and explained you had . . . er . . .-retired early. He understood perfectly. He wished me a . . . er . . . successful night! He was also kind enough to offer me advice on the duties of a husband."

He could contain himself no longer, and together we laughed heartily. Then, shaking his head, he said, "Oh, do you know Lord and Lady William?"

We laughed afresh and it felt good. I was young and tired of unhappiness and tears. Sir Leslie must have sensed this and felt much the same, for he said quietly, "Heather, must we hate each other? Can't we learn to rub along together? I do not suggest more than companionship, but surely that would be more pleasant than . . ."

The laughter died in me. With dignity I drew myself to my feet and answered, "Impossible. What has happened cannot be erased. In public we shall assuredly be cordial with one another. But in private, there can be nothing to say."

Trembling slightly, I walked out of the room without a backward glance and did not halt until I had reached my chamber. On the bed lay a nightdress Ellen had chosen for me. It was embroidered and of a fine lawn. At the sight of it, I began to cry. Was there ever a bride with a more unhappy wedding day? Reluctant to face Ellen, I thrust away the dress and drew out another, more demure one myself. I bolted both doors, then, with trembling hands, undid my gown and tossed it with my other garments on the chair. I pulled pins from my hair, but did not brush or plait it. Then I climbed into my bed, that hateful bed! And blowing out the candle, I cried myself to sleep.

Chapter 4

Thus began my marriage. Our days soon fell into a pattern. Though Leslie and I rose at the same hour, I would be served tea in my chamber, and he would eat in the dining hall. I would then spend the morning with Mrs. Morgan making inventories and seeing to other household duties. Sir Leslie had neglected to introduce me to the servants and so, on the morning after my marriage, I asked Mrs. Morgan to assemble them briefly. She presented me and I said a few words to the effect that I looked forward to knowing them and that I soon hoped to learn all their names. I praised the efficiency and discretion of the staff and said that I did not intend to overset their routines.

And so I came to cuffs with Sir Leslie. We would ordinarily see each other only for the midday and evening meals. How Leslie spent his days I neither knew nor cared. But that first day, he knocked at my door shortly after tea in the afternoon. Ellen opened the door immediately, assuming it was one of the servants. Sir Leslie dismissed her peremptorily, saying, "You may leave your mistress with me."

I turned to face him. There was anger in his voice and I wondered at the cause. "So you have already begun meddling with my servants!" he said.

At this I took courage, knowing I had the right of it. "It was your notion, sir, that we must be married. And your notion that to outward appearances ours must be an ordinary marriage. Very well, sir. In ordinary circumstances I would clearly be the new mistress of the household, and as such would be presented to the servants by you. Since you did not choose to do so, I preserved appearances as best I could. It would seem very strange, sir, if your wife did not interest herself in household affairs!"

He bit his lower lip. "I see. Perhaps you have a point. Very well, do as you please, only pray, do not institute any changes without consulting me."

I curtsied and smiled sweetly. "I assure you, sir, I have no intention of acting otherwise."

He frowned, but only replied, "Very well, madam. I shall see you in the drawing room this evening." He paused, halfway out of my door. "My valet, Peter, informs me the servants were favourably impressed." And then he was gone.

The incident was not referred to again. When I was not occupied with household matters, I often took long walks or read in the library, curled up in a chair. I also began the process of mending linen and garments (Sir Leslie's) that hitherto had been ignored due to lack of someone with time to see to the task. They had merely been allowed to gather in a pile, with some being given to servants.

My first social appearance as Lady Kinwell came that Sunday. I dressed in a new gown, pelisse, and poke bonnet. Leslie also took care and wore a new coat of Bath superfine with pale pantaloons and a satin waistcoat. We set out in the tilbury. At the church everyone turned to stare. I overheard someone refer to us as a "handsome couple." Startled, I looked at Sir Leslie. Yes, I suppose some might call him handsome. A bitter smile played about my lips. What would they say if they knew the truth? As he had promised, Mr. Watly invoked a special blessing for us and announced the reception for the afternoon. Of course, this came as no surprise to the congregation, for everyone knew the castle servants had begun laying in provisions three days past. The service over, we stood in the doorway to be congratulated. Though all must have suspected there was something havey-cavey about the event, none spoke as though it were other than the most ordinary of marriages. I was relieved when Sir Leslie finally said we might return to the castle.

The servants had already set out the tables and food, and guests were arriving. There was no time to rest before we must again stand side by side to receive congratulations. A keg of ale was tapped and soon toasts were being drunk to our health and happiness. The hypocrisy of my position upset me, but there was nought I could do. So I smiled and danced with Sir Leslie the first dance. He had engaged musicians for the occasion, and I was grateful to Mrs. Gilwen for her insistence that all the young ladies under her care learn to dance. Though I was by no means an expert, I did not disgrace myself.

I danced not only with my husband, but as was the custom, with many men from the estate and nearby. By the time I retired to join Leslie at the table, my feet were sore; as much from being stepped upon as from the actual dancing.

The celebration continued well past nightfall, and of course, Sir Leslie and I could not retire before the last guest left. The departing men shot back lewd jests which I bore as best I might. How I longed to tell them that never would Sir Leslie share my bed, and that short of an immaculate conception the estate would never see me with child! Sir Leslie must have felt as I did, for as we returned to the castle he said wearily, "At last the farce is over!"

I paused on the steps long enough to say, "Oh? I was of the opinion it had just begun."

He turned away, headed, no doubt, for the liquor cabinet. I smiled and ascended to my chamber where Ellen waited to prepare me for bed. As she chattered about how nice I had looked and all the compliments paid me, I was tempted to offer to trade places with her. I wondered how she would answer. But that was absurd. I knew full well she considered me fortunate. How could she feel otherwise when she had no notion of what had passed between Sir Leslie and myself? But perhaps she did know. At the very least, Margaret and Mrs. Morgan had seen the evidence of the sheets. I was foolish to assume that neither had told any of the other servants. And who had washed the bed linen? No, in truth, Ellen might well know or have guessed what had taken place. And yet she still believed me fortunate. Truly the world was a strange place when people could view my position in such a way! With a sigh, I dismissed Ellen and began to brush my hair.

I had just checked the door to Sir Leslie's chamber to be sure it was bolted when there came a brief pounding at my door. I pulled my dressing gown closer about me and was prepared to answer when the door opened. Sir Leslie stood there cursing. In fear I backed away, wondering if there were ought at hand with which to defend myself. "Prepare your-self, madam," he thundered, "my sister arrives tomorrow and *you* must entertain her!" Pacing angrily, he said, "And if I know my sister, she'll bring that brat, her son! And *I'll* be expected to keep him occupied!"

Relief swept over me, and at the image of Sir Leslie playing with a small boy I began to laugh. He was not amused. "You will not find it so humourous after you have met her. She will pry until she learns the truth. I have told her nothing save the bare fact of our marriage. Tomorrow, before she arrives, we must settle on a suitable story."

I faced him, sobered now. "Is her husband coming as well?" Leslie shook his head. "Then, sir, I think you must chance the truth. You are a sapskull if you believe she will not ferret it out of the servants. It would be wisest, perhaps, to admit all to her and ask her aid in the matter. Unless, of course, she dislikes you and would use the knowledge dangerously."

"No, she is fond of me. Too fond. She will want to meddle." He sighed with exasperation. "In truth, she *would* ferret out what had happened. With anyone else I'd trust my servants, but not with Mary! Very well, I shall tell her myself. Later, you may tell her your version, if you wish."

With that, he turned and strode from my room, the door slamming behind him. I could not refrain from laughing. Sir Leslie had looked too much like a small boy who awaited a scolding. Nevertheless, I carefully bolted the door.

I rose earlier than was my habit, the next morning. I wished to be certain all would be in readiness for Sir Leslie's sister, Mary. Fortunately, Mrs. Morgan had given orders for the airing of the family rooms. "And the nursery?" I enquired.

"Whatever for?" she replied.

"Sir Leslie seemed to think his nephew would be coming also," I said.

Mrs. Morgan smiled. "Oh, he'll come, but he's not a child anymore. Why, he's older than yerself! Ye see, Sir Leslie was the youngest. Almost an afterthought, and certainly un-expected. Mary was the second youngest and he's always been close to her, but not the two elder sisters. Ye might have thought the late baronet would have been happy to have a son after three girls, but it seems he'd made up his mind he'd never have one, and when the master was born he looked upon the boy simply as a nuisance. Then there was the fact that the laying in was difficult for Lady Kinwell and she never fully recovered her health. I think the late baronet blamed Leslie for that. The poor lad, he—"

"Must you stand there gossiping?" an angry voice snapped. "I've just been to the kitchen and there's a crisis brewing!"

"Oh, dear," Mrs. Morgan exclaimed, "I'd best see to it at once."

"I shall accompany you," I said, anxious to be away from Sir Leslie's condemning gaze.

"No, you will not," he said. "If I know Mary, she'll arrive before noon. Mrs. Morgan is quite capable of coping with crises. You will return to your chamber and dress to receive my sister. Ellen is waiting. Thank God Mademoiselle Suzette is efficient! You'll find a suitable dress laid out for you."

I complied. I was becoming extremely curious to see this woman who could make Sir Leslie so sharp set. Somehow it made him seem less terrifying, knowing that someone existed who could do so.

Leslie had judged his sister well. I had scarcely changed and arranged my hair when her post-chaise and four halted outside the castle. I hurriedly descended to greet my new *belle-soeur*. I was in time to see her embrace Sir Leslie. She was almost as tall as he, and quite plump. "Where is your bride?" I heard her demand.

"Here I am," I answered and advanced with a smile. I sincerely hoped Mary would prove an ally. "How shocking of me not to be downstairs to greet you."

We embraced and then she began to chatter, "How pretty you are, my dear. And such a surprise. Leslie gave no hint he was dangling after anyone. How did you meet? Where were you married? How ever did your family react? Will you be going anywhere for your—"

"My dear Mary," Sir Leslie interrupted her, "you may ask Heather all those questions later. At the moment, I should like to speak with you in the library. I need your advice on one or two small matters."

"Why certainly, Leslie. Though it seems to me that you never heed the advice I give you. . . ."

She followed him down the hallway and as I turned to look

for Mrs. Morgan a voice stopped me. "Hallo. Could you tell me what happened to my mother?"

The speaker was a tall young man of about twenty years. He was well dressed and handsome, in a boyish sort of way. His shirt points were high, his shoulders padded, and his neckcloth tied in an ambitious but not altogether successful manner. He had, moreover, Sir Leslie's dark eyes, but in this young man they seemed friendly and gentle. "She is in the library with Sir Leslie, I believe," I answered.

"Oh. Well I shan't disturb them. My uncle ain't overly fond of me," he confided. "But you're new here, ain't you?" I signified I was. "M'mother says Uncle Leslie has gotten himself leg-shackled. Tenant-for-life! Has he?" I nodded and the boy went on, "Is she pretty?"

I suppressed a smile. "I believe some consider her to be."

"Is *she* like *him*? You know, rather prosy and forbidding?"

"I should hardly call Sir Leslie prosy though I agree he is forbidding at times." I grinned. "As for his wife, I believe neither is true."

"Then why did he marry her?" the young man persisted. "Is she an heiress? No, that's silly, he's rich as Croesus, though a bit of a nip-farthing."

"It was . . . one of those things," I said in a voice that sounded unsteady even to me. "Perhaps I ought to tell you, *I* am Sir Leslie's new wife. My name is Heather."

"You're roasting me!" he exclaimed. "He's old enough to be your father!"

I laughed, "Not unless he entered fatherhood at the age of twelve."

"Well, I suppose not. But look here, this is the outside of enough! You can not really be married to him."

The dismay was evident in his voice. I was beginning to like my husband's nephew. Yet it was curious. In that, our first meeting, I felt the elder, though I knew in years I was the younger. "Won't you tell me your name?" I asked.

He flushed. "Philip. Philip Gainesfield." He began to regain his composure. "Of course, I ought to be at the university at the moment. But when Mother heard of your marriage, she said I ought to come pay my respects. I had no notion my uncle had married someone so, well, like you!"

"I'm sorry I disrupted your studies," I said with some amusement.

Philip shifted uneasily, "Not your fault! Anyway, glad of an excuse for a vacation."

I smiled in sympathy. I was too soon out of the schoolroom not to understand how Philip felt. "Well, shall we retire to the drawing room? Sir Leslie and your mother will presumably join us there shortly," was all I said, however.

He nodded and offered me his arm. As we entered the drawing room I asked Philip if he wished any sort of refreshment. He indicated he would like a bit of something from the liquor cabinet, but I was uncertain as to what Sir Leslie's response would have been. At what age was it acceptable for young men to drink? Still, it would be rude to refuse. As he sipped from his glass Philip said, "Tell me. How does it feel to be married to Uncle Leslie?"

"Unusual," I replied, "and still somewhat unreal."

He grunted. "That I can well believe!"

"I understand all newlywed couples feel that way," Sir Leslie said from the doorway. "Isn't it a bit early in the day to be drinking, Philip? My dear Heather, you must not indulge the *boy*."

I stiffened at Sir Leslie's manner. "I had always thought young men of university age to be quite capable of making their own decisions," I retorted quietly.

"Oh, indeed, they *ought* to be," my husband replied.

Philip flushed and would have spoken, but Mary did not let him. "Heather, dear, I want a comfortable case with you! Shall we nip up to my room until lunch? I want to truly welcome you into the family."

I nodded and Sir Leslie stepped aside to let me pass. Arm in arm, as Mary chattered about her journey we proceeded to her chamber. Her things had already been put away and Mary dismissed her maid. As the door closed behind the woman Mary turned to me. "My poor child! Leslie is a beast! He told me what happened and you may be quite sure I told him precisely what I thought of his behaviour. Are you quite overset? Has he maltreated you? If he does, let me know at once and I will put a stop to that. Just like a man to feel he must force you into marriage and that that would resolve everything! If he had only come to me . . . But this thing is done and cannot be undone, so we must make the best of it. I have already told Leslie he must legally settle a competence on you. And that you must enter the *ton* under my wing. Men! Are they all fools, or only the ones I know?''

I grinned. If I had liked Philip, I liked his mother far better. Yes, she would be a formidable ally. She continued, ''It is too early to know, of course, but if you are, well, breeding, have Leslie notify me at once. I daresay you will be so angry at him you shan't want to see him. And if you preferred, you could come stay with me until the child was born. Oh, my poor dear, you must be dreadfully cast down! Though I must say, I should have had no notion of it from the way you greeted me.''

I sighed. ''I am learning to act a part. Sir Leslie has assured me that in private we need have nought to do with each other, but that in public our marriage must appear normal.''

''Sensible,'' Mary replied, ''though I cannot help but feel it is an unfair burden on you. But you seem to be a sensible young woman. However did you land in the briars like this?''

''I *might* be sensible, but I was very green,'' I said wryly. ''It never occurred to me that Mr. Thornsby's establishment was other than an ordinary domestic agency. Or that the word 'companion' might mean . . .''

''Quite!'' Mary said. ''We are supposed to be naive and innocent and then this sort of thing happens. If I had a daughter, you may be sure she would know precisely what dangers to expect from men.''

''Philip is your only child?'' I asked in surprise.

''Goodness, no. I've three other boys, but they are much younger,'' she said confidingly. ''You see, for a time after Philip was born, my husband and I were, well, at outs with one another. Later we reconciled and now we are reasonably content. He is a dear, sweet fellow who denies me nothing. And I look after him.''

It seemed a rather strange way to view one's husband, but I was scarcely in a position to know what was ordinary. Before I could settle upon a suitable response, she spoke again. ''My dear, I would not tell anyone else the details of your . . . er . . . marriage to Leslie. Particularly Philip. They are not fond of one another even now, and Philip might, well, do something. He might even be so goosish as to tell his friends and I needn't tell you, my dear, that that would not help your reputation.''

I nodded. "I suspected Sir Leslie and Philip were at dagger point and I'm afraid I did not help matters."

"Oh, fustian. Regardless of what you might say or do, they would come to cuffs," Mary said regretfully. "Indeed, I suppose we ought to rejoin them."

I agreed. Privately, however, I wondered at Mary's insistence upon Philip's company here when she knew Sir Leslie so disliked him. Leslie was alone in the drawing room, and at Mary's questioning glance, he said, "I had Mrs. Morgan show the halfling to his room so that he might wash before lunch."

"You didn't quarrel, did you, Leslie?" she asked.

Leslie smiled wryly, "Do I ever quarrel? I am sorry, Mary, but it disturbs me to see Philip's heedlessness. I promise I shall try, however, to be more tolerant."

Clearly Mary was not satisfied, but there was little she could say. Sir Leslie had not, after all, invited Mary or Philip. We stood thus when Philip reentered. "My dear *Aunt Heather*," he said, "I am terribly sorry if I have kept you waiting."

From the corner of my eye, I could see Sir Leslie's scowl. I replied sweetly, "You are not late at all, *nephew*. Shall we go in to lunch?"

Philip offered me his arm and I was about to take it when Sir Leslie stepped between us. "A bridegroom does not relinquish such privileges easily," he said calmly, and offered *his* arm.

Reluctantly I took it and he placed his other hand over mine. As we moved to the dining hall he squeezed my hand harshly and murmured, "I warn you to take care, madam. I will not tolerate you joining with my scapegrace nephew to mock me."

Subdued, I stared at the floor. I had no notion of the nature of the conflict between Sir Leslie and his nephew and it was unfair of me to take sides. Indeed, it was foolish. Mary had counselled me not to confide in Philip. If I continued in this manner would he not guess that something was amiss between Leslie and myself? Meekly I allowed myself to be seated, avoiding Philip's questioning gaze and Leslie's penetrating stare. There was no lack of conversation, however, as Mary told us all the recent activities of her three younger sons. Of Philip she spoke little and I wondered at the omission. But perhaps she was simply reluctant to speak of him when he was present. Sir Leslie unbent sufficiently to give the proper responses. As for me, I was truly interested. Never having known a brother, I was curious as to how they behaved. Philip was bored, but that was to be expected. Then Mary began to discuss Mrs. Gilwen's school. "A most well thought of establishment, my dear. I presume her emphasis on the proprieties and etiquette is as strong as ever? Excellent. And if the reputation of the school is justified, you are an accomplished needlewoman?"

"Well enough," I replied. "Though I prefer tapestry work, I am able to cope with basic stitching needs such as hems and buttons." I could not resist adding mischievously, "Since my arrival I've had quite an opportunity to use my skill. Leslie seems to delight in losing buttons and acquiring small tears in his shirts."

"You've been repairing them?" Leslie exclaimed incredulously.

"Who else?" I asked. "Did you think the fairies or leprechauns had begun visiting the castle?"

Mary laughed. "Good heavens, Leslie, are you kicking up a fuss? Perhaps, Heather, he was glad of the excuse to order new clothes before."

"No, of course not," Leslie said hastily. "I simply was surprised. I have not yet had time to acquaint myself with all of my wife's accomplishments. What other surprises have you for me, Heather?"

"Music or perhaps art?" Mary suggested.

I shook my head regretfully. "I am afraid I have no skill in either."

"Riding?" Philip asked.

I laughed. "I had no opportunity to learn in the center of London."

"Well, you must now," Philip said eagerly, "and I should be pleased to teach you."

"I believe that is my privilege," Leslie said dryly. "I have a mare that is an extremely gentle mount, Heather."

I murmured assent. I dared not say that I would prefer Philip as a tutor. Mary spoke next, "It is really an excellent establishment, Leslie."

"Yes, but did she learn anything aside from needlework there?" he asked impatiently.

Stung, I retorted, "Nothing you would consider of consequence. Simply a smattering of history, the classics, science, politics, French, German, and geography. I am very sorry but I was more interested in my books than in learning how to please *men*!"

Close to tears, I stared down at my plate as the others regarded me in shocked silence. Nor did Philip's subsequent words improve matters. "Well, you seem to have pleased at least one man. After all, Uncle Leslie married you, didn't he?"

Mary spoke hastily, "Politics, Heather? I was not aware it was taught in schools for young ladies."

"Well, of course it is not a regular subject," I explained. "However, one of the teachers was very interested in politics and we often discussed current events. On occasion, we would acquire all the pamphlets printed concerning a particular issue and discuss them. Though I am afraid Miss Hall never seemed to understand them very well."

"Frankly"—Philip yawned—"I don't see why an attractive young woman would want to bother about such things."

"Why not?" I retorted.

"Well, because such topics are much too weighty," he replied, surprised at my question.

Sir Leslie chuckled and I glared at him. I suppose he expected me to be a docile little wet-goose. Well I was very sorry but I could not accommodate him! At my fierce expression, Leslie laughed harder. "Be careful, Philip. My wife can be a tigress when angry."

Philip inclined his head toward me. "Oh, very well. Clearly, Aunt Heather, you are exceptional."

I smiled, but without warmth. I knew Mrs. Gilwen would have condemned my behaviour as most unladylike. But I did not care. There were some matters on which I could not yield. One of these was the demand by any man that his preferences precede all others. Mary was, as soon we came to expect her to be, the peacemaker. "Well, Leslie," she said. "You always said you wanted an unusual wife. You certainly have found one. Heather, I am delighted to know my new *belle-soeur* is not a ninnyhammer. Philip, a pretty face is not all that matters. Now, I am tired of the topic and I forbid it for the rest of the meal."

"What would you suggest we discuss?" Leslie asked meekly.

"Well, I am sure I do not know." Mary huffed. "Think of something."

"Have you met our vicar, Mr. Watly yet, Heather? I mean Aunt Heather," Philip asked with a grin.

"Oh, yes," I replied, "he officiated at our wedding."

"And he gave you advice on the responsibilities of marriage, I'll wager." Philip laughed. When I nodded, he began to imitate the vicar's voice. "Marriage is like a seed one plants. Given careful tending, it grows and flourishes. . . ."

"Do you think the advice so absurd?" Leslie asked.

"No," Philip answered honestly, "of course not. It is Mr. Watly I find absurd."

"You know him well?" I asked in surprise.

Philip grinned. "Does one need to?"

"Philip!" Mary exclaimed angrily. "Whatever your opinion of him, he is a man of the cloth and due respect."

"But tell me," I persisted, "how is it you know his marriage speech? Surely *you* have not been married."

"No, but I was at Uncle's first wedding."

I blanched. "F-first wedding?" I stammered, feeling a trifle faint.

"Philip, you may leave the table at once!" Sir Leslie said in deadly calm.

We waited until Philip sauntered from the room smiling. "Heather," Mary began tentatively.

"There was no first wedding," Sir Leslie said harshly. "I was betrothed. The young woman changed her mind. In the church. Mr. Watly tried to convince her to go on with the ceremony. She refused. I am surprised that even in school you did not hear of it. It was quite an *on-dit!*"

With that, he rose and strode from the room. "Oh, dear," Mary exclaimed. "I had hoped you need not hear of this, Heather. Leslie was younger then. . . . Pray forget it, my dear."

"But why?" I asked. "I mean, why did she wait until the church? And what happened to her?"

"I don't know." Mary fluttered. "My dear, you must excuse me."

And then I was alone, feeling slightly ill.

Chapter 5

Ellen greeted me at the door of my room. "My lady! You look so pale!"

I flushed and drew myself straighter. "I am merely tired, Ellen. Ellen, have you heard about Sir Leslie's prior betrothal?"

"Ah, so that's what overset you. Well," she said confidingly, "of course I was too young at the time to remember it myself. But . . . the servants here told me about it. I thought Sir Leslie had probably explained himself and if not, well, it wouldn't be my place to tell tales." Ellen hesitated, "But since you asked me . . . It seems Sir Leslie fell in love with a young woman, Jane—I think her name was. Well! Jane was in love with some young care-for-nothing her parents refused to let her marry. Why they didn't just elope *I* can't say, but it seems the young man refused. Well! Jane agreed to marry Sir Leslie. Everyone was happy, except Jane and the young man of course, and the arrangements were made. It was to be a lovely wedding. Then, that day, in the church, she said she wouldn't! Well! There she was in her wedding gown and all the guests. The vicar tried to convince her to marry Sir Leslie, but Jane refused. Everyone was quite shocked and wondered what Sir Leslie had done to make Jane cry off. But one of the maids happened to hear Jane telling her parents. Well! It seems she never actually meant to marry Sir Leslie. She had decided that if she did what she did, her parents would have to agree she was ruined and let her marry her young man. And they did of course. Though not immediately. And poor Sir Leslie! He really had been in love with her, it seems. And I needn't tell you he was eyed askance after that affair. I mean, everyone assumed he must have done something to scare the lady off. It was sometime after that he started having young women sent up . . . . oh! I'm sorry, my lady. I didn't mean to remind you . . ."

So Ellen did know what had happened to me. "It seems the servants are rather free with their words," I said reprovingly.

"Oh, never outside the castle. I swear. They all think too highly of Sir Leslie to—"

"Too highly!" I ejaculated.

"Well, of course, in that respect they . . . But in other ways . . ."

"Enough, Ellen," I said. "I would rather not hear anyone sing Sir Leslie's praises. In fact I would rather not hear any discussions of him."

"Yes, of course. Would you care to rest, my lady?"

I was tempted. But I might be needed. "No, Ellen. I shall be in the library," I replied.

As was my habit, I chose a book and ensconced in a chair, my feet tucked under me. Sir Leslie rarely used the library at this hour and I knew I should have privacy. I cannot say why the library seemed such a refuge to me but it did. Thus I was engrossed in a book when someone entered. I glanced up. At the same moment, Sir Leslie saw me and started. Then, calmly, he walked over and sat in a chair near me. "Are you also hiding from my family?" he asked.

In spite of myself, I smiled. "In a way."

He sighed. "I love my sister dearly, but her visits always cut up my peace. What are you reading?"

I showed him the cover of my book. Leslie was surprised. "Mitford's *History of Greece*? So you truly meant it earlier when you said you were a bluestocking?"

I stiffened. I would not tolerate any disparaging remarks from Sir Leslie. He eyed me oddly. "You seem to have startled Philip." When I shrugged, he laughed.

"I daresay most of the young women he knows are bubble-headed things," I countered.

"True," Sir Leslie conceded, "but do you believe he prefers a scholar?"

"Of—of course," I responded uncertainly.

Sir Leslie snorted, "You truly are green about men!"

"And you about women," I retorted angrily, "if Jane and I are examples! I believe the reason you dislike Philip is that he reminds you of incidents you would prefer to forget."

52

Leslie stared at me for a moment, then stood, towering over me. "So someone has been gossiping. I neither know nor wish to know what Banbury tales you have been told. Clearly you would not believe the truth so I shall not waste my time in futile explanation. But pray have care with your tongue, madam. I also am capable of wounding with words."

I half rose from my chair in protest. I did not mean the words in the manner he had interpreted them. But it was too late. The slammed door announced he was gone before my apology was even half framed. I was too agitated to read and I set my book aside. I must apologise to Sir Leslie. But how? He was sufficiently overset that I knew he would not listen to any words I might try to say. I did not like Sir Leslie, and I had good cause to harbour ill will. But in this, if I were honest with myself, I had wronged him. And in truth, in the matter of Jane, my sympathies resided with Sir Leslie. I knew from my school years how feckless a young woman might be. I was beginning to recognise that for Sir Leslie, as for myself, the situation was neither a happy nor an easy one. And my behaviour did not aid matters.

I searched his desk and, finding paper, pen, and ink, set myself to the task of composing a suitable note. How to begin? I could scarcely write: *My Dearest Leslie*, or any similar form of address. Though I searched my memory, I knew there was no protocol in such a case. *Sir Leslie* was too formal and *Leslie* still seemed to intimate. The use of *my husband* could only serve to remind him he was shackled to me. At last I settled upon a letter that did not please me, but would, nonetheless, serve the purpose.

Leslie,

No doubt you believe me to be unspeakably rude and unthinking. I cannot say you are without justification. My behaviour this afternoon was unpardonable. You believed me to have been told falsehoods. I have not even that excuse, for your servants are too loyal to speak other than with complete fairness of you. I knew that in the matter of Jane you were in no way at fault. I should not have spoken of it when I could not help but know it would be distasteful to you.

In the future I shall endeavour to curb my tongue,

but I fear I shall not always be successful. I pray that on this occasion you will accept my apology.

Heather

Nervously, I surveyed what I had written. It would have to suffice. How to deliver it? If I summoned a servant, the entire household would know by nightfall. I must place it either in Leslie's or his valet's hands myself. I folded it carefully, determined not to delay the matter.

I knocked hesitantly, twice, before his chamber door opened. "Yes, my lady?" Peter asked coldly but respectfully.

I held out my note, "I do not wish to disturb Sir Leslie, but pray give him this as soon as it is convenient to do so."

"My lady," he said, taking the note, "if I may say so, Sir Leslie is sadly out of curl at the moment. If this will disturb him further—"

I brought Peter up short. "It should not. It may even improve matters."

"Very well, my lady," he said dubiously, "do you expect an answer?"

"No," I turned to withdraw, then paused to say, "Thank you, Peter."

The valet bowed and closed the door. I imagined him approaching Leslie with the note, in trepidation. Or perhaps he would read it first. Certainly he was in Leslie's confidence. I only hoped he was as discreet as Leslie believed him to be. I was debating whether I might have time for a walk before tea when Mrs. Morgan encountered me in the hallway. "My lady," she said, "will ye have tea in yer chamber this afternoon? As the others are?"

She seemed distressed so I replied soothingly, "It means extra work, doesn't it? Separate pots of tea and all. Well, you needn't bother with mine. I shall not take tea today."

"Not take tea?" she exclaimed.

"No, I am going for a walk," I said and departed, leaving her staring after me.

I walked directly to the copse of trees, for sitting by the stream always soothed me. And within the copse I could not be seen from the castle and thus no one could come to call me back. I had come to love the estate, and in different circumstances might have been happy here. As matters stood, the serenity of the fields and woods kept me from complete despair.

It was late when I retraced my steps to the castle, and I was fortified with the resolution to behave more reasonably in the future. I went immediately to my chamber in order to dress for dinner. To my surprise, a spray of roses sat in a bowl on the table beside my bed. "What? How?" I exclaimed.

Ellen was as mystified as I. "I don't quite know, my lady. Peter, Sir Leslie's valet, brought them. Said they were the first from the garden. The master's orders. But why, I wouldn't know, my lady."

I smiled. "The blue gown, this evening," I merely said. "I would not have Lady Mary believe me to still be a green schoolgirl."

By the time I reached the drawing room, Mary was already there. "You look lovely," she said as she greeted me.

"Thank you and good evening," I replied. "Did you rest well after your journey?"

"Yes, but—Good evening, Leslie," she broke off.

I turned to see my husband standing in the doorway. As he greeted us my eyes met his for a moment and he smiled. I glanced away hastily. I had apologised for my rude behaviour but I did not wish Sir Leslie to believe I meant more than that. In the next moment, to my relief, Philip joined us. "Good evening everyone. I'm not late, am I?" he asked.

A measure of Leslie's improved mood was that he answered affably, "Not at all, Philip."

Philip stared at him in surprise. We *were,* however, somewhat late, so I placed my hand on Leslie's arm and said, "Shall we go in to table?"

Aware of Leslie's eyes on me, I stared at the floor. Neither of us spoke; neither of us referred to the afternoon or my subsequent note. When, after we were seated, I dared glance at him, Sir Leslie was no longer staring at me and I relaxed. Philip, enjoying the favourable mood, regaled us with stories of university life.

"But when do you have time for your studies?" I asked at one point.

"Oh, no one *studies.* One goes to the university to learn about *life.* One cannot get that from books!" Philip shrugged.

Leslie raised an eyebrow but said nothing. Mary shook her

head but smiled. I was not satisfied with the answer, but instead of persisting, I asked, "Which university are you at, Philip? You've not said."

Philip shifted uncomfortably and Leslie and Mary looked uneasy. "Well, my dear, actually . . ." Mary began.

"Philip is rusticating at the moment," Leslie said abruptly. "He was sent down from Oxford last week."

"And I suppose you never kicked up a lark when you were there!" Philip retorted.

Leslie chuckled, "Ah, but I was never caught." After a moment, he continued, "I remember once we managed to bar the dean into his office just before he was due to give an important speech. We would certainly have been sent down if the fellow had only known who we were."

Mary began to laugh. "Leslie! You never told us! But I remember the incident because Father was visiting me and he had heard of it. Though I am quite sure he had no notion you had been involved. He gave quite a sermon on responsibility and the lack of it among university students. Indeed he said he was happy to know *his* son would never do anything of the sort!"

Philip grinned. "It is still talked of at Oxford. It seems the dean was so overset that, immediately he was released, he appeared with his wig askew. What else did you accomplish while there?"

Leslie shook his head, "Now, now. I'll not give you ideas. You must think of your own pranks. After you've finished with the university we can compare notes."

A thought suddenly occurred to Philip. "You weren't involved in the bathing scandal?"

One look at Leslie's face was sufficient to confirm the suspicion. "What was the bathing scandal?" I asked, delighted.

"I don't wish to hear about it!" Mary exclaimed.

Philip ignored her. "It seems that in Uncle Leslie's day. . ."

Leslie stopped him. "If she must know, I'd better explain it. I am not certain what version is circulating now. Well, Heather, there was a somewhat eccentric don who used to bathe in nearby lakes and rivers. One day, one of my friends spied him and shared the knowledge with a group of us. I am afraid we were on a spree for we conceived the following plan. For several days, we watched the spot until finally the don returned to bathe there. We waited until he shed his clothes and entered the water. Alone. It never seems to have occurred to the fellow that it might be foolish to leave his clothes unguarded. At any rate, we scooped them up and carried them off with us."

Philip was laughing, as was I. Mary asked, "How did the poor fellow contrive?"

Leslie laughed. "That was the best part of it. The don was resourceful and fashioned a sort of covering from leaves and branches. Then, keeping to hedges and so on, proceeded to walk home. At some point someone noticed him and, deciding the fellow was mad and ought to be clapped up in bedlam, gave chase. The don was near home and decided to run for it. As he crossed the field to his lodging the covering dropped away and he was in the buff for all the world to see. He had a great deal of difficulty convincing the authorities he was sane and ought not to be carted away!"

"Leslie!" Mary said reprovingly, "how disgraceful."

Although I agreed, I also could not help wishing I had been born a man so that I could attend Oxford and take part in such things. I must have voiced part of the thought aloud for Philip exclaimed, "What a henwitted notion! And I daresay Uncle Leslie feels so more strongly than I!"

Leslie replied, after a moment, "Well, I certainly shouldn't have married Heather in that event."

"I am quite happy not to have been born a man," Mary said with dignity. "I don't think I should have enjoyed it at all."

I reached for my wineglass and, finding it empty, turned to ask to have it refilled. As I did so Leslie caught my eye and discreetly shook his head. For a moment I was angry: how dare he presume to say I could not have more? But then I realised he might have cause. My head felt light, my hand a trifle unsteady, and words tripped a little too quickly off my tongue. I glanced at Leslie guiltily, but he smiled reassuringly.

". . . not set Philip a bad example, Leslie," Mary was saying.

"I'm sorry, Mary," he said and, turning to Philip, admonished, "You are not to take my behaviour as a model." A twinkle in his eyes belied the stiffness of his words. "Except, of course, in the fact that I was never caught!"

"Leslie!" Mary said despairingly. "I swear, Heather, that I am glad he is not *my* husband."

And I wish he were not mine! I wanted to say, but did not. Reminded of my situation, I could no longer enjoy the comfortable atmosphere. Philip must have noticed, for he spoke hastily, "I say, Aunt Heather, don't cut up stiff! Mother's only roasting you."

I forced myself to smile and say lightly, "Of course. And since she is *not* married to Leslie, it scarcely matters, does it?"

Leslie regarded me grimly over the rim of his wineglass. But he spoke lightly also, "I am afraid, Heather, that all my life Mary has been trying to take care of me and keep me out of trouble. A thankless task."

Philip seemed amused by the exchange. I wondered if he now considered Leslie more human. I hoped so, for the tensions earlier in the day distressed me. And, selfishly, I welcomed Philip's company and felt that if the two were at ease with each other, Philip might remain longer. Mary also, of course, but while over the years I had had a surfeit of female companions, I felt starved for male companionship. Particularly male companionship that carried with it no possible complications and no emotional demands.

The men remained behind with their port while Mary and I withdrew. "My dear," she said, when we were alone, "I am happy to see Leslie in a better frame of mind. I wonder what might have happened? Well, no matter. Tell me, my dear. Have you any plans for refurbishing the castle?"

I shook my head. "I hardly feel it my place to make such changes. I cannot feel I have the right."

"Nonsense!" she said firmly. "You are Lady Kinwell! You've every right to do as you choose. And if Leslie questions that I shall tell him so to his head. You must not let Leslie overset you!"

"But I am not sure I wish to make any changes," I protested.

"Of course you do," she retorted. "Tomorrow we shall go around the castle together and form our plans."

I stared at her helplessly. Mary simply did not understand how I felt. She spoke soothingly, "There, there. Truly, Leslie is not an ogre, as you would discover if you but gave him the opportunity to show you his gentler side."

Perhaps. But I could not see how Mary's scheme could do other than set up his back. Though no doubt she knew Leslie better than I. I was freed from finding an answer by the timely entry of the men. I was soon placed, however, in a more awkward position. "Heather," Mary said, "perhaps you might entertain us? With some music?"

It was not, of course, her fault that she did not remember. "You must excuse me," I replied as patiently as I was able, "but I have no ability, either with my voice or any other instrument."

"How fortunate," Leslie said dryly, "for there are few things I detest more than the sort of inane musical accomplishments most young ladies obtain. I would far rather spend the evening quietly reading."

My relief at Leslie's intervention was so great that I smiled at him. Mary was not so pleased. "Well, you shall not be so unsociable *this* evening, Leslie. Heather, are you familiar with ecarté?"

I signified I was and she called for a card table. Leslie and I were to be partners, it seemed. I dearly hoped he was not the sort of fellow who treated cards as a crucial matter. As the evening progressed, however, I discovered there was no need for concern. We were both competent players and frequently we trounced Mary and Philip. Indeed, it was Mary who called a halt to the cards in obvious poor temper. "It is rather late," she said, "I think I shall retire."

Philip was cheerful despite the losses. "You are quite good, Heather. Have you and Uncle Leslie been practising?"

I smiled and shook my head. Leslie replied, "I am as surprised as you are, Philip. It is another of her accomplishments that my wife neglected to inform me of."

"If you knew so little about her," Philip bantered, "why did you marry her?"

Leslie hesitated, "It was . . . one of those things."

Philip frowned. "That's exactly what Aunt Heather said. Really . . ."

"Really," Leslie said wearily, "aren't you being rather ungallant? The proper response would be that seeing Heather you had no need to ask why one would offer for her."

Philip flushed. "Well, of course. I meant . . ."

"Philip," Mary said firmly, "we shall *both* retire now. No doubt Leslie and Heather would prefer privacy."

She swept out of the room, Philip at her heels. I felt it a shame that Mary and Leslie should still treat him as a child. And if *he* were a child, then what of me? When they had gone, Leslie turned to stare at the empty fireplace. "I must apologise for my family," he said. "It seems they have never learned the art of tact. Philip in particular. But then, he is young."

"No younger than I," I retorted.

He turned to face me. "No. No younger than you. Confound it, girl, must you always be so niffy-naffy?" he demanded.

I stiffened. "And why should I not be? Neither you nor Mary appear to give Philip the respect or consideration due him."

"You've a high opinion of Philip, haven't you?" Leslie asked quietly.

"And why not?" I demanded hotly. "He has been kinder to me than anyone else I've met since I left school."

Leslie flushed. "Does that include my sister? Or Mrs. Morgan? Don't you simply mean he has been kinder to you than I have?"

I threw my head back. "All right. Yes. That is precisely what I mean."

"Why?" Leslie asked harshly. "Because he hasn't ravished you? Give him half a chance and he will."

I opened my mouth to reply but I was too shocked to speak. I turned and started to leave the room. Before I could take more than a few steps, a hand closed on the back of my neck and halted me. "Why do you insist on provoking me?" Leslie whispered from above. "Lord knows I resolve to be patient. But always you cause me to forget my resolve." His hand closed tighter. "I would dearly love to shake you as you deserve! But that would scarcely improve matters. Nothing short of removing your tongue . . . and even then you would find some way of expressing your contempt and hatred for me! You said that your behaviour is unpardonable and unspeakably rude. You are quite correct, madam. You also said you were afraid you could not curb your tongue. Well, I suggest you try or I shall not be able to curb my temper!" He released me. "Go to bed," he said contemptuously.

I turned and stared up at him. "I hate you!" I whispered. "I hate you and I always shall!"

And then I fled up the stairs to my chamber. Behind me the door slammed shut and I frantically bolted it. Finally I threw myself on the bed to cry.

Chapter 6

I woke early the next morning. The scent of roses assailed me as I realised I must have at some point undressed. In the calm of morning my hysteria of the night before seemed unjustified. I did not excuse Leslie's behaviour, but I could admit that I had provoked him. I rang for morning tea, unwilling to descend and face anyone over the dining table so early in the day. Ellen arrived with Margaret. "My lady," she said excitedly, "the trunks from Mademoiselle have arrived! Shall I have them sent up?"

"After I've dressed," I said smiling, for Ellen seemed more pleased than I could feel. "Tell me, Ellen. Have the others risen yet?"

"Oh, yes, my lady," she replied. "Master Philip is out riding; Sir Leslie is dining; and his sister is taking tea in her chamber. Margaret said she asked the same question."

I sighed. I truly hoped Mary had forgotten her determination to help me refurbish the castle. For in truth I liked the household as it was. Nor did I wish to antagonise Leslie. I hated him and did not wish to weaken my position in any way by putting myself in the wrong. Ellen helped me dress, choosing the green morning costume. I then relaxed over tea, postponing the moment when I must face Mary. Ellen directed John as he brought the trunks of clothes to my chamber. I could not say Leslie had been ungenerous. There were four trunks and, according to Ellen, four more to come later. At last, I could delay no longer, and leaving Ellen to put away my new outfits, I descended to the morning room. Mary was, as I expected, waiting for me. "Good morning, my dear," she said. "How delighted I am to see you are an early riser. Have you eaten? Good. Did you sleep well? Excellent. Well, shall we begin with here?''

"Mary, I . . ." I began, then I saw Leslie in the doorway.

The memory of the previous evening caused me to stiffen with fear. What if he were angry still? "Good morning Mary, Heather," he said impassively. "Mary, whatever your plans, you must delay them. I have decided to give Heather her first riding lesson."

"I—I have no habit," I stammered.

"It is among the things delivered today," Leslie said inflexibly.

"Leslie, don't ride roughshod over the child!" Mary said angrily.

Without answering her, Leslie said to me, "Go change to your habit."

I was afraid, but preferred to face Leslie now if he must be faced. I could not gauge his mood, but did not believe he would threaten me with more than words. And I did not wish him to believe me pudding hearted. While in sight of the morning room, I ascended the stairs slowly. After that, however, I fairly fled to my chamber. Ellen was still unpacking. "My riding habit!" I ordered.

"Just a moment," she said, "I haven't found it yet. Ah, here it is."

The outfit was a beautiful shade of blue and when I tried it on, I could see it was of the first stare. I might have envied the experience of choosing my own clothes, but I had to admit that between them, Leslie and Mademoiselle Suzette had excellent taste. No other riding costume could have suited me better. Ellen also was pleased. "You look that lovely, my lady," she said.

I sighed. If only there were some man to whom it might matter. Perhaps in time . . . no. Leslie spoke of affairs, but to what point? I could not envision finding pleasure in the act I had experienced with Leslie. And that was the usual goal of affairs, was it not? Ellen broke into my reverie, "My lady, is someone waiting for you?"

"Oh!" I gasped, "Sir Leslie!"

I hurried to join him. He was standing by the morning-room door and Mary still stood inside. She was frowning at him. "You'll remember what I said, Leslie?" she demanded.

"I'll not have you mistreating Heather. And you had better have a gentle mare for her."

"Yes, Mary," Leslie replied crisply, "I have heard all you said. Come, Heather."

He turned and strode away. Leslie had long limbs and it was with difficulty that I kept pace with him. I was beginning to regret giving my assent to this riding lesson. In the stable yard, two horses stood waiting. I had not the least knowledge of horses, but the love and respect with which the groom stroked them told me these were prime blood. Even the smaller horse, however, seemed of overwhelming size. My heart began to pound and I swallowed. I could not mount this beast! But Leslie was waiting and I would not cry craven. I moved forward, then was being helped up. And then I was seated on the mare. I forced myself to sit calmly, not wanting to communicate my unease to the mare. I held the reins loosely and waited as Leslie mounted. The horses began to move slowly. As I realised my perch was not as precarious as it seemed, I began to gain confidence. And finally I could breathe normally again. I even found the courage to smile. Leslie had been watching me carefully, for now he smiled also and nodded. "Good girl. You've a sound seat for someone who has never ridden before." He regarded me oddly for a moment. "You were very much afraid of mounting, weren't you?"

"Was it that obvious?" I asked.

He laughed. "Not if one ignored the expression on your face or its abnormal pallor. You've more courage than I would expect of a young woman of your background. Most young ladies your age seem to prefer fainting to facing matters squarely. What I can not understand is why you are so afraid to face me."

I turned to eye him. "I would have thought the answer obvious. But very well, I am not afraid to face you. What is it you wish to discuss? Last evening's words?"

He looked weary. "To what point? You have already made your feelings clear to me through Mary. I understand that I might have overset you, but I wish you had not chosen to run to my sister to complain of Turkish treatment."

For a moment I was speechless, veering between anger and amazement. Anger prevailed. "What sort of a ninnyhammer do you take me for?" I demanded. "To complain to Mary

64

would only add one more complication to my life. Oh, do not be deceived, sir, I count Mary an ally, but not one to be called upon for every trifle! If I wish to protest, I shall do so to you directly or I shall not do so at all!''

I was breathing heavily then and my mare began to grow uneasy. Leslie reached out and laid a steadying hand on her neck. "It seems I misunderstood my sister," he said calmly. "She is very concerned about you. One of the servants must have told her I have been ill-treating you."

Although this was none of my doing, I felt guilty. I wanted to protest that I had not gossiped indiscreetly with the servants, but could not be certain I had never spoken too freely. Then Leslie said, "I apologise for ordering you to have this riding lesson, but I could not feel you truly wished to spend the morning with my sister. Drastic measures were necessary."

I laughed. "In truth, you were quite correct!" Impulsively I said, "Oh, Leslie, she wants me to change all the rooms about. And I haven't the faintest wish to do so! Mary talks about papers and fabrics and never seems to hear or believe me when I say that I prefer things as they are."

Leslie laughed deeply. "Heather, you will drive Mary to distraction! For years she has been eager to refurbish the castle for me. I daresay she cannot understand a woman who does not care for such things."

"Shall I let her then?" I asked.

"Lord no!" he replied.

I nodded, satisfied, then hesitantly said, "I also felt that perhaps it was not, well, quite my place to meddle."

Leslie halted his horse, blocking mine as he did so. "Heather, I know ours is not an ordinary marriage. But I do not ever wish you to feel that the privileges and rights of a wife are something you must bargain for. It *is* your place to make changes about the castle if you wish to do so. I shall not begrudge you the expense."

He stared at me and I answered honestly, "But I don't! As for my position, you are very generous. I should not have been surprised if you had felt I was due less."

Leslie sighed. "I cannot chide you for how you feel about me. The reason is too obvious." Then he added earnestly, "You understand, Heather, that if what happened could be undone, I would have it so."

I looked away, shuddering. "Please. I do not wish to discuss it. Of what use is your regret now? Though I can accept that you would not have acted as you did had you known . . . this cannot change what I feel.''

He turned his horse and we began to ride again. At first, Leslie did not speak. What answer could he have given to my words? And I? I was gaining confidence and beginning to enjoy the sensation of being on horseback. It was a beautiful sunny day, and I almost began to feel friendly toward Leslie. It is difficult to hate someone who shares one's love of nature. "Tomorrow," he said at last, "I shall take you to some of the cottages on my estate. It means pretending, I am afraid, that we are an ordinary couple. But such courtesy calls are customary and would please my people.''

"Of course," I said. Then added mischievously, " 'Twill be a good excuse to escape Mary and her schemes. Truly, what shall I do about her, Leslie? Should she be offended if I spoke plainly?''

"Probably," he said, "but I suspect it will be necessary. Besides, she will no doubt lay the blame at my feet and cease being angry with you quickly enough.''

I could not bear the bitterness in Leslie's voice and was afraid to speak further of the matter. Instead, I said, "This mare is truly gentle.''

"So you have ceased to fear her?" Leslie asked. I nodded and his voice became harsh, "I would you could find it as easy to grow at ease with people!''

I halted my mare and said in a quiet voice, "If you choose to be so disagreeable I shall have to say 'good day' and leave you. No doubt the horse knows her way back to the castle.''

He flushed, then laughed. "And I have chided you for prickliness! Very well, I shall endeavour to be more agreeable. Lord, what a strange couple we make, Heather! My mother would have been horrified by you. She felt a woman's place was to defer absolutely to her husband.''

"I presume you feel the same?" I asked.

He smiled again. "If that were so, do you truly believe matters would be as they are?''

"I suppose not," I conceded.

We continued to ride in a companionable silence. When we neared a stream, Leslie suggested we stop for a while. I agreed and we approached the water. He dismounted first and came to help me. I could scarcely keep from flinching as his hands circled my waist to lift me down and as my feet touched earth again I shuddered. But Leslie did not immediately release me. "So small to be so forceful," he murmured.

I pulled free and moved to stand by the water as he tethered our horses. From my reflection I knew my hair was slightly dishevelled, but I carried no comb to repair the damage. It was difficult to believe that the young woman who stared back at me was myself. I wondered again, as I often had this past week, if it were not perhaps a dream that I should soon wake from to find myself once more safely in Mrs. Gilwen's school. Or was that too a dream? Another reflection joined mine and I realised Leslie stood beside me. "What are you thinking?" he asked.

"If any of this exists. You. The castle. This stream," I said quietly.

"And I wonder if you exist," he said with a hint of laughter in his voice, "for I know the rest does. Including this rock which I would suggest that you sit upon. Unless you prefer to stand?"

Since my limbs felt strangely unsteady, I chose to sit. I could not explain this to Leslie and I answered his questioning gaze simply with a smile. But for once he did not smile in return. This surprised me and I wondered if he were preparing to be disagreeable again. He seemed to be searching for certain words and I realised that perhaps he wondered if I were breeding. I blushed deeply at the thought, aware that from this morning I could set his mind at peace. Yet modesty made it difficult for me to speak of such a thing even to my husband. Nevertheless, it was his right to know. "Leslie," I spoke hesitantly, "I thought it best you know. There . . . there will be no child from . . . from . . ."

"You are sure?" he asked urgently.

"Yes, my . . . the . . . yes," I replied.

He glanced away, at war with himself, I realised. Though he felt relief that this would not be another problem in our lives, he also felt disappointment. He knew it had been his only chance for an heir. Yet when Leslie spoke, the words were proper enough. "I am glad, Heather. It would have been one more reason for you to hate me. And even if you did not resent the infant, I would not wish a child to grow up in such a home as ours will be. Children are quick to sense moods and ours might have felt torn between us."

I felt unaccountably bold as I asked, "Yet if matters had been different you would have wished for children?"

He answered frankly, "Yes . . . if matters had been different."

I became bolder still, "And you have none?"

He flushed. "None. In general I am a careful man. I would not wish for the birth of a child as handicapped as a by-blow must be. But Heather, you should not speak of such things."

"They should be outside my knowledge?" I suggested sarcastically. "Oh, I know well enough not to ask such questions of anyone else. But I felt that with you I might be frank." He did not answer and I sighed. "Very well. I don't understand, but I shall endeavour not to shock you in the future."

Leslie laughed. "Heather! There never was such a woman as you! What would Mrs. Gilwen say if she could hear you?"

"Don't speak to me of Mrs. Gilwen," I retorted. "She taught me to believe the world was gentle and that one could never find oneself in a position too difficult to cope with!"

Leslie did not answer, nor did I truly expect him to. His words, when he did speak, were of an entirely different matter. "I ought to warn you, Heather, I expect another guest within the week."

"More family?" I asked in dismay.

"Are they so difficult to bear?" he asked laughing.

I blushed. "No, of course not, it is simply, well, a bit of a strain occasionally."

"Well, you need not fear. This guest is no relation of mine. In truth, I do not know him very well. He is coming from London on a business matter. The Earl of Pellen. He shall not be staying above a day or two," Leslie explained.

"Well," I said equably, "perhaps he will prove a calming influence."

"Hmmm," was all he said.

"What tale will you tell him of our marriage?" I asked.

Leslie, shrugged, staring at the ground. "None. There will be no need. He is not the sort to ask such questions and his wife will not be with him."

"But if he should?" I persisted.

"I shall tell him the truth: that I married you straight from the schoolroom."

I was far from reassured, but there was that in Leslie's

manner which warned me not to pursue the matter. And in truth I could not say Leslie was mistaken concerning Lord Pellen. I had so little knowledge of men that I could ill gauge how the earl would react. How bitterly aware I was of the differences between my upbringing and that of other young women! I felt only anger toward my unknown father. How unfair that I must suffer because of his carelessness! Had Leslie fathered a child out of wedlock, I should have welcomed it into my home as my own rather than see it follow the course I had. Or worse. I had seldom felt so alone as I did in that moment. For always before, I had been able to believe that one day all would be well. One day I would find love. Now I had no such hope. For the briefest moment I felt a hand on my shoulder. I turned and looked up to see Leslie beside me. He cleared his throat and said, "Perhaps we should go back."

I nodded and rose. As I approached my mare I felt none of the trepidation I had known earlier. Leslie lifted me easily to my perch and again I was unable to repress a shudder. He appeared not to notice, however, and I was relieved he did not reproach me. Still lost in self-pity, I preferred not to speak. My silence nettled him for after a time, Leslie said, "Do you expect me to disappear simply because you ignore me?"

I flushed. I could not admit he was right. What I should have said in reply I do not know, for it was at that moment I spied Philip. He was cantering toward us and I remember thinking that he looked very handsome. Why could I not have been married to him? I wondered bitterly. I waved to Philip, my eagerness restrained only by the unease I felt as to my seat. A glance at Leslie's face sufficed. He was not pleased. Yet he forced himself to greet Philip pleasantly enough. "Good morning, nephew. You've a fine horse there. One of Bradley's breakdowns, I collect?"

Philip grinned, "Yes, prime blood ain't he? You needn't read me a jobation about expense, either, for I won him in a wager."

"And the counterbid?" Leslie asked easily.

Unaccountably, Philip flushed. "Well, I shouldn't like to say in front of Heather."

My curiosity whetted, I said airily, "Such fustian! Go ahead and tell us."

Leslie started to object then, oddly, changed his mind for he said, "Yes, tell us, Philip."

Still flushing, Philip spoke to Leslie, "Well, you recall the opera dancer you said I must be rid of? I had just come round to the same point of view when Thomas offered me a wager. I'd nothing else to bid so it was this horse against the key to the girl's place. Well, I'd have given it to him for nothing at that point and instead I won this gelding."

"And the girl?" I asked faintly. "She didn't mind?"

"Why should she?" Philip asked, frowning. "Thomas is devilishly handsome and has more of the ready than I do. I thought myself rather clever."

Leslie seemed to be laughing. "I am afraid my wife does not understand these things, Philip."

"No, I do not!" I retorted. "And I wonder you encourage him, Leslie!"

"Oh, I neither encourage nor discourage," he replied easily. "I avoid meddling in Philip's affairs as much as possible."

"Oh, I say, Aunt Heather, don't nab the rust," Philip said, "I daresay the girl was as tired of me as I was of her. Besides, she was only an opera dancer, they expect such things."

He had placed a hand on the mare. I drew her back and said icily, "Since the two of you find it so amusing, I leave you to yourselves. Leslie is quite correct, I do *not* understand such matters!"

With dignity and a skill with horses I did not suspect, I carefully drew my horse away from theirs and set off for the castle. Inwardly I seethed. Were all men so horrid? I had yet to meet one who was not! I was sufficiently angry that when my mare desired to break into a fast pace, I forgot all sense of fear and encouraged her. Thus it was I arrived at the stables with my hair flying behind me, the pins scattered somewhere, and out of breath. With difficulty, I halted the mare. A groom ran forward and grasped the reins and held the mare steady as I slid to the ground. "Did she run away wi' ye?" the fellow asked anxiously. "She's normally sich a gentle 'un."

Feeling exultant after my ride, I laughed. "No, she did not run away with me. I wished to see how fast she was."

"And Sir Leslie?" he continued, still anxious.

I was by this time headed to the house and I called carelessly over my shoulder, "Oh, he is somewhere with Master Philip."

I was as astonished as the poor groom when, in the next moment, Leslie's horse galloped into the courtyard. He dismounted immediately, tossing the reins over to the alarmed groom. Frozen in amazement, I could only watch as he strode toward me, his face an unreadable mask. He grasped my arm fiercely and demanded, "Are you all right? How came your mare to bolt like that?"

I laughed uneasily, "Oh, she did not bolt, Leslie. I urged her to the pace myself."

As I spoke, disbelief crossed his face, then he shook me angrily. "You fool! You've never sat on a horse before today and you . . . you *crammed* her? I suppose you would have enjoyed being thrown? Well, you'll not ride alone, do you hear? And if you try such a trick again I'll have you barred from the horses altogether!"

I grew angry. What right had he to dictate to me? Rebellion grew as I retorted, "I shall do as I please!" Then, in an instant, I knew how to wound him. Smiling and lowering my voice so only his ears could catch my words, I said, "Why should you object? Surely it would serve your plans best were I to be found dead in a field somewhere, my horse bolted."

Leslie turned white with fury and I pulled back, afraid he was about to strike me. Philip's voice halted both of us. "I say, Aunt Heather! What a neck-or-nothing ride! Leslie was worried your mare had bolted, but I said you knew what you were about. You both look quite furious. Has Leslie been ringing a peal over you, Aunt Heather?"

Before I could respond, Leslie had released me and was striding to the house. And the port, I told myself. I forced a smile at Philip who had handed his horse over to the groom— who was pretending to have noticed nothing. Philip offered me his arm saying, "Let me escort you in. I daresay you're as famished as I am and no doubt my mother is eagerly awaiting us. Can't think what's gotten into Uncle Leslie, though. Does he often kick up such a fuss? No, don't answer, I shouldn't have asked. But to me it's the outside of enough that you are tenant-for-life with him! I can't help feeling sorry."

I turned and said icily, "I can do without your pity."

"No offense," he said hastily, "only you're so lovely to

be cooped up here. It don't seem fair. If you were my wife, I'd flaunt you all over London.''

The idea was almost pleasant and I laughed, ''Would you? And what else would you do?''

As soon as I had spoken, I regretted my words. They were highly unsuitable and an answering flash in Philip's eyes unnerved me. I began to chatter hastily, ''Never mind. We ought to go find your mother, Philip. And I had best change from my habit. And my hair needs repinning. I'd best go directly up to my chamber. I shall see you later,'' I said, and gathering my skirt, I fled.

Ellen was waiting. An afternoon dress had been laid out on the bed. ''My lady!'' she exclaimed as I came through the door, ''what's happened? Your hair!''

I flushed, aware of the spectacle I presented. I forced myself to enter the room slowly. ''Oh, I had a bit of a run with the mare Sir Leslie gave me. A bath and some new pins in my hair will set all to right.''

''Yes, my lady,'' she said dubiously and went to order bathwater.

I sat at my dressing table staring at the mirror image that was me. All the words spoken that morning passed through my head again and again. Already I regretted my impropriety in encouraging Philip. And the words I had hurled against Leslie in the yard. Was I still such a widgeon that I could never curb my tongue? I felt weary and unwilling to face Leslie. But I was no coward to hide in my room. Mary also must be faced and told the rooms should remain as they were. I felt tears welling in my eyes and cursed myself for a pea-goose. It was the time of month, I told myself, that made my emotions so unsteady. The bath soothed me, as did Ellen's gentle fingers resetting my hair. And I am enough a woman that the new afternoon dress I wore made me feel almost gay. It reflected, as I had come to expect, Mademoiselle's impeccable taste.

Forgetting my earlier words, I went to the library seeking Leslie. He sat at his desk, poring over certain reports. ''Yes?'' he demanded without looking up.

The iciness of his voice halted me and brought back the memory of what I had said. I advanced more slowly. I had almost reached the desk when Leslie looked up impatiently. He obviously expected a servant, for at the sight of me he started. He rose slowly until he towered over me even from behind the desk. "Well, madam, have you come to insult me further?" he asked bitterly. "If so, please spare yourself the effort. I am not interested in your opinion of me."

I flushed but did not lower my eyes. Leslie's arms were folded across his chest and I reached out to place a hand on them. "No," I said gently, "I've come to say I am sorry for the words I spoke earlier."

Beneath my hand, I could feel a little of his stiffness fall away. He shrugged and said roughly, "It is of little consequence."

I shook my head. "I wish it were. But even so I could not have let it pass without apology." I removed my hand from his arm.

Almost he seemed to soften, but before I could be sure, he had turned his back and was staring at a shelf of books. "I have always preferred," he said slowly, "pound dealings. I can not blame you for speaking plainly this morning. If that is how you see me."

I moved to his side and said in sharp protest, "But that is *not* how I see you! It's my wretched temper! I speak without thinking!"

He looked at me, a smile twitching at the corners of his mouth. After a moment he laughed. "Yes, you have a temper! Very well, I accept your apology. But I meant it when I said you must be more careful when you ride."

I nodded gravely, then said shyly, "I also wished to thank you, Leslie, for the clothes you ordered from Mademoiselle Suzette for me."

He smiled. "They please you?" I nodded. "I collect you're wearing one of the new dresses. Stand back so I may see it."

I did as he commanded and turned about slowly so he might see it from every side. He nodded approvingly, "It suits you well. I am glad you are pleased, Heather. If there is aught else you need, tell me."

I shook my head. Already I felt Leslie had been overgenerous, and in truth there was nothing I needed. Leslie, however, disagreed, for he said abruptly, "I've ordered a shipment of books for you, of various sorts. A few novels, but most are somewhat weightier."

I stared at Leslie in amazement. Truly, had we met under other circumstances I might have liked this man. I stammered some form of thanks. Gruffly he replied, "My library is in need of more recent volumes. And in any event, you may not approve my taste."

He glanced away, but not before I had seen the gleam of satisfaction in his eyes. So! I thought, feeling a cold chill. I should have realised. Sir Leslie is very experienced with women and hopes to seduce me with gifts. Well, he shall see if I can be so bought. "Pray forgive me, Leslie," I said in a cold voice, "I have other matters to attend to."

I dropped a brief curtsy and retreated, noting with pleasure the surprise and dismay evident on Leslie's face. Outside the library I permitted myself to smile. I was not quite so green as Leslie believed! I was only angry at myself for having forgotten that this was the man who had ravished me and who had been in the habit of having women sent up. No doubt he was weary of celibacy. But if so, let him look to the village jade for consolation!

Chapter 7

Even in such a large castle there was no privacy. As I turned from closing the library doors, I encountered Mary. "My dear, is anything wrong?" she asked anxiously.

I did my best to smile for I felt reluctant to share my troubles with anyone. "No, of course not. I am simply somewhat fatigued."

Mary shook her head. "Leslie! He should not have kept you riding so long. And Philip said something about a quarrel?"

"No, no quarrel," I said hastily. "Leslie simply scolded me for some carelessness. Well deserved, I assure you."

She looked dissatisfied but chose not to speak further of that matter. "Heather, my dear," she said tentatively, "pray forgive me for speaking frankly, but . . . well, do you think it wise to encourage Philip so? He is an impressionable young man and if you are not careful, you will have him in love with you. That would serve no one's interests, I am convinced. And he is a bit young, my dear, to supply that which Leslie does not."

I was not certain I fully comprehended Mary, but I understood enough to grow angry. "I see Philip simply as my husband's nephew. He is a pleasant companion but that is all. I believe you overrate my charms, ma'am, if you believe Philip could fall in love with me."

"Oh, dear!" she replied, "I have set up your back! I know *you* have no such thoughts, my dear, I simply meant that *Philip* is apt, occasionally, to be rather heedless. And he does find you so very attractive. But there! I am sure there is no need to speak further of the matter. My dear, if I did not like you so well, I would not have bothered to speak of it at all."

I found myself wishing she detested me. But then I chided

myself for such thoughts. After all, she only meant well. And perhaps she was right. "I will remember what you have said," I assured her.

She smiled. "I knew you would understand, my dear. Now, I confess I meant to speak with Leslie, but the matter can wait. Instead, perhaps we can discuss the drawing room? I thought blue curtains—"

"No."

"NO? Well, perhaps gold?"

"Please, Lady Mary," I persisted, "I would rather leave the curtains as they are. In fact, I would prefer to leave the entire room as it is. As well as the rest of the castle. I've no wish to change anything."

Mary regarded me stubbornly and I met her gaze unwaveringly. At last she lowered her eyes complaining, "Oh, very well. But it's so unfair, you know. I've hoped for years to have a hand in refurbishing the place."

I was amused. "So Leslie told me."

"Leslie told you?" She seemed incredulous. "You and he seem to be on remarkably close terms in view of . . . of . . . well, I must say it surprises me."

I bit my lip. "We are not on such very close terms as you think, Lady Mary," I said, not wishing to deceive her or raise false hopes. "Every encounter seems to end at dagger point! And as for . . . well, I do not believe we shall ever share a bed. Though I suspect Leslie bamboozles himself into thinking it may be so."

"Oh, dear," Mary clucked, "I had hoped the two of you might eventually be reconciled. What of children? Don't you wish for any?"

I stared at the floor. "What I would prefer is unimportant. I could not bear the thought of . . . Not even to have children." I raised my head proudly, "And I would not stoop to be unfaithful."

Mary sighed. "Well, of course the two of you must resolve such matters. And I do understand your point of view. Remember, I shan't put up with Leslie mistreating you. If you've problems, come to me."

I spoke honestly. "It comforts me to have an ally. Yet I prefer to cope with Leslie myself."

She nodded sagely. "Of course, of course, my dear."

I had forgotten where we stood and felt an icy chill as

Leslie spoke from the library door. "Of course *what*?" he asked.

I cursed Mary silently as she flushed and said in a guilty voice, "Oh, nothing, Leslie."

His eyes swept over me mockingly as he bowed ironically. "Then may I suggest we seek the dining hall for some refreshment?"

I wished nothing more than to flee to my bedchamber but could not. Whatever else he believed, Leslie should not have cause to call me faint-hearted. Leslie offered his sister his arm and she took it, fluttering still. I walked behind, feeling keenly my hatred for this man who could inspire such embarrassment where there ought to be none, and I clenched my teeth. In the doorway of the dining hall, he allowed Mary to enter first and stood aside for me. As I passed him he whispered, "How fierce you look. Is the table to be a battleground then?"

I smiled sweetly. "Not unless you choose to make it one."

He smiled grimly. "Oh, not I. I am a pacifist."

The sally lasted but a moment and Mary noticed none of it. A fact for which I was grateful. Philip did not put in an appearance and I, conscious of Mary's words, was relieved. Leslie virtually ignored me to talk with Mary and I felt nettled, for he questioned her on matters I felt quite sure could not interest him. Mary, oblivious to such things, chattered happily about her husband's estate and her other children. My only consolation was that Leslie must find the conversation even more tedious than I did. I was about to excuse myself from the table when Mary changed her topic of discourse. ". . . quieter than you were, Leslie. Eleanor and Katherine thought you unruly, spoiled, and a nuisance. But you weren't truly bad, simply high-spirited. As for spoiled. . ."

"As for spoiled," Leslie broke in, speaking evenly, "I never had the chance to be. Mother would pay her duty calls to the nursery once a week to see me, but I scarcely call that effusive. As for Father! We both know how he felt."

"Yes, but Leslie, surely it would have helped had there not been those *incidents*," Mary protested.

Leslie's voice was steel. "I was *not* responsible!"

"Now, now, Leslie. I never blamed you. And certainly I sympathised with your dislike of the cat, for example . . ."

77

Something in Leslie's face made even Mary pause. "Yes, well, after all these years it doesn't matter."

Leslie rose. "I am not in the habit of telling Banbury tales, Mary. Nor do I choose to discuss further such a distasteful subject. Particularly in front of Heather."

Mary looked at me as though she had forgotten my existence and she hastened to apologise. "I am sorry, my dear. So dreadful for you. I hope you don't misunderstand . . . such incidents were not frequent . . ."

"*Mary!*" Leslie's voice was a warning and she fell silent.

He spoke to her, but his eyes were on me. They did not, as I expected, plead with me to believe him, but challenged me, with cool contempt, to disbelieve. Yet I could not. I cannot say why except perhaps that I thought I knew him well enough to be sure that had he been responsible for those "incidents" he would not lie about it now. I lowered my eyes. At this Leslie laughed bitterly. As he strode from the room he called, "Well, my dear, I hope you are pleased. You've turned Heather even further from me!"

Agonised, Mary said, "I didn't mean . . ."

I cut her off. "Please. I understand. And Leslie is mistaken. If you will excuse me . . . a slight headache . . ."

No longer concerned about whether I was being rude, I rose hastily and fled to my chamber. Ellen was waiting and clucked over me. I accepted her suggestion of a nap eagerly. On no account was I to be disturbed until I rang for tea. In truth, it was not sleep I needed, but privacy. As the door closed behind Ellen, I chose a novel from the bookshelf and tried to read.

I stayed in my room that afternoon, not caring if anyone felt me rude. Mary would understand and she was the only one who mattered. I did not even consider the possibility that anyone had come to call. The local gentry knew of our marriage, but most were away. And none would call until they were certain that I had the proper background. Which, of course, I did not. Not even Mrs. Gilwen's excellent school could efface the unfortunate circumstances of my birth. Perhaps in London there might be hostesses who would receive me, but not in this conservative country milieu. I had left cards, at Leslie's insistence, but it came as no surprise to me that the gesture was not reciprocated.

The afternoon's respite was enough to calm me and I could look forward to the evening. And wearing yet another new gown. I was not such a fool as to concern myself only with dresses and trinkets and such. But for so many years I had had nothing and I could not feel it wrong to enjoy my new possessions. It felt wonderful and strange to know I had a closetful of dresses and that none needed patching, none needed refitting. I am sure Mr. Watly would have been shocked, but I could not suppress the thought that if my fate must be so, it was as well Sir Leslie were wealthy and generous. But I still felt keenly that poverty should have been preferable to my present state.

Ellen dressed my hair with special care and helped me into my gown. In the mirror I seemed older, for the dress had been designed for a young matron. As usual, Ellen was pleased. "My lady, I'd not have known you for the girl who showed up that day at Mademoiselle Suzette's. You look that lovely now. If Sir Leslie does not have a *tendre*, then he be blind. And his nephew."

I smiled. Dear Ellen! I wondered if she ever imagined herself in my place. I think she would not have hesitated to forgive Leslie. Every morning she glanced at the door to Leslie's chamber and, I have no doubt, checked to see if it were still bolted. Sometimes I half expected her to scold me. I could not know about the other servants, but Mrs. Morgan clearly shared Ellen's opinion. She had accepted me as mistress of the household, and even held a grudging respect for me. But often she would gaze at me with sadly chiding eyes until I wanted to tell her to stop! That it was not her affair.

I arrived at the drawing room early and found only Leslie. He bowed stiffly and said coolly, "Madam. Good evening."

I replied as coolly, with the faintest of curtsies, "Sir."

He flushed slightly at the insult. "I hope, madam, you were not unduly distressed by my sister, earlier. Mary occasionally forgets herself." I murmured a denial. "Of course. I had forgotten. Your opinion of my character is such that no tale could shock you further."

I moved toward him and placed a hand on his arm saying impulsively, "Leslie, I cannot believe the things Mary implied."

His eyes searched mine for a moment, then he asked mockingly, "Why ever not?"

Stung, I sought for a suitable retort, but none came. And even as I searched, Mary's voice intruded. "Good evening, my dears. Leslie, when you take Heather to London, you shall have to be careful. All the young men will flock around her."

We greeted her in turn, both I believe, relieved by her neutral presence. Then Philip entered the room. He was, as always, dressed with exquisite care. I was too green to know he aspired to the dandy set but thought he cut a dashing figure. As he greeted me I remembered Mary's warning and felt unaccountably shy. Nor did the romance I had been reading do aught to steady me. "Good evening, Philip," I managed, conscious of a slight flush as he insisted on kissing my hand with a courtly gesture. "How have you spent the day?"

"Oh, out and about," he replied carelessly. "I visited the village. Quite provincial, of course, but with one or two good inns. But then, you know what it's like."

I felt a hand on my shoulder as Leslie replied for me. "Actually, Heather hasn't seen it yet." As disbelief crossed Philip's face Leslie continued smoothly, "I've been too eager for my bride's company to give her time to explore the local countryside."

"But on visits before you were married?" Philip persisted, puzzled.

"My dear boy," Leslie said, "I married Heather straight out of a London schoolroom. I was too eager for the ceremony to worry about conventional visits and such."

Philip sighed. "I never would have guessed you to be so romantic, Uncle." Then he grinned. "Or were you worried about competition? Rightly so, I must say! Heather, you look ravishing."

Poor Philip! He looked so astonished at the faces Leslie and I made. How was he to know how unfortunate his choice of words had been. Mary was the one to bridge the awkward moment. "Philip, lead Heather in to dinner."

Leslie stood behind my shoulder and I could not see his reaction to Mary's command. Nor could he see my face or the shyness I felt as I took Philip's arm. Wanting to be kind to the boy, I chose a topic I was sure would please him. I asked about his new horse. Flushed with pleasure, he answered eagerly. This carried us as far as the table. Unfortunately, it also carried us through the first course. Mary was an excellent horsewoman and Leslie quite a top-sawyer, in fact. It was to be expected then that, overhearing my conversation with Philip, they should continue it. I felt very much an outsider. Surprisingly Mary was the first to notice my silence. "Leslie," she said hesitantly, "I don't think Heather is enjoying the topic."

I would have denied it had Leslie not turned to regard me so intently. Philip spoke before Leslie could. "I'd forgotten you were a London girl. How green of us. But after seeing you ride this morning, it's difficult to remember you are a novice. Ain't it, Uncle?"

Leslie seemed engrossed by his wine as he replied offhandedly, "I was in no danger of forgetting. But yes, she does rather well for a *beginner*."

"Nipcheese with your compliments, are you?" Philip asked frankly. "If you were like this when you were dangling after Heather, I'm surprised she married you."

Feeling on dangerous ground, I said with careful lightness, "Oh, he swept me off my feet, Philip."

I could not repress a smile as that drew a quick glare from Leslie. Mary felt obliged to intervene. "Really, Philip! Except perhaps to you, Leslie seems quite the nonesuch!"

At this, Leslie turned to her with an upraised eyebrow. "I had no idea you thought so, Mary. I recall you always roasted me about how ugly I was."

She grinned and for a moment I saw a hint of a mischievous nature. "Of course I did. What are sisters for if not to prevent their brothers from becoming too puffed up in their own conceit?"

Leslie laughed and I said with mock gravity, "Why, thank you, madam, for helping to prepare him for the state of matrimony."

We all laughed then, though I suspect Philip was somewhat bemused by our banter. For my part, I considered Mary more carefully. There was much I did not know about her and I began to think I had underestimated Mary. Her next words were on a different matter. "Matrimony is very well, my dear, but I have not had enough of your company, Heather. Perhaps tomorrow we might go to the village together. I grant you it is small, but there is a shop with excellent ribbons and silks."

It sounded like a delightful plan, and I started to say so when Leslie intruded, speaking bluntly. "I am sorry, Mary, but Heather has agreed to visit some of my tenants tomorrow."

"You might let the child speak for herself!" Mary bristled. "And you ought not to bearlead her! Let Heather make her own decisions."

"It is not a matter of bullying," Leslie said through clenched teeth. "It is a matter of prior engagements and good manners!"

Philip entered the brangle. "Oh, Mother! Of course Aunt Heather must go with Uncle if she promised to. Anyway, why you want to go shopping is beyond me. If Heather is like you, she has more ribands and furbelows than she can use!"

"Well, I only thought it would be pleasant for her," Mary began defensively, "always cooped up in this gloomy castle. . ."

I could restrain myself no longer. In an icy voice I said, "May *I* speak? Or don't any of you feel I have a right to an opinion? I trust I have no need of advice on the subject of manners, Leslie. There is no question of cancelling our plans." I turned to Philip, "Your rudeness surprises me; however I excuse you since you are clearly incapable of comprehending aught except your own point of view. Madam, if you are agreeable, we could go the day after. I should enjoy it very much, and particularly in your company."

Mary was smiling again. "Of course, my dear. I shall be delighted!"

Philip shifted uneasily and Leslie said to him, in an amused tone, "I warned you to be wary of crossing my wife. She can be a tigress."

Somehow, he managed to reply gallantly, "But always a charming one."

I? I felt pleased with myself. For once I had not allowed the three of them to overset me and I had even enjoyed the encounter. It was excellent practice for my entry into the *ton*. Leslie still looked amused, approvingly so, and this added to my courage. Suddenly, I recalled a matter I had meant to discuss with my *belle-soeur*. "Mary," I said eagerly, "perhaps you might help me. There is a tapestry I wish to mend and could use your advice. I need to find the proper wool and somewhere there must be a tapestry frame in the castle . . ." I paused, noting the amusement on Philip's face and Mary's apparent dismay.

"Oh dear," she said, "I'm afraid . . ."

Leslie cut her off, saying, "You will find my sister has little skill with a needle, Heather. At the time she should have been learning such things, she was climbing trees and riding instead. One might almost have thought her a boy."

"Leslie, if you are implying I am not feminine . . ." Mary bristled.

"Oh, no," he replied easily, "later you obviously turned into a lady. And no one could doubt you are thoroughly a woman. I simply meant that at one time you were too high-spirited to spend hours bending over needlework."

"How wonderful!" Philip exclaimed, clearly impressed with this new view of his mother.

Somewhat mollified by Philip's admiration, Mary sniffed. "Well, I admit I chafed at all the restrictions placed on young ladies. But I never forgot I was a woman."

A thought struck Philip and, I confess, crossed my mind as well. "But how did you manage trees in skirts?"

Mary flushed, "That was while I was still in short skirts, of course. And what Leslie didn't tell you is that while I climbed the tree myself, the gardener had to get me down. Of course, I was forbidden to ever do such a thing again."

Leslie laughed. "Confess! That didn't stop you, did it?"

"No," she conceded good-naturedly. "It didn't. I simply became more careful. Only the advent of long skirts and an increase in the number of petticoats halted me. And, of course, the realisation that it was time I began to act like a young lady."

We all smiled. Yet, looking at the plump woman before me, it was hard to visualise the young girl who had led such an unorthodox existence. "So you see, Aunt Heather," Philip intruded, triumphantly, "all the family tends to be a bit wild. Though Mary and my aunts and Leslie have settled down by now."

"Are you so sure?" Leslie asked mischievously.

Philip looked disconcerted as we laughed, but replied quickly enough, "Certainly. Now that you're all leg-shackled."

It was my turn and I asked, "Do I look so staid and sober, then?"

"The very portrait of respectability," Leslie teased, and I flushed.

"You should not joke about such things!" Mary protested.

Philip cocked a head toward her, "You see what I mean? Never mind, Mother, we love you as you are."

We all became abruptly aware of the servants as the covers from the previous course were removed. Leslie cleared his throat. "Yes, well, all of this does not mean one should not attempt to curb one's impulses, Philip. A bit of spirit is good, certainly, but it is important to be able to control it. I still wish, for example, that you had not been sent down from Oxford."

"Oh, for God's sake!" Philip flushed angrily. "Please don't preach propriety to me. I'm not sorry about the incident, only that I was caught."

Their eyes met and held, neither wanting to give way. But Leslie was the stronger, and at last, Philip glanced away sullenly. The atmosphere was no longer relaxed and I was relieved when it came time for Mary and me to withdraw. Mary was as disturbed as I. "I do wish Leslie and Philip came to cuffs less often," she said. "I've always hoped they could be friends. But then Leslie has never paid any attention to his nephews or nieces."

"Has he many?"

"Well, there are my four boys, of course," she said, "and Eleanor's three girls. Katherine also has two daughters. Though it's not to be wondered at that Leslie never sees *them*. Eleanor and Katherine were never fond of him, so he has no reason to care about their children. And such simpering chits! So unlike Philip or my other boys. I always suspected my sisters resented Leslie because they couldn't inherit the estate. Which was absurd because Father dealt quite generously with us all."

I digested this information. If true, I could see why Leslie might have grown up feeling lonely. I wondered why Mary had not shared in the general resentment, then decided I was being unkind. Mary was simply a generous person who loved her brother. I changed the subject, however, by asking Mary her opinion of next season's fashion. It was a topic she greatly enjoyed and had not exhausted by the time Leslie and Philip joined us.

"Clothes!" Philip snorted, as soon as he was near enough to hear our words.

Leslie raised an eyebrow. "I was under the impression,

Nephew, that you paid a great deal of attention to your raiment.''

Philip flushed, ''Well, a man has to be well dressed, don't he?''

I stepped in with an irate look at my husband. ''Actually, Leslie, dear,'' I said coolly, ''I thought you might ask Philip the name of his tailor. I believe you are overdue for a few new coats.''

Leslie smiled grimly. ''Too late, my dear. I've already ordered them from Weston. I trust they will meet your approval. In any event, I've no wish to look like a man-milliner, whatever Philip chooses for himself!''

Why I baited Leslie then, I could not say. Only that I had an irrepressible urge to do so. But the glint in Leslie's eyes warned me to carry the game no further. So, biting my lip, I replied with no appreciable delay, ''Ah, then there is no need for Philip's man. Naturally I trust your taste, Leslie. It is impeccable.''

My response startled Leslie as my earlier barb had not. Philip exclaimed, ''How disgustingly domestic the two of you sound. Smelling of April and May! *I* shall retire to the game room.''

''I'll join you shortly for a game of billiards,'' Leslie told him.

''And I shall retire to write letters,'' Mary said from her chair.

We waited until they had left, Leslie and I, and still the silence remained. I suspected that I knew his thoughts and so I spoke first. ''Do you mean to chide me for taking Philip's part so readily?'' I asked. ''I only did so because it seems he has no other ally.''

Leslie looked at me carefully. ''Nevertheless, it would be more suitable if you supported your *husband*.''

I laughed bitterly, perhaps because of the dinner wine. ''Yes, I must remember to play propriety, musn't I? But in London it won't matter since surely no one is expected to care about one's husband?''

''Are you so cynical already?'' he asked coolly. ''What will serve for others will not necessarily serve for us. You had no title, no lands, no standing in the *ton*. In short, there are only two possibilities. I married you for love or I married

85

you because I was forced to. You may choose which you prefer to have believed, and act accordingly.''

"Do you truly think you can convince people you love me?" I asked amused.

"With your help, perhaps," he answered seriously. "But I admit it will not be a task I can enjoy."

"Why?"

He regarded me coldly. "Because I find such hypocrisy distasteful. And because if you continue to behave publicly as you have, then I shall be regarded as a lobcock. Think well, madam, before our next guest arrives. And now I presume you wish to retire early due to, shall we say, the headache?"

Astounded by his audacity, I had not the courage to refuse. Nor was I so sure I wished to remain in his company. At last I curtsied so slightly as to almost be insulting and turned and mounted the stairs, conscious of his eyes still on me. Once in my chamber, to Ellen's amazement, I began to cry.

Chapter 8

I woke early, aware of a pervading stiffness and soreness. In addition, there was the discomfort of the time of month. I felt much like staying in bed, but remembering my promise to visit Leslie's tenants, I knew I could not. With a sigh, I roused myself and rang for Ellen, then dressed in my riding habit. To Ellen's questions I replied that for once I would join Leslie for breakfast. She was surprised, but not nearly so surprised as my husband when I appeared in the dining hall a short time later. He regarded me warily as I was seated. A smile twitched at my lips, and after a slight hesitation, I allowed it to show. As my tea was poured I looked at the table and said demurely, "You needn't look at me that way. I've no intention of kicking up a fuss. I thought you might tell me a bit about the various families we are to visit." Glancing up, I saw that he still looked disturbed. "I thought about what you said, Leslie. And it made sense," I said sincerely.

He relaxed and began talking quietly about his tenants. Clearly he knew them well and had sifted out the essential information for me. We would visit his old nurse, the gamekeeper and his wife, and one or two other tenants who had, at some point, served the family. Leslie was still discoursing when Philip entered. "Good morning, Uncle, Aunt Heather. Riding today? Oh, that's right, the tenants."

"Yes, the tenants," Leslie said easily.

As Philip helped himself from the sideboard he addressed me. "Well, I don't envy you. Such a bore! Father drags me off on such visits on our estate about once a year, and I hate them. What do you say, Heather, shall we sneak away somewhere and have a party, al fresco, instead?"

I laughed at Philip's boyishness. "I think not. Besides, I doubt I shall find the calls such a penance. Remember, I have had fewer opportunities for meeting people than you."

"Leslie, why don't you bring Heather to Town?" Philip asked. "You really ought to take her during the Season. I'm sure she would enjoy it."

Leslie was not in the least disconcerted. "So she would and I intend to . . . later. At the moment, it is inconvenient to leave the estate."

"Will you give a ball to present her?" Philip asked eagerly.

"Of course." Leslie smiled. "That's the proper thing, isn't it?"

I was too surprised to speak. I could not imagine myself at such a ball, but I knew Leslie too well to think he was roasting me. I was grateful he felt no urgency to proceed to London. Then I realised Leslie was speaking again, ". . . on the Continent. Heather has never been there and I am anxious to show her Paris and Rome."

"Then I must learn Italian," I said without thinking.

"Why?" Philip asked. "In good inns they know English, and besides, Leslie knows a bit of the language. You've no need to learn."

It seemed pointless to argue with Philip. Irritated, I glanced at Leslie, only to find him watching me with laughter in his eyes. And, it almost seemed, understanding. He spoke lightly, "I shall be glad to teach you, my dear, any words you may need to know."

Feeling thoroughly routed, I rose. "Shall we be going, Leslie? It begins to grow late."

"Oh, assuredly," he replied, getting to his feet. "It must be all of nine o'clock."

I was intolerably aware of how fine Leslie looked in his russet riding-coat and buckskin breeches. We walked to the stables in silence, though I felt his dark eyes on me. Nor, once we had left the dining hall, did he retain a hold on my elbow. He seemed as determined as I to resist a quarrel and waited patiently as I drew on my gloves and tied the strings of my bonnet. Using the groom's laced fingers, I mounted easily and without fear. The mare stood quiet as I stroked her gentle neck. Then Leslie was up beside me and we set off at an easy pace.

It was a cool morning which, in view of the weight of my

habit, was fortunate. My hair was securely pinned atop my head and the breeze felt good on my neck. The first visit was to Leslie's old nurse. She had obviously been warned of our visit for she stood in the doorway waiting: a small, plump, gentle-looking woman. Leslie slid off his horse then lifted me down. I waited as he tethered the horses, then hugged her in greeting. I stepped forward as he presented me. "Nanny. My wife, Heather."

She had not, I recalled, been present at the reception on the lawn. I gave her my cheek to kiss. As she stood a way back to look me over I smiled and she said, "I fancy her, Leslie. Have ye been treatin' her well?"

He didn't answer and I realised that perhaps I should. But the words would not come, and after a moment, Nanny said angrily. "So it's true, Leslie! I'd not have thought it of ye. Come in, child. Let me talk with ye. Leslie, will ye fetch me some water?"

Leslie nodded and hastened off, bucket in hand. My face flaming, I also obeyed the old woman. Her cottage was small but tidy, and on a chair lay her knitting. Scarcely knowing why, I felt at ease there and bold enough to ask, "How did you know?"

She sighed. "Mrs. Morgan often sends me scraps from the castle and the maid who brought the last basket told me the tale. They'd not gossip outside, but after all I belong. I didn't believe the girl until I saw Master Leslie's face today. I cannot understand it! He's always been a gentle enough lad, though spirited. Will ye tell me how it happened?"

And so I did. It was easier than I expected. She waited silently until I had finished and even then paused in thought. At last she said, "Ye'll hurt yerself more than him by yer hatred. Give yerself a chance to know him."

Perhaps she would have said more had Leslie not returned just then. But now it was my turn to be sent out of the cottage to feed the horses some dried apples. Leslie was, I presume, being scolded, for when he emerged a few minutes later, he looked rather sheepish. Nanny kissed us both good-bye, telling Leslie to visit her again soon and to bring me as well. We trotted away waving, but as soon as we were down the road a bit I noticed he was glowering. "Was it so bad?" I asked, half in sympathy, half in amusement.

"Not above half!" he retorted. "Did you know I ought to be whipped!"

"No doubt," I agreed equably.

His sense of humour touched at last, Leslie laughed. "You wouldn't like *all* of the advice she gave me," he warned. "No, I don't think I shall tell you. She may be correct, in which case I shall stand in need of it."

It was too nice a day to argue so I simply shrugged and pretended I had no curiosity. Leslie was not deceived, for he laughed again and said, "I needn't ask what her advice to you was."

I shrugged again provoking more laughter. After a moment, I laughed also. Then Leslie was pointing out the game-keeper's place not far ahead. Like Nanny, the man and his wife were elderly. But Leslie could not bring himself to replace Billy with a younger man. They were waiting outside and Billy held our horses as we dismounted. "Ma wife, Marget," he said as he tethered the horses.

"Lady Kinwell," she said curtsying, "Sir Leslie. Won't you please come in for tea?"

The cottage was larger than Nanny's, having two floors and several rooms. Marget quickly made clear what Leslie had already told me: that she had been born above her station, a vicar's daughter, and had married Billy out of love. She did not seem to ever have regretted the step, which had isolated her from her former friends. Marget was obviously on excellent terms with Leslie. "How did your sisters take the news?" she asked him.

"Marget!" Billy exclaimed reprovingly.

Leslie laughed, "It's all right. I've had a brief note from Eleanor and Kate. Both asking who my bride is. They congratulated me, of course, and asked to meet Heather the next time we happen to be near London or their country homes. You'd have thought one person wrote both notes, they were so alike."

"And Mary?"

"She's here. With Philip. To see Heather, of course," he said.

"And does she approve?" Marget asked.

"Quite," Leslie said casually. Marget looked surprised and Leslie added, "She has been most helpful to Heather."

I was curious and decided to be blunt. "Why do you seem surprised?"

"Oh, I meant no offense, Lady Kinwell. It is simply that I cannot imagine Lady Mary approving of *any* woman Leslie married. Particularly a young, healthy, pretty one," Marget explained.

"Why not?" I persisted.

Marget would have answered, but Leslie had at last caught her eye. She stood up abruptly and went to the kitchen for more scones. Billy seemed embarrassed. "Never ye mind Marget, Lady Kinwell. She's a bit too fond of gossip and forgets her place sometimes."

"Gammon!" Marget chided him fondly, as she returned. And she paused to stroke his hair a moment before sitting and saying, "You'd best keep an eye on the girl when you take her to London, Sir Leslie."

The simple, loving gesture between Marget and Billy overset me. I felt a tightening at my throat and did not hear my husband's reply. Thus I was startled to suddenly feel Leslie's hand over mine. The others laughed and Marget teased, "Faith, Sir Leslie, she's so much in love she spends half her time in the treetops. Ah, but I was like that too, the first few years after I married Billy."

"Ye still are!" her husband retorted.

I laughed also this time and made no effort to withdraw my hand from Leslie's. I would, I must play through this farce! Marget's next question was no surprise. "Well, will you be making a wedding trip?"

Leslie smiled. "Yes, but not for a while. There are matters to cope with here. Then I must show Heather London during the Season. Later we'll spend a few months on the Continent."

"Can you afford it?" Marget demanded bluntly. "You're a generous man and the castle isn't kept cheaply."

Leslie answered seriously, "My great-grandfather left a trust for the upkeep of the castle. The interest is still ample to cover expenses. Nor have I touched my own capital. I shan't outrun the constable!"

Again Billy was shocked into reproving Marget, but Leslie was only amused. I listened with growing unease. Perhaps he was not so plump in the pocket as I thought, and I ought to be keeping a closer eye on expenses.

We chatted awhile longer, then Leslie insisted it was time

to leave, that there were further calls to pay. When we were finally riding away, I heaved a sigh of relief. "Tired?" Leslie asked with concern. I shook my head in denial and he added, "Just two more cottages to visit. I've other tenants, but today we'll only visit those who couldn't come to our reception."

"Leslie," I said, timidly, "*can* we afford to go to the Continent?"

"Don't you wish to go?" he countered.

"Of course, but not if you cannot afford it. And . . . and . . . you needn't buy me so many clothes. . . ."

He cut me off with a laugh. "My dear Heather, I appreciate your concern, but truly we needn't count every farthing."

I nodded, satisfied. "That's as well, then. You never speak of it and Marget made me wonder."

"My mother would have found you incomprehensible." Leslie laughed.

Stung, I retorted, "It's just as well that I don't have to face her then!"

I gathered myself to urge my mare faster and leave Leslie behind. He must have guessed my thoughts for at once his hand shot out and clamped onto the bridle. I glared at him and he said, angrily, "I told you not to behave so childishly when riding. You are not ready to go galloping neck-or-nothing about the countryside!"

I loosened my grip on the reins and stared at the ground. After a moment, Leslie seemed satisfied and he released the bridle. We rode on in silence. Inwardly I seethed. By what right did he treat me as a child? That I knew the answer made me twice as angry as I might otherwise have been. I had little time, however, to dwell on my anger before we reached the next cottage. It belonged to a young man named Jim. He emerged as we rode up and held the horses as we dismounted. "Good day, Lady Kinwell," he said politely. Then, more enthusiastically, he greeted Leslie, "Good day, sir! I must show ye that garden. I've some more new ideas to try."

Leslie laughed and gave me his arm as we followed Jim to his "garden." It was more than a mere garden, however. Jim had plowed and seeded nearly two acres of land. As I watched from the border Leslie and Jim strode among the furrows and occasionally stopped to inspect some plant or other. To my surprise, Leslie seemed interested in all this. I began to fear he would stay the day in the fields. But at last he remembered my existence and spoke to Jim, who glanced over to me, then nodded. He reached me first. "Beggin' yer pardon, me lady, ye might be more comfortable in the shade." He guided me to a wooden bench under an old oak. "Let me fetch ye some water."

Then he was gone and Leslie sat down beside me, deep in thought. Indeed, he was startled when Jim returned with the water. I thanked him and was not surprised when he sat down beside Leslie and once more began to talk of matters I could not understand. By this time, I was beginning to feel short of temper. Neither man noticed as I rose and went off in search of a water closet. Or the nearest thing to one.

When I returned, Leslie was waiting impatiently. "We ought to be leaving, Heather," he said abruptly.

Exasperation robbed me of words. As though it were my idea to stop so long here! Leslie did not await a reply but took my arm and we walked to the horses. Jim endeavoured to congratulate us on our marriage. Reminded of my position, I managed somehow to smile and accept Jim's compliments graciously. Indeed, I even asked him several questions and teased him on the probability of his finding a wife. It would seem I answered too prettily, however, for as soon as we had set off, Leslie taxed me with the matter. "Must you flirt with *every* young man?" he asked evenly.

I could restrain my temper no longer. "Flirt? Because I was civil to the man? 'Twas your idea to visit here! I'd not have joked with him but for your silence over the matter of our nuptials. You *said* we must pretend to be a normal new-wedded couple!" I retorted.

He merely regarded me with evident disbelief and reproof. To my chagrin, I found myself blushing. How dared he treat me in such a manner? We rode in icy silence for a time. But finally curiosity overwhelmed my anger and I asked, "Are you pleased he has cultivated so much of your land?"

"Why not?" he asked. "If he did not it would simply lie unused. And he is an intelligent young man with some unusual ideas."

I was contemplating this answer when I noticed a large house across the fields. "Who lives there?" I asked.

"My great-grandfather built it as a dower house," Leslie explained. "I once thought Mary might wish to use it. But she did not and now my bailiff lives there."

Something in his response puzzled me. "Why should Mary have wished to use it?"

Leslie frowned. "There was a time she and Gainesfield were . . . quarrelling. She thought to return here. They managed, however, to avoid this measure and eventually reached a happy enough arrangement."

I wondered what sort of quarrel could drive mild Mary to consider leaving her husband. But I did not question Leslie further. In any event, we were approaching the next cottage.

No one came out to greet us. Leslie frowned as we approached the door. He knocked and a voice bade us enter. At the far side of the room a young woman lay in bed. It was clear why she had not been at our reception. She was *enceinte* and very close to term. In the next moment I realised that she was, in fact, due now. I hurried across the floor to her side. "Jenny Bartlet? I am Heather Kinwell," I said briskly. "Are you in labour? Has your husband gone for the midwife?"

Jenny shook her head, close to tears. "He's away in town, gone te fetch some things. There be no one te send."

I took her hand. "Don't worry. Sir Leslie will fetch her and I'll stay until he does." I turned to Leslie, "Do you know where to find her?"

He nodded. "Of course. But first I'll send you back to the castle. Mrs. Morgan can find someone to stay with Mrs. Bartlet."

Not wanting to argue beside Jenny, I took Leslie's arm and pulled him outside the cottage. Then I faced him, hands on hips. "Listen to me, Leslie. I'll not leave that poor girl alone. She's no older than I am and half scared to death at the thought of giving birth!"

"And if she should need help? Are you as qualified to help her as someone Mrs. Morgan could send?" he challenged.

"I think I am!" I retorted. "Now please go and fetch the midwife."

For a moment I feared he would forcibly carry me away. But at last he turned and strode toward his horse. I ran after him. "Leslie, give me some silver, please," I said.

Startled, he paused. "Why?"

"For the baby."

He laughed and handed a few coins to me. Clutching them, I ran back to the cottage. I went over to the bed. "Don't worry, Jenny," I said. "Sir Leslie has gone for the midwife. Look, I've brought you the first present for the child."

I showed her the coins and she smiled. Then a grimace crossed her face, and setting the coins on the table, I hurried to pour some cold water into a basin. I found a cloth and bathed Jenny's forehead, for the day had turned very warm. When I had done that, I gave her my hand to hold, which she gripped with surprising strength each time the pains came. They were coming closer together now and Jenny was crying, though she had not yet screamed, as I had heard women were wont to do. Sometime later, she gasped, "I'm afraid, Lady Kinwell. Suppose she don't come in time?"

I was surprised to hear myself say briskly, "Why, then I'll deliver the child."

She regarded me with awe. "Have ye ever done it before?"

"No," I said honestly, "but I know what must be done."

Jenny accepted this and became calmer. I prayed I would not be called upon to cope alone with the birth. I knew, in theory, what must be done, but that was not the same as practice. I had once spent a year where I was much with the school nurse and learned all manner of useful remedies. I had also wheedled out of her very precise information about childbirth by pretending I was greatly afraid of the event and determined never to endure the ordeal. This shocked the poor woman so, that she hastened to explain the "ordeal" in detail and all the various steps that might be taken to ease a woman's suffering. I knew Leslie believed me mad, but I truly felt Jenny needed me and that I could be of use to her. That she was badly frightened seemed clear, and I did not wish to leave her alone even for the time necessary to return to the castle and send someone in my place. I strongly suspected, moreover, that although I had never witnessed a birth, I had better knowledge of what was to be done than a servant who had had no nurse to instruct her. Above all, Jenny most needed to be encouraged. That I was her age and calm would help steady her, I knew.

I moved about the small cottage, tidying it and sweeping the floor. I pulled back the curtains to let in the greatest amount of sunlight and left the door standing open to coax in the breeze. After consulting Jenny's wishes, I laid out a few things for the baby when it should come. Frequently I paused in this work to sit beside Jenny and hold her hand or bathe her forehead or just talk. And then, as the pain grew stronger, I tore my shift (for lack of other material) to provide straps for her to pull on; the other ends being tied beneath the bed. I talked with her, but of what I cannot recall. And I listened for the sound of Leslie's horse returning. I laid aside a knife and some thread in the event the midwife should not come in time. But there was little danger of that since it was Jenny's first and could be expected to be a long time emerging. Yet if the midwife could not be found . . . ? I thrust aside the thought. If Leslie could not find the midwife surely he would summon a doctor.

Fortunately, Jenny had ceased to be so afraid, placing her trust in me. Yet we were both relieved when the sounds of a horse finally reached us. A few minutes later, Leslie entered with Kate, the midwife. She nodded to me curtly and professionally began to examine Jenny as Leslie pulled me outside. "Now will you come home?" he demanded.

Before I could answer, Kate called from the door, "She's asken fer ye, Lady Kinwell."

I nodded and said to Leslie, "No, I will not. I'll return when Jenny ceases to need me. Pray give my regrets to Lady Mary that I shall not be present at dinner."

Leslie was angry but I turned and walked back to the cottage. Behind, I could hear Leslie cursing me. Inside, I joined Kate in preparing Jenny. I smiled at her reassuringly but did not disturb Kate with needless chatter. I was oblivious to time as we worked. At some point Tom Bartlet returned, but Kate chased him out of the cottage saying he would be useless. When he rebelled, I left Jenny's side long enough to allay his fears and suggest he fetch more cold water. Whether it was the calmness of my manner or the fact of my title, I do not know, but Tom quieted and agreed to our instructions. Inside, I teased Jenny over her husband's concern and drew a smile from her. Kate assured me there would be no trouble with the birth and we settled down to wait. When it began to grow dark, I lighted the candles. Kate talked and we listened, Jenny and I. She talked about other births and the families in the nearby countryside. One of her first deliveries had been Leslie.

Then it began and we, none of us, had time to chatter. Kate used the knife and thread I had set aside. Soon I was holding the child and gently bathing it with another strip of cloth torn from my shift. A lusty boy who wanted his mother. And even as I held the child I felt a wave of sadness sweep over me, that I would never hold a child of my own. As the tears obscured my sight I handed the child to its mother. Kate signalled that Jenny was almost ready and I left the cottage in search of Tom. He was just outside. "You've a son, Mr. Bartlet," I said, "and Jenny is well."

He let out a shout of triumph and soundly kissed me before running to the cottage. Laughing, I followed. When I entered the doorway, I saw him bending over to kiss the baby. Then I found myself consenting to their shy request that I stand for the child at its christening. They had begun to discuss names when there was a knock at the door. I hastened to open it. A maid from the castle kitchens stood there, and I realised she carried a large basket of food. "Sir Leslie said I was te bring it," she said shyly.

The basket contained two roast hens, bread, and some elderberry wine as well as some fresh eggs. Tom decided to broach the wine that we might all toast the new baby. I could not refuse, but after the toasts I insisted I must leave. We bade each other good night and I left with the maid, feeling warm and happy.

Outside I discovered she had come in the pony cart. "The maister said I was on no account to let ye ride back in the dark," she said. "We're te tether the mare te the cart."

I smiled and agreed, adding that she must handle the reins as I'd no experience with carts. She, Gail, seemed pleased and more at ease then. And as we rode she asked about Mrs. Bartlet and the baby. I answered her questions as best I might and laughed at her surprise when I said I had torn my shift for straps and to bathe the child. At last, her curiosity satisfied, she sighed. "Well, but 'tis good for ye, I daresay. Ye'll be having yer own babes soon and will know what te expect."

I was glad of the darkness that hid my tears from her. I chided myself silently, saying it was only the fatigue which made me unhappy. Gail chattered on, oblivious to my distress. The servants, she told me, already discussed when the first child might come and whether it would be a boy or girl. From a distance, I heard myself say that a doctor had once told me I might find it difficult to conceive. *That* reduced her to a shocked, sympathetic silence.

I was grateful when we reached the castle. Gail sent me

straight in, saying she would look to the horses. I stumbled up the steps and a startled footman let me in, saying the master awaited me in the library. I went there and rapped on the door. "Come in!" a harsh voice commanded.

I entered. As I did so Leslie rose to his feet with an exclamation, "Good God! Your habit!"

I looked down in surprise. "Oh dear, it's ruined, isn't it? The underskirt also, I fear. I'm sorry, Leslie, I forgot to be careful."

He came and firmly propelled me to a chair and sat me down. "Have you eaten?" he demanded.

I shook my head. "Not since breakfast."

With a muttered curse, he rang for a servant, and when she came ordered a cold tray and a pot of tea for me. Leslie paced back and forth, refusing to let me speak until I had eaten. When the tray had at last been carried away, I began to chatter. I told him how I had come to tear my shift and some of Kate's stories. And I told him of Tom's worry and his kiss. Then I paused. "I agreed we would stand for the child, Leslie. I suppose I should have asked you first, but they were so shy about it. . . ."

A corner of his mouth twitched, but his face remained impassive as he said, "Very well. Go on."

There wasn't much else to tell. Until I came to the lie I had told the maid. I shrank into the chair, afraid of Leslie's anger. But he looked more weary than angry. "Yes," he said, "I suppose that will keep the servants from wondering why there are no children."

He turned around and seemed to be attending to certain papers on his desk. Impulsively I rose and went over to him. Placing a hand on his arm, I said, "I'm sorry, Leslie."

He looked down at me, an expression in his eyes I could not read. He put a hand on my head and said quietly, "Go up to bed, Heather. You've had a busy day."

Confused, I withdrew to my chamber. Immediately, Ellen began to cluck over me and the ruined habit. I let her chatter. The tale of my action had indeed passed throughout the servants' hall, and my behaviour was much remarked upon. Ellen, at least, seemed to approve. After a soothing bath, I dismissed her and sought my bed. Tired, sleep came quickly to me that night.

Chapter 9

Mary's first words to me the next morning were, "My dear! How highly unsuitable!"

This was at breakfast. For the first time we all met at the morning table. I answered shortly, "She had need of me. That was all that was important."

"But you could have sent a servant," she protested.

I shook my head. "The very fact that I was Lady Kinwell helped. Also, I did not wish to leave her alone and I felt I had the necessary knowledge to cope if the child arrived before the midwife."

"How could you?" she asked in a shocked voice. "Surely such things are not taught at Mrs. Gilwen's school?"

I sighed. "No, they are not. Medical texts exist, however."

It was a small lie, but I was afraid that if Mary knew who had taught me she might cause the poor woman's dismissal. Mary confined herself to shaking her head at me. Philip was interested. "Aunt Heather, weren't you squeamish? I mean, it isn't a pleasant process, is it?"

"Philip!" Mary's shocked voice rang out.

"May I suggest," Leslie interrupted, "that this is not a suitable topic for the table."

His words silenced us until I turned to Mary. "The other day, ma'am, you suggested a trip into town. Are you still willing?"

She smiled and unbent perceptibly. "Of course, my dear. Have you many things to buy?"

"A few," I admitted ruefully. "Is there a decent dressmaker in the place? I've need of a new habit."

"A tolerable woman," Mary replied.

"Why do you need a new habit?" Philip was curious. "Thought your blue one all the crack."

I blushed. "I fear I ruined it yesterday."

After breakfast, Leslie called me into the library. From the desk, he produced a small leather pouch of coins. "You will, naturally," he said, "put such things as your new habit on account. You may need, however, cash for tea or small purchases. Or"—he hesitated—"for gifts."

I took the pouch, feeling rather surprised and I stammered, "Th-this is most kind of you, Leslie."

He slammed shut the drawer of his desk and said shortly, "It is nothing of the sort. You were promised a settlement and you shall have it. If you recall, I assured you that you would not lack for spending money."

Dismayed by his tone, I said, "Very well. Then I shall simply say thank you."

He was silent and I hesitated, uncertain if I should stay or leave. Then he spoke with a touch of bitterness in his voice. "Congratulations, Heather. The servants have accepted your tale. This morning my valet, Peter, offered me his sympathy for your condition."

I flushed. "Leslie, I am sorry. But I felt it better they should have no cause to wonder when no children appeared." I bit my lip. "And after all, I could have said *you* were the one unable to have children."

"And if later there should be children?" he demanded.

I grew white angry under his gaze. "I did not tell her conception was impossible, merely difficult. But you need not worry, sir, that I shall present you with"—I hesitated over the word—"a side-slip. Whatever your activities, *I* do not intend to pursue any affairs!"

We glared at each other across the desk. A knock at the library door recalled us to ourselves. "Come in!" Leslie called as I quickly sat down and stared at the floor.

It was a footman. "Young Mr. Bartlet, sir, asks to speak with you, sir."

"Send him up."

"Begging your pardon, sir. I thought that would be your answer and I took the liberty of bringing him with me."

"Very well. Show him in."

Tom was bashful this morning. "Sir Leslie. Lady Kinwell.

've come te thank ye both fer what ye did fer me wife yesterday."

"Why, you are quite welcome," I said frankly. Then asked merrily, "And how is the baby? And the mother?"

He flushed happily. "Oh, famous, ma'm. Jenny's feelin' herself agin, and the babe, well, he's got a powerful strong set o' lungs!"

We all laughed. "When is the christening to be?" Leslie asked with a smile.

"Sunday, a week hence," Tom told us.

"And the child's name?" I queried.

Tom flushed again. "Ken Leslie Bartlet. We'd a named it Heather if it'd a been a girl. Now I won't be wasting any more of yer time, Sir Leslie. I just came te say thank ye and tell ye the day of the christening."

"Will you have something to eat before you go?" Leslie asked. "Mrs. Morgan could . . ."

He laughed. "Mrs. Morgan has already fed me this morning."

We laughed with him again and Tom left, escorted by the footman. When they were gone, I turned to Leslie. "Good day. No doubt Mary awaits me."

Mary was indeed waiting. I paused only long enough to fetch a reticule, gloves, and my hat and to speak to Mrs. Morgan hastily. "Sir Leslie expects another guest this week and does not know the day," I told her.

"Which chamber shall I prepare?" she asked.

"I am not sure," I replied frankly. "The guest is the Earl of Pellen. Best give him the most comfortable one."

"Very well, my lady."

I was glad I had prepared the week's menu in advance and had no need to stop for it that day. Mary was growing impatient. "I'm sorry," I told her when at last we were in the carriage. "I should have warned you had I known Leslie wished to speak with me."

"Was he angry with you?" she asked sympathetically.

"I fear so," I admitted and sighed. Then, needing to confide in someone, I said, "I started a silly rumour among the servants. I told one of the kitchen maids yesterday evening that I could not have children. Goosish of me, no doubt, but I could not bear the thought of speculation belowstairs as to when an heir might arrive."

To my surprise, Mary did not reprove me but said she thought the idea a sensible one. I still did not know my *belle-soeur* very well. We came to a halt in the courtyard of the inn. Having compared our lists of errands, we determined to visit the dressmaker first to order my new riding habit.

It was to be expected that we would be stared at, the villagers being curious about the new Lady Kinwell. We were greeted with deference at the dressmaker's shop, and it was clear she was both surprised and pleased to receive our patronage. After some discussion, I chose a fabric and style much like that of the ruined habit. Miss Markam promised delivery within the week. At the same time, Mary ordered a summer dress and I had the first indication of how long she meant to stay. For the dress could not be ready in less than seven days, and she said they might have a fortnight if need be.

As we walked past the other small shops many of the women paused to greet Mary by name and I was introduced. Even allowing for natural curiosity, I was puzzled by the intentness of many of the stares I received. I could not know that Kate had already spread the tale of my behaviour of the day before. In innocence I agreed with those who asked if I found the country a quiet place.

Laden with bundles, sometime later, we returned to the inn and placed them in the carriage. We had already decided to have nuncheon before returning to the castle. I was frankly elated with my freedom, the new experience of having sufficient funds for all I wished to purchase, and the deference shown me as Lady Kinwell. I should be a liar if I did not admit there were compensations to my new existence. The innkeeper hastened to serve us personally and seat us in a private parlor. We continued to discuss our purchases and the style of boots and shoes I had ordered, this being one article Leslie had been reluctant to choose for me. Indeed, at the moment, I had but one pair of each which must serve on all occasions. We were in complete accord concerning the shawl and lace cap Mary had purchased. I reflected that she, like her brother, possessed excellent taste. Mary confided that often she preferred to shop in such small villages since frequently, if one were careful, one could find very smart articles and the prices were not so shockingly dear as in London. Not that William was clutch-fisted. Quite the contrary. Still, a pound saved was a pound saved and there were all manner of other uses to which it could be put.

Feeling very companionable, Mary and I returned to the courtyard where the coachman waited. As he handed us into the carriage an impressive coach and four pulled up. A moment later, a youngish-looking man of about thirty-five years emerged. He was neatly dressed and carried himself with an air of importance. Beside me, Mary exclaimed, "Why, it seems to be Lord Pellen. Whom can he be coming to visit?"

I was amused. "Us. Or so Leslie has informed me. Do you know him?"

"Oh, dear me, no. But he is everywhere received," she replied. "Of the highest *ton* and in politics, I believe, though rumour has it the family funds are a trifle flat."

"Flat?" I said incredulously. "With that coach and four?"

"Well, in a relative way," she temporised.

Confused, I gave the order to drive home. Confusion passed to anxiety as I wondered if Mrs. Morgan had prepared a room for the earl. I wished I had remembered to warn her yesterday, for I feared we should see him at the castle before nightfall. But the matter was of little concern to Mary and she began to discuss the gifts I had bought for Jenny Bartlet's new son. Soon I was deep in a discussion of the relative merits of various sorts of rattles.

The sight of the castle reminded me of my responsibilities. Leaving the servants to deal with the packages, I apologised to Mary, then went in search of Mrs. Morgan. After a few questions I ascertained that a chamber was aired and ready with dry sheets and that it would be no trouble to lay aside some of the best wine for dinner. Satisfied, I decided to seek out Leslie and warn him our guest might arrive at any moment. He was, as I expected, in the library. As was his habit, he did not look up as I entered, and I was halfway to his desk before he realised I was not a servant. "Ah, Heather. Did you enjoy your visit to the village?" he asked.

I untied my bonnet and drew off my gloves. "Very much," I admitted.

As I sat down in a wing chair he came to sit beside me. "And what did you buy?"

"Well, I ordered the habit, of course—'twill be ready within the week—shoes, and oh, the dearest boots. . . ."

On I chattered happily, pausing now and again to ask if such and such a price had been reasonable.

Each time he gravely assured me it was. And he laughed when I described my dilemma in choosing a gift for the baby. When I had finished and sat staring at him, feeling a bit breathless, Leslie reached out and gently flicked my cheek. "You look quite pleased with yourself," he teased. "And happier than I have ever seen you. I must send you shopping more often."

"Oh, no," I protested earnestly, "that would be terribly foolish. I should spend all your money. . . ."

Abruptly I realised he was roasting me and blushing, I fell silent. "Did you do anything besides shop?" he asked gently.

Eagerly I told him about the splendid luncheon at the inn. And the innkeeper's deferential manner that had made me feel so strange. "Oh, I must tell you," I said after, "your guest will no doubt be arriving today. Someone stopped at the inn with a travelling coach and Mary said it was Lord Pellen. She seemed surprised to learn he would be visiting at the castle, though she said she didn't know him. I've already spoken with Mrs. Morgan. A chamber has been prepared and his comfort shall be seen to. I daresay even the groom has been warned he shall have extra horses to attend to."

Leslie nodded absently, his thoughts clearly on other matters. He seemed disturbed almost. I wondered if he truly welcomed the earl's visit and whether the reason for it were unpleasant. Some of this must have shown on my face, for abruptly Leslie asked if anything had gone wrong. "N-no," I said, blushing, "it simply seemed that you were, well, concerned."

He smiled, but I sensed weariness behind the smile. "You needn't bother your head about it. His lordship is arriving earlier than I expected, and I haven't the least idea how I shall entertain him. That's all."

I wavered, uncertain if Leslie were shamming it. He spoke again, more gently. "Go along now and change, Heather. It's almost teatime, you know."

"Very well," I said, aware there were things which required my attention, "I shall see you shortly."

Ellen was waiting for me. Somehow she always seemed to know when I would need her. My packages were on the table, but resolutely I decided to ignore them for the time.

Suddenly I realised Ellen was regarding me oddly. "Is something wrong?" I asked her.

Hastily she set about helping me change. "Oh, no, my lady. Only . . . well, that Mr. Bartlet this morning, told everything. I mean, we knew you had stayed with Mrs. Bartlet, and I could see from your habit you had helped deliver the child . . . but to tidy the cottage! And standing for the child . . . and . . . and all . . ."

I turned to face her. "Oh, dear, Ellen. Have I shocked the servants terribly? Have I sunk myself beneath reproach? But what else could I have done? She needed me."

Ellen was shocked at my dismay. "Oh, no, my lady! That isn't what I meant. Everyone is saying how wonderful it was . . . and what a proper mistress for the castle you be. Proper sympathetic they are, too, at your position, and saying Sir Leslie had best treat you with respect."

At the image of Leslie's servants taking up the cudgel in my defense, I laughed. "So I am accepted then?" I asked.

"I should say so!" Ellen answered.

I sighed. "Lady Mary believes I acted improperly."

"Don't you be listening to her!" Ellen said firmly. "You've more sense than she does. 'Tis odd, my lady, but though Lady Mary is respected in the castle, I think she is not liked."

I was puzzled. Why should the servants dislike Mary? True, she was a dominating woman, but good-natured enough. I hoped she would not realise how the servants felt (or that Ellen was mistaken), for it would distress the poor soul.

Ellen's voice interrupted my thoughts. "They say in the kitchens we're to have another visitor, my lady."

"Yes. The Earl of Pellen," I said, rolling the title off my tongue. "He is expected today."

"Shall I lay out a special gown for dinner?"

"Yes, though I cannot be sure he will arrive by then."

"Best to be prepared," Ellen admonished.

Downstairs, I discovered that the earl was a considerate man. Lord Pellen had sent a messenger from the inn to inform us of the hour of his arrival. The time had clearly been chosen to cause the minimum of inconvenience and I found myself looking forward to making the acquaintance of a man who would think of such things. Leslie had already been apprised of the note and given the necessary orders, the

105

footman respectfully informed me. I thanked him and proceeded to join the others.

Everyone had gathered for tea. I was somewhat nervous
since, aside from rare occasions at Mrs. Gilwen's school, I
had never poured for others. Yet I was glad of the practice
now, for I knew it could not be long before I should need to
serve as hostess often. Mary smiled at me reassuringly and
Philip roasted us about our shopping expedition. Rather than
setting up my back, his boyish banter made me feel comfortably at ease. Almost he could have been the brother I had
never had but always imagined. Leslie alone was quiet, often
regarding me with an odd look in his eyes. I wondered
whether this were due to the impending arrival of Lord Pellen
or my behaviour of the day before. Annoyed by Leslie's
reticence, I turned my full attention to Philip. He seemed
flattered. So easily had I forgotten my resolution! Mary's
voice, however, soon recalled to us who and where we were.

Tea eventually over, Philip suggested that he and I take a
turn in the garden. I refused, preferring to work at my needle
and fearing his lordship might arrive early. I would also have
nervously sought out Mrs. Morgan save that Leslie assured
me that all was in a state of readiness. I should, of course,
have realised that Lord Pellen would be punctual, arriving
neither early nor late. The footman informed us of the approaching carriage, and Leslie and I waited on the steps to
greet our guest.

The wind tugged at my curls and I felt a flutter inside as
the man I had seen at the inn approached. At the proper
moment, I curtsied and Lord Pellen took my hand, kissing it
in the French manner. Face-to-face, I found the man younger
and handsomer in appearance than I remembered. He stared
rudely at me, as though evaluating a horse or hound. After a
moment, he said to Leslie, "Quite presentable. You took us
all by surprise in London. Didn't know what the devil to
expect."

Leslie raised an eyebrow and shrugged. Angered, I wondered if I must expect all Leslie's friends to make so careful a
scrutiny when we appeared in London. Already I began to
dislike his lordship. But then Pellen turned to me and smiled.
"Forgive me, Lady Kinwell. I do not mean to be rude. I was
simply startled to discover that so lovely a young lady could
exist in London without my knowledge."

I smiled, but there was that in his voice that disturbed me, and I distrusted his cozening tongue. Yet I said, graciously enough, "Ah, but Sir Leslie married me out of the schoolroom, my lord. So it seems unlikely you should have had reason to see me."

Still smiling, he bowed lightly and offered me his arm. We entered the castle and Mary and Philip somehow appeared. As the one made a deep curtsy and the other a bow Leslie said, "My sister, Lady Mary Gainesfield. Her son. Philip. Lord Pellen."

Lord Pellen kissed Mary's hand as gracefully as he had kissed mine and retained it a moment longer than necessary. "I am enchanted," he said. "I have often seen you in Town, have I not? You have a fondness for the opera, I believe."

Mary was flustered by the knowledge that the earl had deigned to notice her. Yes, he certainly had charm, I admitted to myself. And the moment's extra pressure on an older woman's hand could scarcely fail to flatter. It was becoming clear that his lordship was either an accomplished diplomat or a charming rake. He moved on to Philip. "Ah, young Gainesfield. I have heard good things of you, although with a warning that you are a scapegrace! Sometime we must discuss our college experiences. I am curious to discover whether my generation or yours has the most imagination."

Philip flushed with pleasure. I stepped forward, "My lord, may we offer you refreshment?"

"No, no, Lady Kinwell," he replied kindly, "but if I may be shown to my room . . ."

Leslie beckoned to a waiting footman. "The oak room, John," he said.

The hour of his lordship's appearance allowed us an hour and a half to dress for dinner. Thus, as soon as he had disappeared up the stairway we scattered to our own rooms. Ellen had laid out an evening dress of green silk trimmed with flounces that left, it seemed to me, too much of my bosom bare. But I accepted Ellen's assurances that it was the kick of fashion and that no one would consider me immodest. With greater care than usual, she dressed my hair. Then, as I was admiring my reflection in the glass, I heard a knock at the door. "Sir Leslie!" Ellen said in surprise.

I turned to see him standing in the doorway, looking splendid in his evening clothes. For a moment he did not speak, but stared at me. Abruptly, he thrust something into Ellen's hands and said to me, "You are to wear these tonight."

Then he was gone. Much astonished, Ellen closed the door and brought me the box. It was a simple one and did not prepare me for what lay inside: a necklace, bracelet, and earrings. "The Kinwell emeralds!" Ellen whispered.

I laughed. "Truly, Ellen, you are much better informed than I! Tell me what you mean."

As she set about fastening the necklace about my throat she explained, "Well, my lady. They'd said in the kitchen there were a goodly amount of Kinwell jewels. The emeralds in particular are known, though they say Sir Leslie has a set of rubies and diamonds, too. Well! According to tradition, the wife of the eldest son is supposed to receive the jewels. I'd begun to wonder if you would. There, my lady. You be ready."

I stared in the glass again, looking in vain for the shy, penurious young girl who had fled from the schoolroom less than a month before. But I only beheld the image of young Lady Kinwell and felt a stranger to her. I had no time to wonder over this, however, as Ellen reminded me I must not be late.

Fortunately, only Leslie was waiting. He looked at me briefly, before turning away to pour himself a drink. I realised then that he intended to give no explanations. Mary entered a moment later and halted when she saw me. Her mouth gaped open and she said in a strange voice, "You . . . you've given her the emeralds, Leslie?"

He answered curtly, "Yes. Why not? She is, after all, Lady Kinwell."

Mary's eyes narrowed, "Does this mean . . . ?"

The question hung for a moment, unfinished. "Don't be a widgeon," Leslie snapped. "You must know I have no interest in tradition. I simply felt it was time Heather had them." He added coolly, "Besides, Pellen would think it strange if she wore no jewels."

"You could have given her the rubies!" Mary retorted.

There was a tension in the room I could not comprehend. Then Leslie said, "With that dress, sister? Don't be absurd."

Mary turned her back on him and I felt a desire to respond to both in kind. Need they speak so cryptically? The pleasure I had felt over the emeralds began to fade, destroyed by the agitation of Mary and the casual attitude of Leslie. To her the matter was too important. To him, it seemed, not at all. Hearing Philip and Lord Pellen's voices in the hallway, we three turned as one to the doorway, wearing the calm smiles the social occasion demanded of us. As they entered the room I again felt Pellen's appraising stare on me. Good God! I wondered. Can it be he is . . . *interested*? I must discover from Mary if he could be such a loose-screw as that. If so, Leslie must speak to him. Otherwise his visit would be unbearable.

My impression grew as his lordship insisted on escorting me in to dinner. I looked at Leslie questioningly, but he merely smiled and nodded and took Mary's arm. Philip followed alone. I was not altogether surprised to discover that his lordship had been seated next to me, but I began to feel uncomfortably aware of his attention.

From the first moment, Lord Pellen dominated the conversation. It was not that the rest of us were intimidated by him, it was simply that he was capable of turning any subject to the course he wished it to take. Yet unless one watched closely, as I did, it seemed he was deferring to the wishes of those around him. I began to wonder just who this man was whom my husband had invited to visit. I gleaned from his words the knowledge that he was active in the House of Lords. And I had the impression he was considered important. Yet I had never heard of him. I would have questioned him on his views of the Corn Laws, but he early stated that he felt politics an interest totally unsuitable for women. Courtesy forbade my commenting on this as I should have liked to. The talk turned, naturally, to horses but was turned away again when Lord Pellen noted my lack of interest. This consideration, however, only irritated me further, as I had no desire to be so closely observed by this man. He then spoke to Mary of the latest London fashions. I listened with but half an ear since I felt it would be some time before I should need any new clothes. And in any event I trusted Mademoiselle Suzette to choose her styles well. Again I felt as though Lord Pellen were aware of my lack of interest. At one point, Philip questioned him as to his university escapades. His lordship laughed and shook his head. "No, I shall not discuss them here," he said. "We must confer in private. I should not wish to shock your mother or your aunt or uncle."

We all laughed pleasantly. Then, to my surprise, he transferred his attention openly to me. "I understand you attended Mrs. Gilwen's school for young ladies."

"Yes, I did."

Then followed a catechism concerning the subjects I had studied and the accomplishments I had, or rather, had not acquired. Forced to deny any musical or artistic skill, I began to grow embarrassed. Philip startled us with the words, "Well, at any event, she learned how to deliver babies."

Mary's shocked voice rang out in the silence. "Philip!"

I blushed deeply and stared at my plate. Lord Pellen turned an enquiring eye on Leslie, who described my adventure of the day before, making light of the matter. Yet to my ears, there was a note of discomfort in his voice. As it died away I felt Pellen's speculative eye on me again. But all he said was, "Well, well, you are an original, Lady Kinwell."

"Indeed?" I said coldly.

Leslie frowned at me, but his lordship was only amused at my rudeness. "Pray don't be angry with me, Lady Kinwell," he said easily. "I simply find you fascinating. And not only I. I daresay many people in London eagerly await your appearance in the *ton*. After all his years of bachelorhood, everyone wants to see the woman Sir Leslie succumbed to."

My fingers clenched so tightly the nails dug into my palm. I wondered if I appeared as angry as I felt. There was that in Pellen's manner that convinced me he knew the truth, and I felt sick with fear that others knew as well. All that remained was for this man to taunt me for my lack of ancestry. Leslie spoke then, his words light but his voice a warning. "Ah, my lord, they will need but one look at Heather to understand my surrender."

I forced myself to take a sip of wine and this steadied me somewhat. Yet I was still upset and even now cannot remember aught of what was said between then and when we rose from the table. The men declined port and we all left together. As though sensing my feelings (though perhaps they were obvious), Leslie took my arm before Lord Pellen could offer to escort me out. His lordship merely smiled and bowed to Mary, who was suitably appreciative of his graciousness.

The earl, it appeared, was extremely fond of whist. I was delighted, as this would easily occupy the others all evening and I would be free to do my needlework. I had not anticipated Mary or Lord Pellen's reaction to this suggestion. "Oh, but Heather, dear," Mary protested. "I am not overly fond of cards. Surely you would prefer to play?"

Determined not to be so trapped, I replied, "Ah, but I have no knowledge of the game."

"How terrible!" Pellen exclaimed. "Then there can be no dispute, Lady Kinwell. You must join us and we shall teach you. You cannot enter the *ton* ignorant of whist."

I looked at Leslie, pleadingly, but he agreed with the earl. Seeing no escape, I gave in graciously. So the table was set up and the cards brought. I grew increasingly upset with myself. Not only must I still play, I should also be forced to listen to them explaining rules I well knew. And I should have to be careful to play as a novice would. I had lied to no purpose.

The first few rounds were as boring as was to be expected as the others attempted to show me how best to play. Gradually, however, the play began in earnest. Pellen concentrated on his cards and gave no further excuse for me to take offense. Leslie was my partner, and once or twice, I saw him glance at me quizzically and I would take care to play poorly for a while. Philip, now and again, would speak encouragingly and compliment me on taking up the game so quickly. We played till quite late, halting only when a footman informed us a late supper had been laid out. This time I could not evade Lord Pellen and I took his arm. Cards had relaxed me, however, and I felt less of my earlier antipathy toward him. "You've a head for cards," he said.

"The credit must be given to good teaching," I replied.

"Well, I believe Heather will do very well in London!" Mary's voice intruded. "She will be more popular with a little skill than if she were an expert."

The talk became more general as Leslie asked Pellen the *on-dits* of London. Foolishly, I barely listened, forgetting that what seemed trivial here might well be important when we arrived in Town ourselves. At last our guest announced a desire to retire, adding as an afterthought, "Oh, I believe you may expect callers in the morning."

With no further explanation, he went upstairs, followed by Mary and Philip. When they were no longer in view, Leslie turned to me. "You should not have lied to Lord Pellen about the cards."

To cover my confusion, I lifted my chin, "I dislike the man."

"Nevertheless, he is not stupid." Seeing this made no impression on me, he added in exasperation, "You cannot always choose your companions! Quite frequently you shall have to deal with people you dislike."

"I have already discovered that!" I muttered.

He flushed, but ignored the insult. Continuing, he said, "You are really not being fair to his lordship, Heather."

At this injustice, I could bear no more and fled to my chamber in tears. Behind the bolted door, I pounded a pillow with my fist. All through dinner the man had taunted me and I-I-*I* was being unfair! Ellen tried to soothe me, insisting I undress. Then she brushed and plaited my hair. By the time I was ready for bed, the fury had drained out of me, leaving only weariness. But sleep was elusive and it was some time before I found its shelter.

Chapter 10

I woke early, as usual, but determined not to face Lord Pellen before I must, I rang for Margaret to bring a light breakfast to my room. Grimly mindful of his lordship's warning that I could expect callers, I told Ellen to bring out my best morning dress. Had matters been otherwise, I might have been excited at the prospect of someone new to meet and pleased that the barriers had been broken. As it was, I resented that Lord Pellen felt free to invite anyone he wished without asking if it were convenient for Leslie or myself. I also was angry that people would come to see Lord Pellen when they had avoided calling to see me heretofore. Perhaps I was unjust to the man, I told myself. Perhaps he simply assumed people would come to call, having heard he was here. No doubt the *ton* usually did when he went visiting.

Privately I wondered how I would deal with his lordship during the remainder (undetermined in length) of his stay. I had understood Leslie quite well. This man was not to be offended. Yet what was I to do? He seemed to delight in taunting me, and I could not bear the touch of his hand on my arm. And he always seemed to want to hold my arm or kiss my hand or stare at me in an intimate way. Could Leslie not see this? Was it possible he did not care?

The next few hours were a nightmare for me, and looking back, it is difficult to remember all the events that took place, all of the words that were spoken. I had waited until the last possible moment before leaving the refuge of my chamber and descending to the morning room. I noted with relief that his lordship was not in evidence. Leslie and Philip, Mary informed me, were out riding. And Mary and I? What were we to do as we waited for the arrival of callers? Mary shook her head. "My dear Heather, you must not allow yourself to be overset. You are looking well today and need not bother about refreshments since the servants are well trained. Really, my dear, what you need is to be busy. But not with mending. Perhaps some delicate needlework . . . ?" she suggested.

I agreed, knowing her advice to be sensible. As we worked, Mary and I discussed many of the women who had greeted us in the village. (By mutual consent, we did not speak of Lord Pellen.) The time passed agreeably enough and I was quite calm when Mr. and Mrs. Bentworth, of the neighboring estate, were announced. I sent a footman in search of Lord Pellen and Leslie as the Bentworths were shown in. I was greeted coolly by Mrs. Bentworth, who scarcely seemed to notice me. Mr. Bentworth was kinder and felicitated me on my marriage before turning to Mary. "May I offer you tea?" I asked. Mrs. Bentworth inclined her head and I rang for a servant.

When the maid arrived, I gave the proper orders, then turned my attention to my guests once more. "I do not remember seeing you during the last London season," Mrs. Bentworth said to me.

I began to feel ill. Mary spoke hastily. "Well, of course not. Leslie married the child straight out of the schoolroom."

"Which school, if I may ask?"

"Mrs. Gilwen's School for Young Ladies," I replied.

"Ah, yes," she said. "I have heard it is a . . . serviceable establishment. I believe Mr. Watly sent one of his daughters there."

I wished that the tea tray would arrive. I could think of naught to say. Mrs. Bentworth, however, felt no such loss. "Have you met many of the local gentry, Lady Kinwell?"

"Not . . . not yet," I stammered.

"You see, Heather and Leslie are so recently married they feel no need for other company," Mary inserted.

Mrs. Bentworth smiled. "And then, of course, one must be *so* careful. It would not do to form an . . . er . . . *unsuitable* acquaintance. One must be quite certain of people one doesn't know before calling."

The tea tray arrived before I could speak. When I did, it was with deliberate misunderstanding. "I am gratified to see you have resolved the question in my case."

She drew herself erect and spoke coldly. "I see I must

speak plainly, Lady Kinwell. I am not in the least satisfied as to your background. However I felt that your guest, Lord Pellen, deserved the consideration of a call from us.''

I was white with anger and would have retorted sharply, when a voice from the doorway forestalled me. ''Madam, if you cannot speak with common courtesy to my daughter, you will please leave at once!''

We all stared, our mouths agape. Lord Pellen, followed by Leslie, calmly strolled into the room. An extremely flustered Mrs. Bentworth dropped a deep curtsy. To cover my confusion, I poured tea, hoping no one would notice my trembling hands. Someone passed the full cups around and his lordship sat next to me, taking the next but last cup. He spoke, ostensibly to me, but with a quiet voice that carried to every corner of the room. ''My dear Heather, you must learn not to allow such impertinence. I am aware you dislike to be rude, but really I think you are far too tolerant.''

Mrs. Bentworth had regained her tongue, however, and said indignantly, ''Lord Pellen! Why . . . why *everyone* knows you have no daughters!''

The earl regarded her with deceptive mildness and delicately yawned. ''Indeed? Then *everyone* is mistaken.''

Suddenly a thought occurred to Mrs. Bentworth. ''Are you boasting, my lord, that you have a daughter born the wrong side of the blanket?''

Before any reply could be made, I rose to my feet and, setting down my teacup, said with all the dignity I could muster, ''If you will please excuse me, Mrs. Morgan has need of me in the kitchen.''

My eyes appeared to look at each of them, but in reality I saw nothing. I withdrew, forcing my steps to the slowest pace they were capable of. I continued down the hall and through the kitchens, my head erect, greeting those I passed but not pausing. I calmly walked out of the castle and toward my favorite copse of trees. Halfway there I broke and ran into their sheltering midst, sobbing as I ran. Over and over the words chased through my head, ''My father . . . my father. . .''

I reached out to steady myself against a tree, almost blind with tears. I leaned against it, my head tilted back. ''My father . . . my father . . .''

I still could not fully accept what I had heard. All my life, until a month before, I had believed my father dead. And my mother. Was it possible my mother . . . ? I forced myself not to consider the thought. My father. A month ago I had learned he had not died but deserted me . . . his illegitimate daughter. I was never to see him or know his name. And now . . . now I had met him. He was a man I did not like and did not want to know. Why, why had he come? I no longer needed him, and I could not bear his boasting to the world of my shameful birth. How could my mother have loved such a man? Or was she, as Mrs. Gilwen had implied, a lightskirt who cared only for the gifts a man might bring? I felt bewildered. None of my assumptions had been true, it seemed, and I knew not where to begin again. I felt dizzy and leaned harder against the tree, my head aching.

After some time, I moved to a rock at the water's edge and sat. I was exhausted, drained of my fury and tears. I must think, I told myself, and determine what was to be done. There was no one I might turn to. Mary? Even if she did not reject me now, she was well meaning but not very wise. Leslie? The name was bitter in my mouth. My husband! He had known and not told me. Nor had he stopped my father from speaking. Well he should suffer for it! He had been so concerned that none guess the cause of our marriage. Well, here was far greater shame for him to face! Why had he let my father come? What, dear God, could I do? Run away? Where could I go? Who would receive me after this?

Over and over the thoughts went round my head. Looking in the water, a tear-swollen face stared back at me, and I bathed it in the cool water. This calmed me some, and my thoughts became more coherent, then turned wild again as the hopelessness of my position bore relentlessly in on me. At times I paced under the trees, and at times I stood and stared at the water. I considered the possibility of refusing to see Lord Pellen during the rest of his visit, and I considered speaking with him long enough to ask him to leave. But these emotions also passed, and finally I was left standing, staring at the water, with a quiet resignation. Soon, I would return to the castle and face what must be faced.

I stood thus for some time, how long I cannot say. Then from behind me came a voice, "Don't, Heather!"

I turned to see Leslie only a few feet away. As my brain strove to digest the knowledge he came and pulled me roughly toward him. I stumbled and fell against his chest and his arms immediately encircled me. After a moment, the shock wore away, however, and I tore myself free. An arm's length away, I stared up at him. His face was distorted by an emotion I did not know. I saw him anxiously glance past me to the water, then at my face. And I understood. I moved away from the stream, careful not to approach any closer to him. In a voice tinged with contempt, I said, "You need not fear. I have no intention of killing myself." His tense shoulders relaxed and I continued, "Whatever else you may believe me to be, I am not such a coward."

"Oh? You ran from your guests and left the castle."

I looked down. "I believe I had a good cause to leave. Nor did I *run*."

His voice, when it came, was heavy with anger and sarcasm. "Well, Heather, if you are quite finished with your childish games, shall we return to the castle? You need not fear, the Bentworths have left."

"Childish games!" I exclaimed in disbelief.

"Yes, children's games," he retorted. "Running out of the castle and hiding in the woods. Philip and Peter are also out searching for you. There would be others except that I did not wish this latest foolishness bandied about, among the servants."

"They have enough other cause to gossip," I laughed bitterly.

Leslie ignored me. "Why didn't you answer when I called your name?"

"I didn't hear you," I said sulkily.

"Not hear me!" he exclaimed. "I did not realise my voice was so softly pitched. Come, madam, admit you did not wish to hear me."

The injustice of this accusation angered me further. "Had I heard you, sir," I said between clenched teeth, "I should have answered."

He stared at me for a moment, then said quietly, "Shall we go in? Your father wishes to speak with you."

"How dare you invite him here?" I demanded. "I don't *wish* to speak with him!"

Leslie's voice was sharp. "You forget yourself. This is still my castle and I invite whom I wish. As for speaking with Lord Pellen, you have no choice. If you will not come willingly, I shall carry you. It will be a most undignified experience for you."

Aghast, I stepped back and turned to run. A hand closed harshly about one wrist and the other arm around my waist. From over my shoulder, as my heart pounded, came his voice. "Well? Which is it to be?"

I forced my head up. "I'll come."

After a moment, apparently satisfied, Leslie released my waist but not my wrist. He did not speak as he dragged me out of the copse and I could not understand what was happening. Even of Leslie I would not have expected such Turkish treatment. "Can we not walk slower?" I gasped.

"We have kept your father waiting long enough!" he tossed back at me.

"You knew!" I accused bitterly.

"Yes, I knew," he said grimly.

The effort to keep pace with Leslie reduced me to silence. Only when we reached the castle did he slow. "Smile," he warned.

Mrs. Morgan met us at the door. "If Master Philip or Peter return," he told her softly, "tell them Lady Kinwell is found."

She nodded, and pretending an amiability neither of us felt, Leslie and I proceeded to the library. Lord Pellen was seated at the desk, waiting. He stood as we entered and Leslie, not content with dragging me here, thrust me into a chair. Pellen waited for Leslie to shut the library door, then shook his head at me. "My dear child, I am disappointed. I thought you were made of sterner stuff. Nevertheless, your behaviour was not a disaster. Mrs. Bentworth quite naturally assumed you were a well-bred young lady who disdained to reply to her insult."

Though stunned, I now found my tongue. "Indeed? How fortunate. Yet I wonder how she reacted to your reply. I am very sorry, *father*, but somehow I could not bear to stay and hear you confirm her suspicions. Was it necessary to tell her I was your by-blow? But then what should I have expected of a man who deserted me at birth, spending barely enough to keep me at school and allow me two dresses a year? And who should cease even this meagre aid upon my eighteenth birthday!"

"That will be quite enough!" Pellen's voice rang out. "You speak from ignorance. First, as I told Mrs. Bentworth, you are not illegitimate. Your mother, Elizabeth Wade, and I eloped and though underage, were married nineteen years ago. If you care to see them, I have the marriage lines." I nodded and he passed a paper over to me, and I saw the names and the fact of their marriage stated there. At last I looked at my father questioningly. "That's better," he said. "Elizabeth's father opposed the match and he disowned her. My parents were more incensed and physically dragged me home. Elizabeth was the daughter of a clergyman. I, the future earl, betrothed to a wealthy heiress from an eminent family. My parents tried to annul the marriage, but Elizabeth was pregnant. I was kept locked at home until you were born, while my parents hushed up the elopement and, unknown to me, did not break my engagement. Elizabeth died giving birth to you, Heather. That much I know to be true. But I was also told you had died. Within a year I allowed myself to be married to the heiress, who had no notion this was my second marriage. Secretly my mother arranged for your care and education, determined no one should ever know of your existence. She was afraid it would destroy my marriage. I did not learn of you until Sir Leslie came to inform me he intended to marry you."

I sat in shock, finally managing to say, "But Mrs. Gilwen said I was illegitimate."

Leslie answered. "She thought you were. Lord Pellen's mother claimed to be your guardian but swore Mrs. Gilwen to secrecy. She scented a scandal."

"You must not judge my mother too harshly," Pellen said, "She felt she was doing the best for me and doing her duty by you. When Mrs. Gilwen offered to give you a position at the school, my mother felt it would be suitable."

"Suitable!" I exclaimed. "An unpaid teacher?"

"She did not realise this was the sort of position meant," he said soothingly.

"And now?" I asked.

"Now? Now I shall recognise you, of course," he replied. "After this morning the entire countryside will soon know you are my daughter by a prior marriage, one which lasted a regrettably short time. In London, an announcement has been placed to the effect that Sir Leslie Kinwell and Lady Heather, daughter of the Earl of Pellen, have been married."

"Don't you think someone will wonder why I have never been seen at your house with you?" I demanded sarcastically.

He sighed. "You are being difficult, Heather. The answer is really quite simple. I was away when my wife, Elizabeth, gave birth. Due to some confusion, I was told both Elizabeth and the baby had died. I have just recently been united with my long-lost daughter whom I discovered because she has been given (due to a clerical error) the name Heather *Wade*. Such a touching and romantic story."

"And who had been caring for me?"

"A childless woman, who believed you to have been abandoned, anonymously provided the money for you to be sent to school. Alas, you have never known the name of your benefactress. Nor, despite my efforts, have I been able to discover it." He smiled. "Later this Season I shall introduce to society my charming daughter who is now Lady Kinwell. You will be veritably inundated with respectability and will be able to claim your rightful place in the *ton*."

He was very pleased with himself and I was forced to admit the tale was clever, the ruse might work. Ruse? It was essentially the truth. I *was* respectable. And yet I disliked the idea of even this amount of deception. "And if I do not choose to play out the farce?" I asked.

Leslie moved to stand beside Lord Pellen. "You have no choice, Heather," my husband replied. "I do not intend to let you set foot in London until you have agreed. Remember, my position is at stake also." My eyes narrowed and he hastened to add, "But you will gain—or lose—the most. It is to your advantage to secure an unsullied reputation so easily."

"Very well," I said at last, "I see I have no alternative. And upon reflection, I am grateful, Lord Pellen. You could easily have continued to ignore my existence."

Leslie smiled oddly and Pellen coughed. "Yes, well . . . er . . . never mind that." He hesitated. "I think it best if you call me Father." I nodded and he grew bolder. "I must say, Heather, I am quite pleased with you. When Sir Leslie told me you existed, I had no notion what to expect. After all, I'd never seen you, had I? Oh, of course I knew you'd been sent to excellent schools; still such training is no guarantee. But I am definitely pleased. You recall that last night I seemed to be quite rude? No doubt you felt I was extremely impertinent? Well, of course you were right. You see, I was testing you. I wished to see how composed you would remain. You have dignity, my dear, you have dignity. I was disappointed this morning when you fled the room, but even then it might have been worse. A little experience and you shall deal quite well in society. You must be presented at court, naturally, and I shall undertake to arrange that myself. My wife, Lady Phyllis, will coach you."

"Are you sure she will wish to?" I asked skeptically.

Lord Pellen seemed surprised at the question. "Of course. Phyllis is a sensible woman. She will see the importance of it. And she knows protocol as well as I."

For the next several minutes, Leslie and my father discussed how best to manage the affair. When should I arrive in London? Whom should I see? Decisions on matters such as these were made. As they talked I tried to think over what had been said. I still could not quite believe all I had heard. Then I found myself wondering, "What did you tell Mrs. Bentworth?"

Pellen looked up, startled. "Eh? Oh, why, I told her our touching story. She was quite embarrassed and most apologetic for her . . . rudeness. I was, at first, stiffly cool, then allowed myself to be coaxed into amiability. I believe it is safe to wager that by week's end everyone will have heard the tale. You may expect a great many bride-visits, my dear. As for Mrs. Bentworth, I am sure you will see her again, suitably respectful the next time." At the sight of my face, he added, "Yes, I know. I detest the woman myself. But you must learn to be polite to such people. Handled properly, they often prove to be quite useful."

I nodded since he seemed to expect it, but I was not happy. Leslie and my father began to talk again. I was startled to hear the words, ". . . marriage settlement, Sir Leslie. It ought to be arranged before I leave here."

"Marriage settlement?" I asked stupidly.

"Of course. I must settle something on you," Lord Robert explained. "It would seem odd otherwise."

"I do not want your money," I heard myself say.

"My dear child, that is for your *husband* to decide. Now, Sir Leslie . . ."

I swallowed, foolishly hurt and angry that Leslie had not refused. I felt ill and very small and I found myself wondering why my mother had married this man. Or had he been different then? Gentler, kinder perhaps? Why had my mother's father opposed the match? Why had Lord Pellen allowed himself to be dragged home? Well, perhaps he hadn't a choice. But why marry the other girl, less than a year after my mother's death? If my mother had not died, what then should my father's family have done? Had I not been born Robert's parents might well have contrived an annulment. What of my mother then? My mother. Did she believe herself simply deserted? Or did she know or guess that her husband had been removed against his will? Lord Pellen's voice scattered my melancholy thoughts. "Well, Heather, have you any questions?"

"What did she look like?"

"Who?"

"My mother!" There was impatience in my voice. Whom else could I have meant?

"Oh. Very much like you, I believe. The same sort of hair and eyes. A somewhat softer chin and mouth. She was a bit more feminine and delicate perhaps," he answered with a shrug.

More submissive? I wondered silently. "Did you love her?" I asked aloud.

"Love her? I must have thought I did or I should not have eloped with her against the wishes of our families," my father said.

"And Phyllis? Did you love her?" I persisted.

"No, of course not. What an absurd notion."

I could not hide my shock. "Absurd? Why?"

Lord Pellen sighed, but his patience was unshakeable. "My dear child, I can see that someone unwisely has allowed you to read novels. You must realise that love is a very poor foundation for marriage. Consider Elizabeth and myself. We only had two weeks together before we were found, and yet we succeeded in making each other extremely unhappy. Of necessity, we had differing opinions on many subjects and this distressed us. We each felt the need to convert the other. And naturally it was impossible. We could not, moreover, bear to be apart even for the very shortest period of time. That may do during a short honeymoon, but believe me, very soon one tires of such restrictions and wants more freedom. Then, of course, one has jealousy. It is simply impossible to avoid and is a great strain on one's emotions. One is constantly seeking reassurance of the other's love. My dear, the best sort of marriage is one without this nonsense of love. Easier on everyone.

"Consider my marriage with Phyllis. We liked each other, in a general sort of way. But none of this 'love.' We were of the same social background and had common interests and common friends. This was the most important factor, not emotions. Well, we dealt very well with each other. Since we were not in love, we felt no zeal to change each other's opinions. Nor did we feel the need to hold each other accountable for our movements. Since we had always been friends, we provided a suitable companionship for each other. Without the annoying problem of one or the other taking offence over some silly little matter. And since Phyl was never in love with me, she was not in the least disturbed when I found it necessary to supplement our marital activities with . . . er . . . companionship elsewhere. The only demand she made was that I should be discreet. That's reasonable enough, ain't it?"

"Quite!" I murmured sarcastically.

He glanced at me sharply, but as I continued to watch him demurely, he continued, "We've similar wants, Phyl and I, and she's very reasonable about helping me get them. Consider, for example, the matter of your existence. Had we been in love, Phyl might well have kicked up a fuss. She might even have refused to receive you. But this way she can be quite sensible. I can trust her to confirm anything I say. And if Phyl confirms my story, no one else will dare question it. They'd be insulting Phyl if they did, you see. Had I known then what I know now, I'd never have run off with Elizabeth. Silly thing to do. The best marriages have nothing to do with love. Only causes problems, my dear. Why, consider you and Leslie. No love there when you married, was there? But you're dealing quite well with each other, I'd say."

"Would you?" I asked with raised eyebrows.

"Would you rather be ruined?" Lord Pellen demanded. "I'd wager not. You've a good social position, respectability, money, and in a few years, children. What else could you want?"

"There will be no children," I said as I met his gaze full on.

"No children? Why the devil not? You've given yourself no time to discover that," Pellen replied in astonishment.

"A woman who sleeps alone rarely conceives," I said bluntly. Avoiding Leslie's angry eyes, I added, "I believe my *father* ought to know what to expect. Or, rather, what not to expect. Well, father, on our wedding day Leslie promised not to force himself on me."

Lord Pellen whirled to look at Leslie. "That was a damn fool promise! You ought to have begun as you meant to go on. If you'll accept my advice, you'll forget that promise. The girl is simply frightened. All brides are. They soon accustom themselves to the inevitable. Will you next be living under the cat's paw? You're the master of the household and you'd best be sure she understands that." My father was clearly deeply shocked. "We can discuss those other matters later, Sir Leslie. Now I think I ought to leave you alone with Heather. It would seem you've some things to settle."

He left before we could stop him. Leslie glared at me and I tried to hide in my chair. His voice was sharp and angry. "Was it absolutely necessary to tell him?" I stared back, helpless to answer. "I warn you, Heather, if *you* cannot keep your tongue between your teeth, *I* cannot answer for the consequences. Good God, woman! Don't you understand? If anyone should hear of this, not only would they not believe I married you for love, but other rumours would start as well."

Leslie was white with anger and very near to hitting me. I leaned farther and farther back into the chair as he stood above me with smouldering eyes. Then, abruptly, he turned and strode from the room saying, "Damn you!"

It was awhile after the library door slammed before I could force myself to move. And then I only drew my handkerchief out as I broke into tears. I had never seen Leslie so angry, nor angry with such good cause.

The sound of servants' voices made me start. With surprise, I saw it was well past noon. I must return to my room and change. Lord Pellen might well be expecting more callers. And by now, Mrs. Bentworth's tongue would be at work. Whatever came I must be prepared.

Chapter 11

The servants, Ellen informed me when she answered my summons, were discussing how marvelous it was that I was the daughter of an earl. "Who would have thought it, my lady?" she said as she helped me change. "And such a romantic story! After all these years!"

"You *know* what happened?" I asked with some surprise.

"Oh, yes, my lady. Sir Leslie discovered that one of the maids had overheard Lord Pellen say he was your father. Well! Sir Leslie felt it would be best if everyone knew the truth instead of rumours. So he told Mrs. Morgan and told her to tell us! No need to be ashamed of *your* birth."

I laughed. "Truly, Ellen, I am amazed how well informed the servants always are. What else do you know?"

"Well, nothing certain, my lady. But the head footman said that, surely now, Sir Leslie must arrange for you to be presented at court," she said hesitantly. "And they are saying, my lady, since you asked, that it is a shame, it is, that you cannot have children."

I frowned. "It's not impossible, Ellen. Simply unlikely."

"Yes, my lady. Well! Everyone says that if it were not for that, you and Sir Leslie would be very happy. Since you asked, my lady."

I flushed. Happy! If they knew . . . there would be no talk of happiness. "Yes, well, please leave me now, Ellen."

She nodded sympathetically and departed. I dressed my hair myself, no difficult task, since until a few weeks before I had never had anyone to do it for me. A smile twitched at my lips, for I could easily picture Ellen in the kitchen listening to gossip. Or, perhaps she would be telling how I had dismissed her, wanting to be alone because I was so unhappy at the thought I could have no children.

I was composed when I entered the drawing room. Leslie glanced at me quickly, then looked away. My father regarded me more carefully before nodding gravely. I understood that he had signified his approval. Philip, of course, was staring with undisguised astonishment. I smiled at the two strange women in the room. Mary was speaking, ". . . Lady Kinwell. Heather, may I present Louise and Irma Connelly?"

They murmured a polite greeting and I spoke with the combination of warmth and self-assurance that was appropriate, though feigned. "I am delighted to make your acquaintance. I presume Mary has already introduced you to my father, Lord Pellen. And, of course, you know Sir Leslie and perhaps Mary's son Philip as well. Shocking of me not to be here to greet you. I was unfortunately delayed with a household matter."

And why, I wondered silently, had no one informed me of this arrival sooner? Irma was speaking and I endeavoured to concentrate my attention on her. ". . . us about you and your father, Lady Kinwell. Such a romantic tale! How happy you must feel to be reunited!"

I smiled, but was saved the necessity of hypocrisy by Miss Louise. "I must admit, Lady Kinwell, that we have been somewhat concerned as to your parentage. It seemed quite unusual that no one knew your family. Now, of course, we are perfectly satisfied."

My anger grew as I listened, and I might have spoken had Lord Pellen not forestalled me. "My dear woman," he said, "I hope you are not trying to say that had my connection to Lady Kinwell not been known she should have been unacceptable. Even lacking such credentials, the veriest fool must have seen Lady Kinwell is quite unexceptionable! Her very carriage and bearing proclaim her to be bon *ton*!"

Under his fierce gaze, Louise and Irma Connelly distinctly quailed. I felt grateful indeed to my father. And the arrival, just then, of the tea tray provided a welcome diversion. I was relieved to be able to sit aloof, pouring tea as the others talked. Once again, Leslie was describing his plans for our trip to London, and later, to the Continent. Then Mary was

126

explaining I had been educated at Mrs. Gilwen's school. By the time I had finished pouring tea, conversation had turned its attention to Philip. I felt sorry for him as the admission that he had been sent down from Oxford was extracted. Happily the two sisters soon recalled that my father was come straight from London and they begged him for news of acquaintances. Lord Pellen and the Connelly sisters did not move in the same circles, and he deftly turned away questions he could not answer by volunteering gossip. When his supply of *on-dits* ran short, he shifted to the topic of London fashions. *This* subject was inexhaustible and seemed further to inflate my father's worth in their eyes, for at one point Miss Louise said, "My lord, how very clever you are. Few men would have noted so many details or described them so well."

Lord Pellen smiled. "You are much too kind, Miss Connelly. I am sure there are many details I have forgotten and which you will tax me with should we meet again after your next visit to London."

"Do you intend to visit here often?" she asked eagerly.

He continued to smile and glanced at me. "Can you doubt the answer, my dear lady? I have so recently discovered my daughter. Shall I now relinquish her?"

"How touching!" Irma sighed.

Lord Pellen glanced again at me, mockingly. I understood. Whether he visited or not, it could not but help my social position if it were generally believed he would. I smiled at him. "And of course my father shall always be welcome here. We have many years of not knowing each other to make up for."

Leslie looked at me sharply, but I avoided his eyes. And when he spoke, it was to Irma. "How is Mr. Connelly?" he asked.

"Oh, my," she began, "you know of course my husband's knee. . . ."

I ceased to listen, needing the time to compose myself again. Irma had no children to discuss, but when the subject of her husband was finally exhausted, it was also time for the ladies to leave. "Will you be at church, Sunday, Lady Kinwell?" Louise asked.

"We will all be at church," Lord Pellen replied smoothly. "May I escort you to your carriage, ladies?"

127

Amid flutters and polite farewells, they withdrew. When they were well out of earshot, Mary exclaimed, "Concerned about Heather's credentials indeed! And who is Mrs. Connelly to cavil? Married her own cousin. And for that matter, the family is Irish!"

Leslie laughed. "The first Connelly came to England three centuries ago."

"The Irish blood is still there!" Mary insisted. "You know very well that the Connellys have often sent to Ireland for brides for the men. Questioning Heather's background like that! The fact that she is your wife ought to have been sufficient, Leslie."

"Ah, but I am so eccentric," Leslie teased. "How could they be sure I had not married an opera dancer?"

"Leslie!" rang out Mary's shocked voice. "I beg of you not to speak so lightly of such an important matter."

"Oh, Mother," Philip said impatiently, "everyone knows Uncle Leslie is too top-lofty to marry an opera dancer."

At Philip's words, Leslie raised an eyebrow in amusement. I wondered, not for the first time, how Philip had acquired such an absurd notion of Leslie. Well, that was not my affair. Philip grinned at me. "Your father rang a peal over Mrs. Bentworth this morning for her rudeness."

Mary intruded, "Philip! Show a proper respect for your elders!" She turned to me, "Are you well, Heather, dear? I thought perhaps you might not wish to see anyone this afternoon or I should have informed you the Connellys had arrived for tea."

"But I was informed," I said with some surprise, "albeit a trifle late."

"Quite right," a voice behind me said. I turned to see my father standing in the doorway. "Forgive me, Lady Mary, I did not know of your intentions. I simply asked one of the maids to tell Heather she was late. I thought my daughter shy, perhaps, and felt it necessary she overcome such missishness. When she is presented to the *ton*, neither fatigue nor nerves will excuse rudeness, *nor any action which might be construed as rudeness.*"

Mary flushed under Pellen's gaze and I wondered again at my father's ability to bend others to his will. But I pondered too deeply, for he found it necessary to speak my name sharply before I attended to his words. "Heather! I pray you will listen for a moment, daughter. I wish to discuss Sunday. It is of the utmost importance our arrival be properly timed. We do not wish to arrive so late that we disturb the service; however it is imperative we should be the last to enter.''

"Why?" Philip broke in.

My father smiled and answered patiently. "Because we wish everyone to have the opportunity to gossip about Heather. And they will. Also, I have an aversion to standing about when people around are gossiping about *me*. After church, it must be borne since we must greet as many gentry as possible. They will expect it of us.'' He paused and frowned, "You and Heather *do* attend regularly, do you not, Sir Leslie?"

Leslie smiled, but I noted his eyes were grim. "We've had but one opportunity, thus far, and we were there. One could hardly say 'regularly,' yet. But we will.''

My father nodded as though satisfied, but I suspected Leslie's irritation had not escaped him. It was not to be wondered at that so autocratic a man as my husband should chafe at having his actions determined by another. Lord Pellen turned to me again. "Well, Heather, I was pleased to see you had regained your composure. I believe you shall deal well in London, very well indeed. Particularly as Lady Phyllis will be there to guide you. Sir Leslie has informed me you patronise Mademoiselle Suzette. I might have recommended another, but that does not matter. Mademoiselle Suzette obviously understands what suits you. Phyllis will ensure you receive all the important invitations. *And* she will tell you which ones to refuse.''

"Oh?" I said dangerously. "Why must I refuse any?"

"Because you must show everyone that you consider yourself as important as you are. *That* means that for your début, at least, you must be a snob," my father answered quite practically, his eyes warning me there should be no protest. His voice softened. "Of course, if it is a matter of an old friend from school, you may tell Lady Phyllis and I am certain she would not object.''

"How kind!" I murmured.

My father chose to ignore my sarcasm. He looked at me critically. "You are in need of rest, my dear. In London you must have a care. Neglect your rest and you will endanger your appearance. Upstairs with you now.''

I was relieved to be dismissed at last, for it was a clear

dismissal. I nodded and gathered my skirts to leave when Leslie spoke, "I would like a moment with you first in the library, Heather."

Though tired and unequal to being lectured further, I could not refuse. I nodded and followed. I think he might have taken my arm, save that I drew away when he moved to my side. In silence we walked, and in silence he held the library door for me. Only when I was inside and seated did he speak. And even then it was not easy for him. "Heather," his voice was taut, "if you choose, we need not follow your father's plans for London."

I sighed. "I admit I am not altogether pleased with my father's proposals, but I have seen that he is an expert at dealing with people. I suppose, therefore, that his advice must be sound."

He turned and stood with his back to me. "I see. Very well, I shall go ahead with the arrangements your father wishes me to make."

He paused and, on impulse, I asked, "Leslie, what is this settlement my father spoke of?"

Leslie was tired, very tired, or he should never have answered so frankly. "Your father is deeding you one of his estates. The smallest one. In return, I shall pay off the mortgage on the estate and—"

"My father is deeding us a *mortgaged* estate?" I demanded in shock. "What sort of gift is that?"

Leslie answered wearily, "It's not meant to be a gift. It's a gesture your father feels is necessary for appearances. Ostensibily your father will pay the mortgage himself and only the three of us will know otherwise."

"But this is absurd!" I protested. "You must refuse. I have cost you too much money already."

Leslie chuckled bitterly. "You do not understand, my dear. I cannot refuse. But I appreciate your concern."

A suspicion grew in my mind. "Mary said Lord Pellen was scorched. Are you giving him other money also?" Leslie did not speak, but his face answered for him. "Leslie! I will not have it, do you hear? I will not have you franking my father. I would rather do without his goodwill!"

Leslie faced me squarely and his voice brooked no dispute. "*You* will not have it? This time you've gone your length, madam. I shall do as I choose with *my* blunt! Your father was

quite right, you have forgotten who is master of this estate."
I stared at him, shaken by the force of his anger. "You will
go to your room and rest," he said in the same manner, "and
ponder what your father and I have said today."

I had no choice than to do what he wished. Shakily I rose
and withdrew. It was difficult not to run, but I was learning
to keep in step with my role as Lady Kinwell, and it was with
dignity intact that I reached my chamber. Nor did I tremble
when, later as she helped me dress, Ellen clasped the emeralds about my throat.

It was at dinner that I began to truly feel I should be able to
deal with London society. For nothing could have been more
difficult than that meal. Mary was again disturbed over the
emeralds and I feared Leslie almost regretted the gift. Philip
was curious and asked me questions for which I had no
answer. It was left to my father to reply, and though he did so
with ease, I grew more and more distressed with the curious
mixture of truth and falsehood he spoke. I believe Leslie felt
as I did, but I could not be sure, for we avoided each other's
eyes and indeed conversation so far as it was possible to do
so. Nor could I feel at ease with my father after all I had
learned that day. Yet I believe an outsider would have thought
all was well, so smoothly did the conversation flow. If our
smiles were without true warmth, I think few would have
guessed it. And more than once, my father nodded his approval to me. If this was to be an example of my future, I
should not be happy, but I knew I should be capable.

After the meal, my father suggested a game of whist, to
which we all agreed. somehow it was arranged that my father
should partner me and I became quickly aware he was testing
me. How well could I play if my partner were a fool? How
well if he were skilled? Did I lose gracefully? Did I win
graciously? Could I both converse and play at the same time?
Did I appear to consider the cards too lengthily? Too lightly?
He tested me until I grew weary of it. I considered warning
him that I knew what he was about and was on guard to
please him. But I did not do so for fear he should devise a
more devious test. From time to time, Leslie regarded me
anxiously, it seemed. But I would not let him see my weariness. Philip, I am convinced, noted none of this and Mary
placidly wrote letters, oblivious to the rest of us.

Leslie had again ordered a cold supper to be served at

midnight. I thought it ironic that Lord Pellen ascribed the efficiency to me. For the first time that evening, Leslie and I exchanged truly amused smiles. So little escapes my father that he noted even that and nodded to himself, as though with satisfaction. Mary bade us good evening in a rather abrupt manner and I wondered what had overset her. Perhaps she did not welcome Lord Pellen's presence in the household, disrupting as it did our previous quiet existence. And yet, I should have thought her pleased at the right to claim such close ties to someone so important. Perhaps she feared my newfound father would claim all my affection and I should have no time for herself. I determined to find an opportunity to reassure her.

I withdrew shortly after Mary, climbing the stairs slowly. To my surprise, Ellen was not waiting to help me undress. Instead, as I looked about Mary came out of the shadows. "Mary!" I exclaimed. "What's wrong?"

"Hush," she whispered, and made haste to shut the door. Then she smiled, but spoke little louder, "I'm sorry, my dear, I dismissed your maid because I wanted to warn you to bolt your doors tonight, if you could, and if not to sleep in my room."

"I shall assuredly bolt the doors, as always," I said in puzzlement, "but I do not understand your distress. What has happened?"

Mary sighed unhappily. "My poor child! Leslie spoke with me this afternoon. He told me your father had bade him ignore the promise he made to leave you in peace. And when I asked if he meant to do so, he said he was sorely tempted . . . that your father was, after all, a man of sense. I was shocked, my dear, and told him be reasonable, but he seemed too angry to listen. So I came to warn you, my dear, to bolt your doors. Though I believe it was an empty threat."

I stood for a moment, rooted in shocked silence, then strove to reassure Mary. "My doors shall be bolted and Leslie expects them so. I know he is angry with me, but I cannot believe he will try to force himself on me."

"Heather," Mary said in distress, "you forget what passed your first night under this roof!"

"But—" I stood, mouth agape. "I thank you for your warning, Mary, but I think this a different matter. Nonetheless, I shall be careful. Is there anything else you wished to speak of?"

She hesitated. "Your father. I fear I can not trust the man altogether."

"Nor I," I said grimly, "and I shall continue to need your advice."

Mary smiled and I knew I had pleased her. "I shall always be available, should you need me," she said. "You are tired, my dear, let me help you undress."

I protested that I did not wish to trouble her, but she insisted and in truth I was glad of every assistance. As Mary undid the buttons she said grimly, "It's unpleasant enough fulfilling one's marital duties when one has wed willingly. Unbearable if one has not! Should Leslie determine to force his rights, no bolts would protect you, nor any laws. You must promise to come to me should Leslie go too far. I swear I would protect you."

She was agitated and I said, "Is marriage always so unpleasant, then?"

Mary paused. "Usually, I fear. Even Richard and I . . . we've a good enough marriage now, but . . . well . . . at first it was difficult. Men demand so much and often are not faithful even so. If Leslie respects your privacy, then yours will be an enviable existence."

Enviable? I thought in wonderment. But it lacked so much and seemed so empty, this marriage of mine. I could not think what to say to Mary. But she did not seem disturbed by my silence. "You are tired and perhaps I have shocked you. I shall leave you now," she said. "Try to sleep *and bolt the doors*."

I promised I would and she waited as I shut and bolted the door after her. Yet, surely, it was absurd to think Leslie would intrude? Perhaps not so absurd, for scarcely had I gotten into bed and blown out the candle than it seemed I heard a hand softly try my door.

Saturday was another day of callers. Although my father and Leslie were visibly pleased, I found the day wearying. And after dinner, there were cards to be played, this time with Philip as my partner. Fortunately he cared no more than I whether we won or lost. Determined not to be cast down by anyone, I encouraged Philip's natural gaiety. I also discovered that he was not so shallow as I thought, for later, as the cards were put away he said softly, "You seem very tired, Heather. Let me escort you upstairs."

I was about to assent when Lord Pellen said, "When you are in Town, Heather, you cannot keep such country hours."

Before I could answer, Philip retorted, "Well, this is not London. This is Heather's home, and there are no guests, only family present. So she is free to do as she wishes. Shall we go up, Aunt Heather?"

Avoiding the eyes of the others, I took Philip's arm. And with an exchange of "good night" we swept out of the room.

Chapter 12

Sunday. I dressed with special care, aware that I would face a more careful scrutiny than ever before. My dress was demure, yet fashionable, and my straw hat vastly becoming. Ellen took pains with my curls, and when she had finished I knew I should pass muster.

Leslie came to my room when it was time to leave for church. He surveyed me carefully and childishly I waited for his compliments. But when he spoke, it was curtly, "Your father ought to be satisfied."

Annoyed at this lack of gallantry, I gathered my skirts and swept out of the room, but I was not so foolish as to refuse his arm on the stairs. I well knew it would annoy my father to detect such an obvious sign of discord between Leslie and myself. As matters were, my father was pleased. "Good morning, Heather. I trust you slept well? Excellent. Your dress is enchanting. You will give precisely the correct impression today. Simply be calm and remember that if anyone gossips it is from envy. *You've* nothing to be embarrassed about."

I smiled and spoke truthfully, "Indeed, I am calm, Father."

"Good." He nodded. Then, past me, he said, "Good morning, Lady Mary. How nice you look! And young Philip? I should say that I am glad to see you are not irreverent as so many of your generation. I will not, however, as I suspect you are motivated less by piety than by a desire to see the reaction of the countryside to the news Heather is my daughter. 'Tis only natural."

Philip grinned and did not dispute Lord Pellen's analysis. Mary appeared less pleased, but was placated when his lordship offered her his arm. And soon he had teased a smile from her as well.

As we approached the churchyard, I could see the parishioners being herded inside. It seemed my father should have his wish . . . we would be the last to enter. With Mary on his arm, my father led us in. Leslie and I followed next with Philip last. As I expected, all eyes turned to scrutinise us. With creditable dignity, we reached the family pew in front. Mr. Watly had heard the news but a short time before, it seemed, for he was flustered as he gave the announcements and made a point of welcoming the Earl of Pellen, Lady Kinwell's father. I was amused. Was Watly afraid I should complain to my powerful father of his cavalier treatment of me on my wedding day? Didn't he realise my father should be more likely to thank him than to nab the rust? Or perhaps it was not that at all. After all, I had no notion what Leslie had told Watly of my birth.

I cannot remember the sermon as it was unutterably boring. (Though later Philip said he believed a bit of it had been directed at me.) As a young woman, I felt no closer to the church than I had as a child. Church attendance was a ritual to be observed, much as was taking tea or leaving calling cards. Of what use was religion to me when it could not provide the love I had ever lacked? Never had a curate even noticed me save to lecture over one or another of my failings. I surreptitiously glanced about, studying faces and hats and the altar and . . . Then I felt a hand close over mine in warning. It was my father, of course, reminding me of my position. I resentfully tried to concentrate on Mr. Watly, but my thoughts would not stay. Of what use was a father if he were never loving or understanding?

And then the service was over, and as Lord Pellen had predicted, it was necessary to stand and greet everyone. Mrs. Bentworth wished us to meet her daughters, and the Connellys wished to introduce us to friends. "Wasn't Mr. Watly's sermon so uplifting?" Miss Louise Connelly demanded. "Of course, all of his sermons are inspiring."

Neither I nor Mary could reply, so astonished were we at this view of Watly. Fortunately, my father, ever the diplomat, answered, "Indeed, he has a style quite his own and I confess myself impressed. Mr. Connelly, I trust you are well?"

Mr. Connelly seemed surprised at Lord Pellen's question.

"Oh, indeed, my lord, indeed. Are you enjoying your visit to our neighborhood?"

My father smiled and nodded his head in my direction. "Reunited with my daughter, how could it be otherwise?"

Mr. Connelly turned to me. "Lady Kinwell, I can easily understand your father's delight."

I smiled at this attempt at gallantry. Mrs. Connelly was not so pleased and she soon hurried him away. As they receded, Mary muttered impatiently, " 'Found the sermon uplifting' indeed! Her difficulty is that she cannot forget the family was popistical but three generations back. And she is afraid everyone else remembers as well. Which of course, they do, as she is at such pains to remind us with her absurdly pious behaviour."

Leslie smiled. "Confess, Mary," he said softly, "in truth you dislike the family because you once had a *tendre* for Mr. Connelly and he spurned you."

"What a bouncer!" she protested.

Leslie merely regarded her with amusement. Philip whispered to me, "Lord, ain't this daffy?"

I nodded and found it easier to smile. After all the others, we still had to face Watly and his wife. Leslie performed the introductions and I added with a touch of malice, "Father, Mr. Watly officiated at our wedding."

My father scrutinised the vicar for a moment before answering. "Ah, yes, I am happy to make your acquaintance, sir. I am sorry I was unable to be present at my daughter's wedding. It was a most *interesting* ceremony, was it not?"

Though the words were spoken mildly, Watly blanched. Leslie chose to rescue him. "He has for some time now presided over all the Kinwell family marriages, burials, and other such occasions."

Lord Pellen nodded and I hoped we should be able to leave. Unfortunately my father appeared to consider Watly in some way important, for he requested a tour of the church and grounds. "Oh, certainly, my lord, I should be delighted." Watly glowed.

With resignation, I prepared to endure the process. We were all to be included in the tour, it seemed. I held back a moment, casting about for an excuse to remain where I was, when I felt a hand on my arm. With surprise I saw that it was Mrs. Watly. She spoke softly. "I cannot think you truly wish to join them. Perhaps we might enjoy a comfortable cose instead?''

I glanced toward the others. They had apparently not noticed my desertion. I smiled. ''I should like that, Mrs. Watly.''

''I must wish you happiness with your marriage, my dear. And tell you we have heard of your help with the Bartlet child. I could not say it in my husband's hearing, but that act has gained you much credit hereabouts.'' She paused to smile. ''Of course, my husband and others felt it unsuitable for a well-bred gentlewoman who has not yet had a child of her own, but I think you cannot care much for such disapproval. And even did you, the news of your father's name will silence the highest sticklers.''

I laughed at the truth of what she said, but shook my head. ''No, not silence them. I fear I shall be much talked of, but it will force them to receive me.''

For a moment, we were silent ourselves, perhaps a bit shy. There was much I would have asked Mrs. Watly of herself, but from politeness could not. How could I ask what strength enabled her to endure a continuous existence with a man such as Watly? How could I ask what was truly being said of Leslie and myself? What if she in turn asked for my story? And did she know the truth about my wedding? ''Have you many children?'' I asked her.

''Six. All but two safely wed and away,'' she replied instantly. ''The eldest, a boy, has followed his father in the church. The next two, girls, have married farmers and live nearby. The third girl attended Mrs. Gilwen's school a few years back. She married well and lives in London now. And then I've the two boys at home. I worry what they'll do, for they have but a small portion each. One is army mad, but the other has no notion what course he wishes to follow.''

''Grandchildren?'' I asked.

She smiled, but a trifle wearily, I thought. ''My eldest has two boys, but as his living is south of London, it's not often I see them. And my daughters have none. The third has been married a short time, so one cannot yet expect . . . but the other two . . . The first has borne and lost two babies and the second girl has had none. Ill luck they've had, those two, for much.''

"How did you come to marry Mr. Watly?" I asked before I could stop my tongue.

"Ah, well, it was a fine offer for the fifth daughter of a deacon," she smiled gently. "His prospects were good and he was a kindly, pious man. And I a plain child. I cannot say I have been unhappy with him, and it is not every woman who needs excitement in her life. Nor have I ever believed contentment comes without work. If one works at it, love comes in time."

Guiltily I wondered if her words were meant as a reproof to me. I did not doubt this woman would have disapproved had she known the course Leslie and I followed. Hers was a far gentler, far more forgiving nature than mine. It was not necessary to answer, however, for she was already talking of other, parish, matters. The time passed agreeably enough in this manner, and I was impressed with all the things Mrs. Watly found time for when I saw the group come round the side of the church. Mr. Watly saw me at the same moment. "Why Lady Kinwell! I had not realised you were not with us."

But Leslie had, I noted by his angry eyes, as had Philip and Mary, who seemed to reproach me silently. I spoke quickly, "I pray you will forgive me. I wished to speak with Mrs. Watly and learn what church projects are afoot."

Watly beamed. "Ah, just so, my child. An excellent notion."

I believe Mrs. Watly and I both smiled with relief. "Say you will stay for luncheon," she asked us.

Leslie answered, "Thank you, but the servants will have laid a meal at the castle and Mrs. Morgan would tax us with waste."

It was said with a smile and we all laughed. After a few more polite exchanges, we climbed into the carriage and were on our way home. Mary and my father discussed the church while we other three sat silent. I was grateful for the company that prevented Leslie from speaking to me. The coachman was as eager as we to be home and reached the castle in good time. As Leslie handed me out of the carriage, his grip was as iron on my arm. I began to grow impatient with this absurd behaviour. In the hall, Leslie hung back to let the others go up, but Philip refused to leave us, and after a moment, Leslie said, "I shall see you at table, shortly, madam. I trust you will not keep us waiting?"

And then he was gone up the stairs. I turned to Philip, who smiled impishly. "I have saved you from a scolding, Aunt Heather. When Uncle noticed your absence, he was all for going and looking for you to be sure you were all right. But Mother wouldn't allow it. She said she was quite sure there was no need for concern. I rather thought Uncle would cut up stiff over it, but not if I were here. And now you're forewarned!"

I grinned in spite of myself. "I thank you, Nephew. And now we'd best both go up and prepare for luncheon. It would not do to further tax his patience."

Philip agreed and we hurried to our rooms. Dear Philip! Perhaps I ought not to encourage such behaviour, but in truth I was grateful. I'd no mind to be taken to task today. Lunch was the usual sort of affair with polite, unimportant conversation. I noted, with relief, that Leslie appeared to have forgotten his annoyance at me. After lunch, Mary withdrew to her room and Philip I am not sure where. I determined to plan the week's menu and to this purpose went to my room. I had not, however, worked long when I realised I had no notion how long my father meant to stay. After he returned to London we should have no need of midnight suppers, as the rest of us preferred country hours. With a sigh, I set down my pen. Best to know the answer before I went further. I walked down the cool corridors to the library and paused at the door, for I could hear voices. ". . . you, Lord Pellen, it is a matter which must be handled gently."

"Gently! And I tell you the solution will not be found that way! You must be firm with her."

The voice became hard. "Let me speak plainly, my lord. I will handle it my way. It is one matter on which I will brook no interference. She is not *your* wife, she is mine."

I waited to hear no more, but fled to the garden. It was intolerable that my father should meddle so far! And Leslie . . . his voice had been so sure of success, whatever the goal they discussed. Well, and why not? He had succeeded in forcing me to marry him. I felt tired suddenly. How could I fight these two men who were so determined to rule my future? "Heather?" a voice said softly near me.

I turned. "Philip!"

"Are you well?" he asked with concern. "You seem very pale. Has Uncle Leslie been angry with you?"

"Leslie? No, why do you ask?"

"I saw you coming this way, and a moment later my uncle, looking quite furious. I thought perhaps . . ."

I smiled at the concern in Philip's voice. "No, all is well between us, I believe. Perhaps he was disturbed by my father. They were closeted together in the library."

Philip nodded with evident relief. "Yes, perhaps that's it. I was worried because I know Uncle has a temper and you are so young. . . . Aunt Heather, you must promise me that if my uncle ever bullies you, you will come to me and I will protect you."

There was that in his voice which warned me I must not laugh. "I thank you, Philip," I said gravely, "but I do not believe there will be a need."

He was silent a moment. Then: "The servants say he did not know you were barren before he married you. I fear that he married you for the sake of an heir and now that he knows you cannot have one . . ."

I smiled sadly. "There is little Leslie did not know about me before we were married. Nor is it certain I am barren, only likely. But this is a matter I ought not to discuss with you. You must excuse me, Philip, I have household matters to attend to."

He nodded but watched me unhappily as I walked back to the castle. It was as well, I thought, he had no notion of how matters truly stood. Philip was a hotheaded boy, too quick to anger, and I had no wish to see an open breach between him and Leslie. The menu sheet I had begun lay on my desk and with a sigh I turned to it. I should plan as though my father were to remain the week. If he left sooner, then I must simply change the orders. This matter occupied me the entire afternoon.

It was a quiet day that ended early, for Mary felt it unsuitable to play at cards on the Sabbath. So, one by one, we drifted upstairs and I found a likely novel and read myself to sleep.

Monday we again had callers, but the pattern had changed. These already knew of my birth and, from the first, were courteous. Indeed, one apologised that she had not called before. I began to feel, cynically, that from a shortage of friends, I should soon have a surfeit. My father, with his careless ease, charmed them all, both men and wives. Even

Mary grew more comfortable with Lord Pellen as she realised how his presence added to her consequence. Nor was Leslie displeased that I was finally to be accepted here. True, it was not London, and that would be a more difficult ordeal, but it was a start. And the men could now laugh with him again and visit easily. I realised for the first time that our marriage had, until now, cost Leslie the companionship of the neighbouring men. (Not that *they* cared whom he had married, but most had been prevented from visiting by their wives.) I no longer wondered that Leslie was so anxious to prove me respectable in the eyes of the world. Only Philip was absent during these visits, for he decided they were sadly flat. I confess I sometimes envied him the freedom to be out riding instead.

As Ellen dressed my hair late one afternoon I discovered that even the servants had a hand in the matter. "They'll be taking back tales, the grooms will," she proudly informed me, "of how good a mistress you be. And the Bentworth coachman has told the Warren housekeeper, and the Giles coachman has sisters in two other households, and . . ."

And so it went. I smiled at the pride with which Ellen spoke. Yet perhaps it was not a misplaced pride, for indeed the story would spread so. It were better to have the servants of a household friendly than against one. I sighed. How strange to be so cosseted as I was now. I shook myself free of such thoughts and turned to the task of dressing. On my table were the Kinwell garnets, and it was these jewels I wore. Perhaps, I thought with a smile, they would disturb Mary less than the emeralds had.

In this I was correct, for Mary was less sharp-set that evening, and indeed, it was a gay party we made at table. My father, at one point, raised his glass and said, "A toast to the future toast of London. My daughter, Heather."

With smiles, Leslie and Philip drank to my health, and Mary sipped at her glass. Philip asked eagerly, "When will you be taking Heather to London?"

Lord Pellen raised an eyebrow. "I? I shall not be taking her to London. Sir Leslie shall, later in the spring. You must ask him the day. I shall be leaving for London tomorrow."

In silence, I heard my voice echo, "Tomorrow?"

He smiled at me gently. "Yes, my child, I am sorry but I must leave. I have business matters to attend to, and I am no longer needed here." Ever the diplomat, he added, "I hope to see you *all* in London. I shall look for you at the opera, Lady Mary."

Mary fluttered and Philip smiled, but Leslie was grave. "I will ride as far as the village with you, if I may, Lord Pellen."

My father nodded just as gravely, "Yes. Perhaps we might take care of a few matters there."

I felt an unaccountable chill at these words. I wished again that I had been told what these matters were and could speak of them with Leslie. My father was talking again, ". . . er's ball. I trust you will be in London then, Lady Mary?"

"Oh, I should think so!" Mary said emphatically. "Philip knew the sons at school and met Celia twice. He thought her well enough then, but she was still in the schoolroom. Now, I hear, she has quite blossomed."

"Quite," Lord Pellen replied.

I glanced at Philip, who was carefully staring at his plate. He was embarrassed, I saw, but not for care of the girl. Rather it was chagrin that his mother should speak so. Which was as well, I thought, for Celia, as I remembered her, was a spoiled chit who cared only for herself. I spoke lightly, "Indeed, at school we thought her a diamond of the first water."

All eyes turned to me, Leslie's concerned and Lord Pellen's piercing. It was my father who spoke. "And did you tell her of your marriage when you left?"

I tried to match the casual tone, "No, I told no one. For I thought I'd no family or anyone truly to care. So one morning I slipped away."

Philip seemed surprised. "But surely they knew he'd been dangling after you?"

"Oh, no. I was always careful, you see. When one is apparently an orphan, one must be over worried of one's reputation," I lied with amazing ease.

Philip seemed satisfied, but Leslie's eyes were drawn together. My father said smoothly, "I think it would be best if one did not dwell on it. Though highly romantic, a schoolroom courtship must, in general, be frowned upon."

"Well, of course I shall be careful!" Philip said indignantly. "I shan't be hinting anything improper. And anyway, everyone knows Leslie is too high in the instep to have seduced Heather."

143

For a moment, there was silence. Then we all were laughing, save Philip. It was that or cry. Again my father chose to answer. "My dear young man, that was not what I meant at all. A schoolroom romance should be frowned upon simply because Heather was so young to be thinking of marriage."

"Oh."

Philip flushed, and I wondered what he had guessed and what he had imagined. But I knew Philip could be trusted. He would not be careless of my reputation no matter what he thought. It was Mary, after all, who turned the talk to safer topics. "Tell me, my lord, have the musicians been chosen yet for the ball?"

It seemed they had not, and for several minutes the discussion was of the merits of various possible choices. The names meant little to me, for I had attended but one dance, and that in a borrowed dress, in the countryside. What else passed at table that night I cannot say, for I confess I did not truly listen. As Mary and I withdrew to leave the men talking over their port she taxed me with it. "My dear Heather," she asked anxiously, "is something wrong?"

I smiled in spite of myself. "No, Mary. Only that I am tired. I fear I am not so accustomed to entertaining as you, and cannot be at ease yet."

"Well, you must learn," she replied instantly. "In Town you will no doubt entertain often. And, should you later have an establishment separate from Leslie, it will be doubly important."

So, I thought, Leslie has already told Mary we shall do so. I felt unaccountably disturbed by the knowledge. But unwilling for Mary to see this, I spoke quickly. "I shall be happy to see London again. And dance. For I love to dance, though I've had little chance other than in school."

Mary hesitated a moment, then said, "There will be occasions, my dear, where it would be considered improper for you to do so."

"But why?" I demanded.

"Because you are a married woman."

"Oh, no!" I protested and stood mouth agape in dismay.

I whirled about as a voice behind me asked with concern, " 'Oh, no' what?"

I ran up to Leslie. "Mary says I may not dance in London because I am a *matron!*"

Leslie threw back his head and laughed, as did Philip and Lord Pellen. But Leslie's arms encircled me as well. Behind me, Mary spoke crossly. "I did not say she could *never* dance, only that upon occasion 'twould be *improper*."

Leslie chuckled anew. With one hand he tilted up my chin. "I shall be careful that you need not endure many such dreadful evenings," he said. "And you need not fear. There will be many balls for you to dance at. We shall even give one, if need be."

I smiled at him gratefully, feeling rather goosish. Then I glanced away as his face took on a strange expression. My father was watching us with open approval. Abruptly I realised where I was and that Leslie's arms still encircled me. I pulled free, blushing deeply, but Leslie only smiled his strange smile. Philip broke the silence, his voice oddly pitched, "Lord Pellen, is it to be cards again this evening?"

"Why, I thought not," my father spoke slowly, "I thought perhaps you and I might play at billiards." He paused to wink. "And compare university life in my day and yours."

Philip fairly glowed. "Oh, I should like that!"

"Good. Then it's settled. Come along, my boy."

As they left the room, I stared at the floor, unable to meet Mary or Leslie's eyes. The silence grew uncomfortably until Mary said, "Well, I shall retire early. Please make my excuses to your father, Heather."

I turned in dismay to stop her, but could think of nothing to say. And in a moment, Leslie and I were alone. I stared at him, my mouth dry. We had not spoken alone since that day I learned Lord Pellen was my father. And then, Leslie had been justly angry with me. He turned to look at the fireplace, where a small fire, suitable to spring, burned. At last he asked, "Are you sorry your father leaves tomorrow?"

"No!" I said truthfully. He looked surprised at my vehemence, and I added, "I mean no disrespect, but life will be quieter when he is gone back to London."

Leslie nodded and turned back to the fire. "I have already told Lord Pellen we shall not follow for a few weeks, that you . . . we . . . are in need of time to prepare."

I nodded, though his back was to me. And again there was a silence. I tried to fill it with chatter. "Mary says that we shall entertain much in London. That I must learn to be a good hostess. Particularly after we have separate establishments. But I . . ."

"Are you looking forward so eagerly to separate establishments?" His voice cut across my words.

I looked at the floor, my mouth dry again. "I . . . well . . . naturally," I said as resolutely as I could, "it is what we both want, is it not?"

He looked at me for a moment with his piercing dark eyes and then, abruptly, strode from the room. I would have followed and caught at his sleeve, but remembered in time and did not. I stood alone in the empty and now chilly room, suddenly very tired. Slowly I climbed the stairs to my chamber. If the men thought me rude, so be it. I could not face them again that night.

We were all at breakfast next morning. My father asked, "Heather, will you give orders that callers are to be told you are not at home? We shall have more time together then, and none shall think you rude."

I readily assented, and it seemed we were more relaxed, all of us, as we talked. After breakfast, my father and I walked to the copse of trees near the castle. He spoke of things I would do, places I would see, and people I would meet in London. And he spoke a little of his own ambitions and the steps (some of them) he had taken in order to achieve them. We talked comfortably, and for the first time I truly began to feel he was my father. And as I did I was aware of disappointment, for I could see that I would never have any real closeness or love from him. As we talked suddenly I felt very old and alone. And yet I knew that in trouble, he would stand by me . . . *if* it did not require much sacrifice of him or threaten his reputation.

After luncheon, my father took his leave with the grace and charm I had come to expect of him. He kissed my hand and Mary's and the compliments were many. Leslie was more abrupt. A few curt words were all he spoke to Mary and Philip. To me he said, "I shall be back late. You need not postpone dinner for me. I shall dine with your father." He paused, then added with a smile, "I shall stop at the dressmaker to see if your riding habit is ready. Have you any other commissions for me to execute in town?"

In truth, I could think of none, and said so. But Mary

charged him with a few. "A packet of pins, and some lace two inches wide. And ask at the dressmaker when my order will be ready. Oh, and . . ."

I ceased to listen. A few minutes later, Leslie was in the saddle, for he would ride beside, not in, my father's coach. As he sat there I moved without thinking and, placing a hand on his arm, said, "Have a care."

He smiled down at me and said quietly, "I shall."

And then they were gone. The rest of the day passed slowly as I stayed in my room and read. Dinner was a quiet affair and we sat about, after, in the drawing room. Mary and I worked with our needles and Philip paced about. The hour grew late and still Leslie had not returned. Mary retired at ten, but Philip waited on with me. At midnight he spoke. "You'd best go up to sleep, Aunt Heather. I fear Uncle will be very late."

He tried to speak lightly and I to reply in kind. "Perhaps. You must sleep as well."

He nodded and together we climbed the stairs. At my door we halted and he said good night. Almost, it seemed, he would speak further, but he did not. Quickly he strode away and I entered to find Ellen waiting to put me to bed.

Chapter 13

It was late when I woke, for it had been late when I had at last slept. Indeed it was only when Margaret brought the tea that I rose. She looked at me oddly while Ellen slammed an unnecessary number of things, I thought, and I chided her for it. Then I learned the reason for the behaviour of my servants. "I'm sorry, my lady. 'Tis the master. He has not yet returned, they are saying in the servants' hall. And Peter, his valet, had no notion Sir Leslie would be gone o'ernight!"

She paused for breath and I said, "Ellen, it is not for the servants to question Sir Leslie's behaviour."

"Well, we do, my lady!" she said hotly, to my surprise. "Scarcely two weeks married and he stays in town the night! With a *woman*, I doubt not!"

"Ellen! That is the outside of enough!" I said sharply. "If the servants must gossip, you may tell them *I* knew Sir Leslie would be gone the night. The only wonder is that he forgot to tell his valet as well. 'Tis nothing out of the ordinary."

She flushed. "Oh, my lady, I'm sorry. I . . ."

We were both silent as she dressed me and I sent her away while I ate. In the empty room I was angry. Why had I lied for Leslie? Well, I knew the answer to that! Because I could not bear the thought the servants should pity me. Nor did I care to know our lives were watched so closely. But where was my husband?

I was descending the stairs when I heard him. I began to hurry, only to pause as I heard Philip's voice. "Uncle, may I speak with you in the library?"

Leslie's answer was both weary and alert. "Certainly, Philip."

I decided to wait to greet my husband as Philip appeared to

148

so be concerned over some matter. And indeed, I was almost glad Philip's voice had halted me, for I realised my haste might have been misunderstood. Slowly I climbed the stairs to my chamber for I had some small matters to attend to there. It was sometime later as I worked at my desk that the door was thrown open with a loud noise. I turned swiftly and saw Leslie standing in the doorway, his face white with anger. He stepped into the room, closing the door behind him. I was frozen in my chair as he advanced. "How dare you, madam?" he demanded softly, "How dare you?"

I stared at him, frightened and speechless. He towered over me. I, too, was pale now. "How dare you send that young whelp to question me?" he asked, his voice growing louder. "You could not greet me yourself and ask, if you must, for an explanation. Instead you send my nephew to demand— *demand!*—an explanation of me! How dare you, madam?"

"I . . . I . . ."

"And what concern is it to you if I should stay away the night?" he lashed out with his voice.

My anger now rescued me. "None, save that I must hear the servants offer me their sympathy that my husband of two weeks seeks women in town!"

He stared at me for a moment, then threw back his head and laughed a bitter laugh. "Indeed, madam?" he asked harshly. "Does this disturb you? But surely you cannot wonder at it if I seek elsewhere for what you will not give! Or do you prefer I follow your father's advice and ravish you each night?" It seems I paled further, for he said bitterly, "I thought not. I shall speak with you later, madam. Now I wish to change. But I warn you, have a care whom you use against me. You hurt my nephew as well as yourself when you use him so."

He gave a mock bow and was gone. For some time, I sat at my desk shaking. When at last I could stand again, I fled my room for the garden. I was still too numb to think, and I wandered aimlessly about. And when a little later I saw Philip approaching, I ran to him. For a moment, his arms encircled me. Then we remembered who and where we were. He led me to a bench and sat me down. We stared at each other. "He thinks . . ." Philip began.

I nodded. Philip clenched a fist, "I only meant to remind him of his duty to you. And he said . . ." I nodded again, helplessly. When he spoke, his voice was puzzled. "He said that if I were married to you, I'd take *his* side quick enough." I flushed. Philip's voice was urgent now, "Why did you marry him, Heather?"

And in that moment, I was myself again. "Why does any woman marry a man?" I parried. "Leslie is not the same to me as he is with you. Often he is very kind and gentle. If, at times, we quarrel, what of it?"

The words were not easy to speak, but I had a part to play, and play it I should. But it was not easy to sit still as Philip's face showed its dismay. "I wish you had told me sooner that you were so *happy!*" he retorted. "Then I should not have made such a cake of myself!"

Angrily, he strode away to the castle. And I could only watch him go.

It was late when I returned to my room. Almost teatime. I would take tea with the others, else the servants would talk. I hurried to change, and Ellen quickly repaired the damage the wind had done to my hair. It was she who told me of the note "on your desk, my lady."

I opened it quickly, the hand unknown to me. Perhaps Philip? No, there was a seal. From my father.

My dearest Heather,

It is my painful duty to write this note. Your husband will not have returned last night, and I doubt not you believe the worst. You had best know the truth of it. After we dined, your husband stayed late, drinking, and it was necessary to put him to bed at the inn. I must leave for Town early, but when he wakes, the innkeeper will send Sir Leslie back to the castle.

Indeed, I cannot approve of such behaviour, but *we both know* its cause. You are fortunate it was not worse. And I counsel you that if you do not school yourself to be a good wife then, in time, it *will* be worse. Sir Leslie well knows I believe him too easy with you and . . .

The letter continued for a page and a half and I read it but quickly. I knew well enough what he would say to me. Of importance was the knowledge there had been no woman. I felt absurdly relieved. Feeling somewhat lighter, I descended

150

for tea. To my surprise, Leslie as well as Mary awaited me, though Philip was nowhere to be seen. Mary looked nervously from Leslie to myself, but could not, I was sure, feel as nervous as I when I greeted him. The anger was still in his eyes, but he spoke quietly enough. "Good afternoon, Heather. Mary has already rung for the tea as we were not sure you would join us."

"Indeed? Well, I confess myself ready for a cup. Has Mary taxed you yet with all your errands?"

Leslie looked surprised at the lightness of my tone. Mary was speaking. ". . . more than just errands! But enough of that; I have promised. Yes, Leslie remembered most of the charges. And your habit, he tells me, is as lovely as the one from London."

I glanced at Leslie, who said, "I have only now sent it up. With all Mary's packages, I'd forgotten to deliver yours. I believe you will be satisfied."

The tea arrived, then, and with it, Philip. He greeted us curtly. Although he apologised to Mary for his tardiness, he would not look at me. Leslie glanced in puzzlement from Philip to myself, and I could not meet his eyes. Let him wonder. *I* should not explain!

We became more and more constrained, the four of us, and tea was quickly over as Leslie and Mary found excuses to withdraw. Only Philip remained longer, and he regarded me sullenly. I could bear it no longer and, in a moment, had undone all I had said before. I rose and walked to the doorway. There I paused and said in a voice that was not altogether steady, "Do not judge me so harshly, Philip, for you have not lived my life."

He sat up abruptly, and under the piercing gaze, so like his uncle's, I fled.

The evening meal passed much as had tea, save that Philip was more thoughtful than sullen. And we all sought our beds early that night.

With the tea tray, next morning, came a note from Philip. He had heard my new habit was ready, should I care to go riding? I should. I did not linger over my breakfast, and soon I was downstairs. Philip's appreciative smile told me I looked my best. The horses were saddled and we were off. The wind in my face was agreeable, and Philip was his usual, charming self again. And I laughed as I had not laughed in days. Philip regaled me with *on-dits* of Oxford. We were laughing over some such tale when we heard a horse behind us. As one, we turned to see Leslie approaching. I stiffened in preparation for his anger. But he only greeted us mildly and said to Philip, "May I borrow my wife, Nephew? You musn't have all the pleasure."

I listened with care but detected no sarcasm in Leslie's voice. I glanced at Philip, but he had no choice save to ride away. Leslie's horse fell in step with mine. "You've a good seat, Heather."

I smiled a brief, wary smile. For a while, we rode in silence. Then he said, "You have turned my servants against me, madam. This morning, *Peter* took me to task!"

Dismay crossed my face. " 'Twas not intended, Leslie, I. . ."

"Yes, I know. You told the servants you knew I expected to be away overnight. But Peter, I fear, did not believe you and said it was one more cause I should not behave as I have."

Leslie's voice lacked anger and I looked at him warily, not trusting this mood. "Leslie," I ventured, "I did not ask Philip to speak with you."

He halted his horse and regarded me seriously. "I know that, Heather. Or rather I realised it yesterday, once I calmed down. I hope I didn't frighten you?"

"No, of course not," I replied boldly. He looked at me with raised eyebrows, and after a moment, I added, "Well, a little, I confess."

He sighed. "I've the devil of a temper, and no amount of effort can school it. A little like your tongue, madam." Leslie laughed as I bristled at his words. "No, I will not come to cuffs with you today, Heather. I mean to apologise for yesterday. I suppose I was angriest because the accusation was unfair!"

I knew he watched to see how I should react. "I know," I said gravely. He was clearly astonished, and now I smiled. "My dear Leslie, do you truly believe my *father* could resist the opportunity to meddle? I had a note of him, late yesterday, in which he explained lest I think the worst. And he spent much time advising me to be a good wife."

"And?"

I looked squarely at Leslie's eyes. "And . . . I do not believe my father is infallible," I retorted, "nor do I believe he understands me very well."

I could not read Leslie's face as we rode on. He began to talk of other matters and told me about various tenants. But it was as though there were a wall between us, and the day felt suddenly cold. When we were in view of the stable, he halted his horse again and said, "This time there was no woman, Heather. But next time it may not be so. I meant what I said: I will seek elsewhere what you will not give. I'll be discreet, but I'll not live the life of a monk."

I could not explain how I felt. I knew his words were reasonable, and yet . . . Resolutely I said, "Of course. That was the agreement, was it not? I was distressed only that you had been (apparently) indiscreet."

I could not meet his eyes and when we began to ride again, I stole a glance of his face. But it was again a mask. We rode without speaking, and in the courtyard, after lifting me down from my horse, Leslie strode away, leaving me to follow as best I might.

Nevertheless, matters were easier, and next morning, the books Leslie had ordered arrived. I was childishly happy as I sorted through them. Leslie had thrown off his dark mood and even laughed with Philip over my delight. I sat on the floor of the library, lifting the books out, one by one. Leslie sat beside me and Philip shelved the books as my husband explained where each belonged. Mary looked in from time to time, but only shook her head and went away again. "What will you do with so many books?" Philip asked in genuine puzzlement.

"Read them!" I said indignantly.

They both laughed and I reached for another book. As it came from the box I froze. It was a book of children's tales. As was the next. Quickly now, I lifted out the rest of the books. They were all for children or of child and baby care. I stared at Leslie, anger rising in me. He, too, was pale. "I ordered them before . . . before I knew . . . there would be no children," he said in the silence.

I stared a moment longer and Philip, clearing his throat, asked, "Shall I shelve the books?"

I handed them to him and rose. Looking at Leslie, I said, "I do not care what you do with them!"

Then I turned and fled the library. Leslie was on his feet before I reached the door, but he did not follow. And Philip looked away.

I would have fled to the grove near the castle, but it was raining and instead I went to the tower. I had never explored it, but I knew there was a room at the top. The staircase wound upward, and though I tired, I would not stop. The lock protested but yielded to my key, and I stepped inside the room. It was dusty, but I did not care for that and sat on the lid of a trunk. For the room had become a storeroom. My anger, which had been all but spent in reaching the room, flared anew. How dare he? What in God's name had he meant by it? Even had I been with child by him, there should have been time enough to order such books later. What had he been thinking of?

Eventually, my anger died and I began to look about me. With a feeling of guilt, I opened a trunk. You are the mistress here, I told myself sternly, you need not feel guilty! And I began to look through the contents. In the second trunk, I found a journal and began to read the small, feminine hand. I was not the first woman in this house to be unhappy, or to be forced into marriage. Laura, her name had been, and the suitor an earl. Her father, an earlier Kinwell baronet, had forced her to accept the man. The journal ranged over only a few months, the half year preceding her marriage. I read with fascination of balls and routs and musical evenings. I read of a London I had never seen, for even then the family moved in the first circles. And as I read I knew that I, too, must leave an account of my misfortune.

I cried as I read the last few pages in which Laura spoke of preferring suicide to marrying this man she had come to hate. I had just closed the journal when I heard steps outside the door. I turned from the window, where I had stood to read, and saw Philip. "Good God!" he exclaimed. "What are you doing *here?*"

"Hiding," I replied, unable to lie. "And you?"

"Looking for you!" he said angrily. "Do you know Uncle Leslie has turned out the whole castle to look for you? And he's out in the rain, himself, right now! I know you were upset, but this is the outside of enough! Come on," he said, grabbing my wrist, "we've got to tell Jeffries to signal you're safe. And hope my uncle hasn't caught a chill looking for you!"

Philip dragged me down the stairs and I could say nothing as his tongue lashed at me. I had no defense. Nor could I speak to him of the true reason I had for anger. At the foot of the stairs, he shouted and a servant came running. She saw me and halted. "Tell Jeffries to sound the bell!" he snapped, and she turned and ran toward the main hall.

In the distance, I could hear the shouts repeated and then a loud ringing. Philip continued to pull me as we made our way to the drawing room where Mary was waiting. She rose as we entered, and the family assemblage was complete. "Well!" she said, "I knew you were young, Heather, but I had not realised you were so thoughtless! My poor brother is out in the rain because of you. And where were you?"

"In the tower," I said meekly.

"The tower!" she repeated. "And what have you in your hand?"

I looked down in surprise. I had forgotten I held it still. "A journal. Of a Laura Kinwell." Then I added defiantly, "Who was forced into an unhappy marriage."

"Her!" Philip snorted contemptuously. "You needn't feel sorry for *her*. She ran away the night before the wedding and married a man she had a *tendre* for."

Mary added, "The silly fool had never mentioned the boy or her father would never have engaged her to the earl. He was of a respectable enough family, though not as good as the Kinwells." She paused, "Though I grant you he was wrong to betroth her to the earl."

"Well, what should he have done?" Philip asked. "She had to be married to someone, didn't she? And the earl was rich and not too old."

"Don't you believe one should marry for love?" I asked.

"Oh, well, if one is in love, with someone eligible, then by all means, one should marry that person. But if by twenty-eight one hasn't fallen in love, one isn't likely to, and one might as well marry an earl."

I would have answered further, but we all turned at the sound of voices. Leslie's could be heard loud and harsh, and a softer voice mingled with it. They were coming toward us, and in a moment, Leslie stood in the room. His eyes were dark and large, weary and angry. He stared at me. "Where?"

"The tower," Philip answered shortly.

Jeffries stood behind Leslie. "Sir, you must change out of your wet things."

Water dripped from Leslie to the floor. And his hair was plastered about his face. "Stubble it!" he said sharply, and with a sigh, Jeffries withdrew. "Mary. Philip. You will leave us."

They hastily withdrew also, and Leslie and I stared at one another, he blocking the door. He stepped forward and I could feel his anger grow. Another step. Then he was towering over me, his eyes stormy. Suddenly, my eyes were full of tears, and the journal slipped from my hands to the floor. I stooped to retrieve it and felt Leslie's hand close over my wrist. Frantically, I tried to pull free, but could not. "Heather!" he said sharply. Then, in a voice more gentle, "Please, Heather." In surprise, I looked up into his face, and saw that the anger was gone from his eyes. As though he sensed my uncertainty, Leslie added, "I'm not going to hurt you."

I stopped pulling and stood straight. He sighed with relief and indicated I should take a seat as he released my wrist. Nervously, he poured a shot of whiskey and I could see that he shivered in his wet clothes. It was not easy for Leslie to speak and he took some time in choosing his words. "Heather, I don't doubt that you are angry with me. The books—I should not have ordered them. I admit that. But as for explanation . . . I can give you none. I knew it was unlikely you were with child from that night. And I knew that if you were not . . . Forget it, can you, Heather?"

I sat stiffly, unwilling to understand, but unable to resist the urgency of his voice. Still, I could not trust myself to speak and I nodded. Leslie's relief was evident and he smiled as he said, "Thank you, Heather."

I in turn, needing to fill the silence that followed, said, "You'd best change to dry things, Leslie. It must soon be time for tea."

He nodded. "You are correct, madam; however you will forgive me if I take my tea alone? Good day."

And he was gone. Only then did I realise how tightly I gripped the journal. I, too, would take tea in my chamber, I decided. And perhaps begin a record of my own.

Ellen was waiting for me and, for once, had taken Leslie's side. "You had us all so worried, my lady! And Sir Leslie. He was truly beside himself, I should say."

"Leave it, Ellen," I said.

She sniffed. "As you wish, my lady. But you could have come here. *I'd* have kept everyone out. You'd have had your privacy, and no one worried."

"Ellen!"

She fell silent then and soon left, having laid out a dress for dinner. With relief, I turned to my desk. If Mary and Philip were to be believed, Laura's journal had omitted much, and I determined mine should not.

It was evening before we were all together again and we spoke as though nothing had occurred. Indeed, the meal was easier than any since my father had arrived at the estate. And the next two days were to be much the same, quiet and easy. I began to feel calmer, and yes, happier. In the mornings I rode, and in the afternoon Mary and I received callers. I sent one of the servants to Jenny Bartlet with presents for the baby. Among these was a christening gown for the ceremony on Sunday. Sunday. If there had been no christening, how different our lives might now be. And yet, it was a day which dawned so quietly.

Chapter 14

"Just a moment more, my lady," Ellen was saying as she gave a last twist to the curl at my neck.

A voice laughed resonantly in the doorway. Ellen and I both turned to see Leslie standing there. "Impatient, Heather?" he asked.

I smiled. "A little, I confess. I haven't seen the child since its birth, and I am curious."

Leslie smiled indulgently in return. "Well, if we don't hurry, we shall be late and you may not have the chance."

At that, I was out of my chair and pulling on my gloves as Ellen fastened the poke bonnet on my head. Then, my hand on his arm, Leslie led me down to the carriage. Philip was waiting beside it, and to my surprise, Mary was also ready. Her lips were pursed in disapproval. "I cannot approve your . . . your help in delivering the child . . . but it would not do for anyone outside the family to see it."

I smiled slightly. Mary could be trusted to preserve family unity at all costs. Which was more, I suspected, than could be said for my father. In spite of Leslie's warning, we arrived well in time at the churchyard. Tom, his wife, and the baby were waiting, and I greeted them with a broad smile. "How are you, Mrs. Bartlet," I asked. "And the baby?"

She smiled also. "Oh, quite well, me lady. And I thank ye for all yer kindliness."

She even managed a half curtsy with the child in her arms. Mary graciously admired the baby, and then we were being herded inside. I fidgeted, I confess, during the (it seemed to me) long wait. Then the time came and I proudly stepped forward to take the child. He wore a simple beribboned dress along with a hood and cloak. The latter were of my giving. I slipped these off the child and cradled him in the soft shawl I had brought for the purpose. As I held the child I felt something stir within me, and suddenly I was close to tears. The baby began to yell with a lusty, healthy cry. Mr. Watly stopped and smiled wryly. "I like a noisy child at a christening," he said, "for it means the baby sets forth its determination from the start. It says it *will* have a place in this world!"

A ripple of amusement flowed through the church, and then silence again prevailed. Watly continued the ceremony. Finally, he handed the child back to me and I kept it in the shawl, making no attempt to exchange this for the hood and cloak. I had no mind to set the child to crying again. And the shawl was meant to be a gift for Jenny Bartlet in any event. Soon we were seated again in our proper pews.

To my surprise, Watly gave a good sermon that day. I remember part of it still. "Motherhood is the most important and most joyous state a woman can obtain. She is then fulfilled and secure in the love of a being she has brought forth. It cannot but bring a husband and wife closer together, and in that closeness the bonds of marriage are woven stronger. For I speak here of motherhood within the sanctity of marriage. Motherhood without such security is surely a disaster, both for mother and child. The woman is alone and must provide for herself and the child, when both should be provided for by a husband and father. And such a woman brings shame upon herself. And this shame is visited upon the child all its life. In time, each must come to hate the other, mother and child. Better the sanctity of *any* marriage than such a fate.

"But motherhood is not a light burden. Nor is there any guarantee of a personal reward. For the child may die young or grow up to leave his parents. For parents do not own the child. They are, rather, given the child in trust. It is a being unto itself, with a right to its own existence. But this is not to say we must ignore the child when it is grown. The responsibilities of a mother and father never end. From its earliest days, the mother must watch over the child and guard its physical existence. As the child grows it becomes necessary to guide and mold the spiritual existence, for if this is neglected, the child will be an everlasting sorrow to its parents, to society, and to God. This is not an easy task, for there are ever temptations and dangers to guard our children from. But with God's help . . ."

At last the service was over and we were outside. I held the child again. And again I felt the tears, and running through me, a terrible loneliness. Suddenly I thrust the child back into its mother's arms. "Are you all right?" Leslie asked with concern.

"No," I said, "I feel rather faint."

"It *is* a very warm day," Mary said sympathetically.

We made our farewells hastily. I was aware of the whispered comments as Leslie handed me into the carriage. Many of the voices were sympathetic. Others, the uninformed, held secret smiles over the condition they falsely believed existed. Mary looked very thoughtful as we rode home. Home! I felt ill as I contemplated a lifetime in the castle. And when we arrived, I immediately went to my room. Ellen was, of course, waiting. "I shall not be going down for luncheon," I told her. "I . . . I am not feeling well."

"Yes, my lady," she said, her eyes wide. "Shall I undress you? No? Shall I bring you some tea?"

"Yes, thank you."

Ellen rang for tea and then undid my hair so that it fell in waves about my shoulders. When the tea arrived, a moment later, I dismissed both girls, saying I should ring when the tray was to be taken away. The cook had provided a few pastries I was particularly fond of, but I had little appetite for them. After a time, I turned from the table to look out the window. I could see some distance from there and the land was green and healthy. Had matters been different . . . But they were not. I was shackled to Leslie, yet not truly his wife, and not wanting to be. And I could never have children. Babies such as Jenny's. Silently I began to cry. Then it grew stronger and I began to sob helplessly as unhappiness washed over me. And in that moment came a knock at the door. "Heather?" Philip's voice called.

"Go away!" I sobbed.

But he would not, and the door opened and he strode quickly to me. "Heather, Heather, what's wrong?" I could only cry. His arms encircled me, "Please, Heather, don't cry. Whatever it is, I'll help you. Please, Heather, I love you!"

And then he kissed me. And, *God help me*, I did not fight

him. In that moment, all that mattered was that someone loved me. Suddenly I was standing alone. I looked up at Philip, then followed his gaze to the door. *Leslie!* I sank into the nearest chair, my face chalk white. Leslie took two steps forward. Philip was trembling, but his chin was thrust out in determination. It seemed an eternity before Leslie spoke, and when he did, his words came as though from far away. "Philip! I shall speak with you in the library shortly. Please go."

"No. I won't leave Heather."

"Please, Philip," I heard myself say, "go."

He looked at me a moment and saw the plea in my eyes, for he left. Then Leslie slowly closed the door. "So," he said softly, as he advanced on me, "I was wrong. Mary said Philip had come up here, but I believed it to be in harmless sympathy. My God, how wrong I was!"

"It *was* harmless!" I cried.

"Harmless!" His anger exploded. "Pray, tell me, madam. Do you *always* receive men with your hair down? Do you *always* encourage men to kiss you? And don't try to say you were resisting, for I saw you! God, how wrong I was about you! I thought I had to marry you to save your honour. What a fool I was! You are no better than a common slut! You don't even provide what you have been paid for. *Were* you a virgin, I wonder? Or was it a chicken's blood in the bed?"

Under the fury of his attack, I was incapable of speech. Leslie took my silence for guilt. He advanced closer and grabbing my wrist, dragged me to my feet. "If you must have kisses," he said savagely, "why not mine?"

And then his mouth was on mine, bruising with its strength. I struggled, but one arm held me firm as the other hand tore at the front of my dress. I was crying, terrified, when suddenly he threw me to the bed. "God damn you!" he swore, and was gone.

I lay, shocked, on the bed. And after a while, I began to cry again. When I could cry no more, I got to my feet and tried to close my dress. But my fingers were too clumsy, and finally I removed it. Trembling, I forced myself to put it away and choose a wrapper. Then I began to pace. If I had felt despair earlier, I felt it threefold now. I had, perhaps, destroyed Philip's relationship with Leslie as well as my own marriage. For there was no doubt that Leslie hated me now.

Hated me and regretted his marriage. It had not been worth it, the kiss. As I paced I knew I could not stay. I must escape. Today. No, tonight. But I must also be careful. Leslie would put paid to my plans if he knew. I must think. What would seem normal? I could not face the family. But that was all right. Mary thought me ill and Leslie and Philip would not question my decision to remain in my room. But the servants, also, must not become suspicious. Well, Ellen already knew I felt ill. I turned to the tea tray where the pastries still rested untouched. I forced myself to sit and eat them. I should need all my strength tonight. When I had done, I rang for Ellen and a maid to clear away the tray. I told Ellen that I had the headache and that I should like the day's meals in my room.

"Yes, my lady," she replied in sympathy. "You'll become quite thin if you don't take care."

I smiled. "Thank you, Ellen. That will be all."

Then I packed. I still had the bag I had left Mrs. Gilwen's school with, and in it I placed a few things. Not many. I would have left all behind, if I could, but I was not so imprudent. Soon I was finished and quickly I hid the bag, afraid someone would enter and see it. It was necessary, somehow, to fill the time until the hour of my escape. In my nervousness I could not read, and I paced. Then my eyes fell on the journal I had begun. I spent the next several hours writing much of this account.

As I expected, no one came to chide me for my absence downstairs. But the hardest time for me was when Ellen came to put me to bed. I dared not alter my routine, so I had to sit patiently as she plaited my hair and helped me undress. Finally, I was in bed with a book, and she tiptoed away. Hurriedly I bolted the door, as was my habit. An hour, no more, to wait. Then I must attempt it. Twice, footsteps paused outside my door. And twice they went away. I dressed quickly. Mentally I had already composed my farewell letters, and now I wrote them. First to Mary.

Dearest Lady Mary,

Circumstances make it impossible for me to remain here. You have been kind enough to offer me aid and shelter, but I fear I cannot accept. The proximity to Philip would be unwise. I thank you for all your kindness and hope that now and then you will think of me with fondness.

Heather

It was more curt than I should have liked, but I was too distraught to write better. Next I determined to make an end to the confusion with Philip. No lies now, but the truth.

Dear Philip,
Circumstances make it impossible for me to remain here. But I wish also for you to understand how I feel. I do not love you, Philip, nor could I ever love you save as a brother or nephew. You will wonder at this morning, and I can only say that it is but now that I understand myself. I thank you for your championship of my cause, but too late I see it was something only Leslie and I could have resolved. You will perhaps believe I write so because I am Leslie's wife. I tell you now that Leslie's wife or no, I could not love you. Make peace with your uncle, if you can, and try not to hate me.
                                        Heather

That should be sufficiently final, I thought. But one letter left and that the hardest one. For what could I write to this man who was my husband? I forced myself to begin.

Leslie,
I am leaving. You must see that this marriage is impossible. I am sorry to sneak away, but otherwise you would not let me go. I do not know the precise nature of the law, but I am sure you can find a means to end our marriage. You will then be free to find a wife who would love you and could give you heirs. I am taking the guineas you gave me because I must, but I shall repay you as soon as I am able.
I know that you must hate me, and I wish it had not been so. But we were never suited. I would not have you deceived about this morning, however. I am not leaving you to join Philip. I have written him, also, explaining that I do not love him, nor desire his attentions. I beg of you to make peace with him, for I would not have such a breach on my conscience also.
Good-bye, Leslie. Had matters been otherwise, I think I might have loved you.
                                        Heather

I sealed the letter quickly before I could change my mind, and set it with the others. It was late and I determined to delay no longer. I had my reticule and the bag with my clothes and my journal. I needed to travel light, for I should have to walk to the village. Not daring to take a candle, I set my keys beside the letters and resolutely stepped into the darkness. My footsteps seemed to echo loudly, but no one came to challenge me. And then I was outside and I ran, needing to be away from there. I ran until, exhausted, I had to stop, my breath coming in painful gasps. And tears began to run down my cheeks. I walked, then. I had no notion of how far I must travel, and after a time, I grew weary. Right foot. Left foot. I must not pause. At last, sometime after midnight, I reached the inn. Mike, the fellow I had met the night I arrived, weeks before, was there alone. "Aye?" he said curtly when he saw me.

"Mike?" my voice trembled.

"Lady Kinwell?" he whispered. "Ye are Lady Kinwell, are ye not?" I nodded. "What the divil are ye doing here?"

"Mike, I need help," I said. "I need to get to London. I've money, but I must be on the first coach through. I must be away by morning."

"There, there, child," he said soothingly. "Of course I'll help ye. And put ye on the mail to London if ye are determined. But ye must not stay here, now. My wife will give ye a cup of tea. Come along, child."

Gently he took my bag and led me to the kitchen of the inn. His wife stood as we entered, her eyes sharp on my face. "Well?" she asked Mike.

" 'Tis Lady Kinwell, run away," he said. "I've said I'll help her te London. But it be hours before the mail coach. She could use a cup of tea, love."

But the last words were unnecessary, for she was already setting the kettle to boil and bringing out cups and the tea. She pointed to a chair, but did not speak until the tea was ready. It was only then I noticed she had put out but two cups. "Mike" I asked, realising he was gone.

"On watch, Lady Kinwell. We've a horse ill."

"Please call me Heather," I said, "the other sounds so strange."

She nodded. "Mike said ye'd not be happy at the castle. I

see it, too. But we thought, when we heard of yer wedding, that Mike'd been wrong.''

"It was not of my choosing, the marriage," I admitted. "Still, I think all might have been well had I not been such a green girl.''

She nodded again. " 'Tis often so. And to be a *wife* in the castle is different than . . . other posts there. Are ye sure, child, ye cannot go back? Begin again? I know yer not lacking in courage. And most ways Sir Leslie is a gentle man.''

I stared at her. "I am sure. I can never go back.''

She sucked in her breath at my tone. "Has he acted so badly? Offended se deeply?''

"It is I who have acted badly," I sighed. "I who have offended.''

"What will ye do?''

"Find a position, perhaps abroad. I've told Sir Leslie to annul our marriage, and I'm not afraid of hard work," I answered. She looked at me and I knew she was troubled. "Promise you won't tell Sir Leslie, or anyone else, what you know," I said.

She hesitated, then with a sigh nodded. "I promise.''

Our talk became strained then, as we pretended it was the most ordinary of conversations. We talked about Leslie, Mary, Philip, and even my father. After a time, however, we ceased to speak. I rested my head on my arms and slept until Mike came to put me on the coach at dawn. "Good luck, lass," he said.

I suppose I slept a little on the coach, but it was not enough and I arrived early Monday afternoon in London, feeling very tired. But I had already made my plans . . . I would go to Mademoiselle Suzette. How different my return to London was from my departure. Then, I had been sure of myself. Now, I felt unalterably cast down. Then, I had been poor, but with a position, albeit no family. Now, I had a father, husband, and a little money. But no position. My father was of no use, for he would but send me back to the husband I sought to escape. The money was only borrowed and, in any case, meagre. Which woman had been more fortunate? I could not say.

I soon discovered I had gained something else in my short marriage: poise. I was incapable of walking to Mademoiselle Suzette's establishment, even had I known how to find it. So I determined to go by hack. There was no question in the coachman's eyes as he handed me in and, later, out of the carriage, as there would have been but six weeks before. Nor did Dragon question my demand to speak privately with Mademoiselle Suzette. Indeed, she did not recognise me, and her first action was to glance at my left hand. I was glad, then, that I had not yielded to impulse and left my wedding ring behind. Already it was providing a shield. And I toyed with the idea of posing as a widow. But no, at my age, that would scarcely be convincing. And then, suddenly, I was facing Mademoiselle Suzette. She recognised me at once, and the expression on my face. *"Mon dieu!"* she exclaimed. "Prudence, leave us." She waited until Dragon had gone, then said, "Well?"

"You said I could come to you for aid," I began to chatter. "I didn't know where else to go. I have left Leslie. Forever. You must know we were married. It was against my will. It was impossible. And now he hates me. And I cannot live with him. He found me with his nephew . . ."

"With his nephew?" Mademoiselle Suzette was shocked. *"In bed?"*

"No, no!" I said hastily. "He was kissing me. We were dressed. But my hair was down. . . ."

She smiled. "Well, if that is all . . . *tiens,* he must simply send away the nephew. And perhaps bed you more often."

"He beds me not at all!" I said before I could stop myself.

We stared at each other in shock. I was horrified at my failure to guard my tongue and she at the revelation. At last she spoke. *"Mon Dieu!* This is very bad. I think you had better tell me all of it."

So I did, omitting nothing, for I knew she was discreet. When I had done, she was silent for a moment, then said, *"Tiens,* I do not wonder you have not gone to your father for aid." She paused and asked shrewdly, "You have not eaten, have you?"

I signified I had not, and she ordered a tray for me. We were both silent, both thoughtful, until it came. I began to feel safe. I knew Leslie well. He would be searching methodically about the castle and grounds for me. Then he would ask in town if I had been seen. Finally, Leslie would try to discover if I had left by mail or post, but I knew Mike would not betray me. I should have two days or more before he would conclude I could only have gone to London. Even then he could not know I had gone to Mademoiselle Suzette. He would come here, but not for two or three days after that. By then I should be gone. Yes, I was safe. When I had done eating, Mademoiselle asked, "What will you do?"

I spoke carefully. "I cannot stay in England. Leslie would find me if I did, and it would be difficult to find a position. I thought to go to France. Surely there are families who would be glad of a governess who might teach their children English. Or perhaps, I might teach in a school for young ladies."

She tilted her head. "You are very sure. And what do you wish of me?"

"Help in finding such a position. As a *modiste* in France, you must have known many good families."

She smiled sadly, "*Tiens*, child, you ask much. There have been many changes since I left France; many families have lost their fortunes."

I was worried, but persisted. "The schools, perhaps, have not changed so much . . . and you could give me a reference, could you not?" Desperately I added, "I would even be a seamstress for a good *modiste!*"

"Child, I wish I could help you," she sighed. "But you must understand. In France, I was not a *modiste*. That is a lie I have used here. In France I was a *femme de chambre* and I left with the son of the house. He established me here. Of the families I know, my reference would ruin you." I stared at her in dismay, and Mademoiselle Suzette hastened to reassure me. "*Mon Dieu*, child, do not to cry. I will help you. But you must to have patience."

Somehow her odd English, in that moment, was very reassuring. And with no protest, I allowed myself to be put to bed. This time she put me in the guest room. I was soon asleep.

I woke slowly, puzzled at the strangeness of the room. Then I remembered. I was out of bed quickly and began pacing, trying to form new plans. Mademoiselle Suzette had said she would help me, but perhaps it would be best not to rely on her entirely. By teatime I had achieved no more than to decide to go to France alone, without references, if need be. Lady Kinwell could always write one, after all. Mademoiselle took tea with me and again counselled patience. She was very curious about my life as Lady Kinwell, and I answered her questions in much detail. At one point she said, "*Tiens,* you do not hate him, then?"

"Only because he ravished me," I said frankly.

"Oh, *mon Dieu,* that is nothing! So many women are ravished on their wedding night! Sir Leslie was only hasty."

"It is everything to me," I said coldly, "this hastiness."

"Could you not begin again?" she asked.

I shook my head vehemently. "Anyway, he does not want me, now."

After a time, she left. I was alone that evening, for Mademoiselle Suzette felt it best I not be seen. And she would not let me aid with the needlework this time, so perforce I had to think. To my surprise, I found I missed my chamber at the castle, with Ellen and my books and the little things I had come to think of as my own. And Leslie. Above all, Leslie. Resolutely, however, I prepared for bed and extinguished the candle. I lay in the darkness, vainly willing myself to sleep. The first light of morning had appeared before I succeeded. And it was noon before I woke to find Mademoiselle Suzette setting a tray on the table. She regarded me carefully, but shrewdly said nothing. And to my questions, she only would reply, "Have patience, *chérie.*"

That day was the longest I had yet known, and in desperation, I at last turned to the books that filled a small bookcase in my room. It was good practice for my French. Though it was difficult to keep my thoughts on what I read, I forced myself, with the sense of one accomplishing something worthwhile. I saw Mademoiselle but briefly, as there were many important clients that day. Yet I was not concerned, for she said she had determined on a plan, though she would not say what it was. I sought my bed early, for want of aught else to do. But sleep was as elusive as the night before. And, senselessly, I cried. My thoughts were many, but all tangled as a spider's web. I slept not at all and, at dawn, rose to write. It was sometime later when someone opened my door. Knowing it was Mademoiselle Suzette, or her maid, I did not turn at once as I said, "Come in."

And then, my heart beating wildly, my pen slid across the page as Leslie said, "Good morning, madam."

Chapter 15

I forced myself to turn slowly to face Leslie. But no force of will could lift me to my feet. "Good morning, Leslie," I said. "May I ask how you found me?"

"Mademoiselle Suzette sent for me," he replied curtly.

"I see."

So, my only ally had betrayed me. I waited for Leslie to speak, for I could not. "Philip and Mary are well," he said, at last. "Though greatly distressed by your disappearance."

"I left letters."

"So you did, madam," he said contemptuously. "Should that lessen the offense?" He was angry now. "We've had two sleepless nights, the servants and I. And we gave out that you'd gone to London early, though I doubt it will silence the tattle-boxes."

I retorted. "Ah, yes, the god you worship . . . respectability . . . might have been disturbed! And nothing else matters, does it?"

"Be quiet, madam!"

"No, I will not. I left you so that you might annul our marriage. You should find your *respectability* easier to maintain without me!"

"Do you think so?" he asked bitterly. "I had not understood you to be so concerned for my welfare! And in any case, your departure would not aid me. Everyone would think you a second Jane and all the evil suspicions would be confirmed."

I was aghast at this notion which had not before occurred to me. "Leslie, I . . ."

"Spare me your protests, madam. Indeed, spare me further

170

speech. We leave for my town house in half an hour. Prepare yourself."

And then he was gone. I still sat, frozen, staring at the door, when Mademoiselle Suzette entered. I regarded her angrily. She stood, hands on hips, and said, "*Tiens!* But he is a fool! So you have had words. And you are angry with me."

"He is concerned only for his reputation!" I spat out.

"*Ma foi!* You are as stupid as he is!" she said bluntly. "He speaks so because he does not know how else to deal with such a woman."

"I should have gone to Lady Mary," I said bitterly. "Though his sister, *she* would not have betrayed me."

"That one!" Mademoiselle tossed her head. "She would not be eager to see this marriage. She thinks her son Philippe his heir. *I* would see you happy."

"Happy? With Sir Leslie? I will not go!"

"You will," she said grimly, "if he must to carry you screaming."

Stiffly I rose and packed my few things. Then I turned to her and said, "I am ready."

She sighed, "*Tiens, mon enfant*, do not be so stiff with him. You are not made of stone!"

"I shall write to you from France," was all I said.

Leslie was waiting and silently handed me into his barouche. As we began to move, Leslie began to lecture, "You came to London early to have a dress fitted by Mademoiselle Suzette. I followed. Will you give me your word, madam, not to run away again?"

"No!"

He was silent, and I smiled to myself. No doubt he would be vigilant, but I would yet escape. "Heather," he said quietly, "can we not call a truce?"

"Very well," I said, hiding the ache I felt, "a truce until I escape?"

He swore and we rode on in silence. The servants were lined up just inside the house. It seemed Leslie had remembered the proprieties, this time, and he introduced me. I fear my greeting was not altogether coherent, but no one seemed to mind and soon I was going upstairs. One of the maids accompanied me. "You seem tired, my lady," she said. "Shall I draw a bath?"

"Please," I said. "I should like that."

The arrangement of my room and Leslie's was much the same as in the castle. Both were large and airy, with two connecting doors. Surreptitiously, I checked for a bolt on my side, and to my relief, I found it. Quietly I closed the door. The bath was in a corner of the room partitioned off with a large screen. As soon as the servants had filled the tub and departed, I undressed and stepped into it. The warm water was soothing and I allowed myself to relax. Once, someone (the maid, I assumed) came into the room briefly, but I did not care. At last, satisfied, I stepped from my bath and dried myself. The maid had thoughtfully placed a dressing gown near the tub and I put that on until I could dress properly. Combing my hair, I walked into the main portion of my room. The maid had removed my clothes. For cleaning, I supposed, and I looked about for my bag. It was not there, and a rapid inspection informed me that my clothes were not in the wardrobe. Puzzled, I rang for the maid, trying to remember her name. When she arrived, I asked mildly, "Meg, where are my things?"

To my surprise, she bobbed a curtsy and said, "Please, my lady, you must ask Sir Leslie."

"*Sir Leslie?*"

"Yes, my lady. Sir Leslie," she said firmly.

"Please tell Sir Leslie that I wish to speak with him," I said as patiently as I could.

"Yes, my lady."

As I waited for Leslie I paced back and forth. I had an uneasy suspicion as to what he would say. And for the moment, I was helpless. Leslie soon arrived, entering my room with a careless air. "I trust your bath was satisfactory?" he asked in a friendly fashion.

"Where are my clothes?" I demanded.

He said nothing and I repeated the question. He smiled as though pleased with himself. "Do you not wish to rest, madam?"

"I wish to have my clothes!" I said, losing my temper.

He grew serious. "You may have your clothes, Heather, when you have given me your word you will not run away again."

"Never!"

"As you choose." He shrugged. "But I cannot think you will be much pleased to spend your life in a dressing gown."

"I won't!"

He shrugged again. "Perhaps not. The choice is yours. Oh, you need not expect help of the servants. They are quite loyal to me and understand I act for *your* welfare."

"Oh? And what will other people say, do you think?" I demanded.

He smiled insolently. "They will say it is such a pity my lovely young wife is ill and cannot even have visitors."

"I swear I'll find my clothes and escape!" I retorted.

"Perhaps. Or perhaps I've hidden them where you would not look."

I regarded him silently, unsure of what he meant. Where would I not look? Gradually a suspicion grew and became certainly as he added, "You might think to look there, I suppose. But as a gentlewoman, you would not."

I hid my satisfaction well. So he thought I would not? "Please leave me," I said with dignity. "I wish to rest."

He gave a mock bow and withdrew. Then I permitted myself to smile. I would wait for my opportunity. Knowing I should need my strength later, I slept.

Meg woke me, sometime later. "My lady, 'tis time for luncheon. I've brought your tray."

I sat up quickly, for I found I was quite hungry. Meg placed the tray on the table beside my bed. It held only a bowl of broth. "Meg," I asked evenly, "where is my meal?"

"Here, my lady."

"Meg, I see only a bowl of broth."

"Yes, my lady. Just as Sir Leslie ordered, my lady."

"Meg, take away the broth and bring me some food."

"No, my lady."

"Meg. Do as I have said, or fetch Sir Leslie. Else I shall not be responsible for what I do."

"Yes, my lady."

She hurried away to fetch Leslie, and I clenched and unclenched my fists. Leslie arrived, alone, and closed the door behind him. Then he folded his arms across his chest and, leaning against the door, regarded me calmly. "What is this?" I demanded, pointing to the tray.

"Broth, I believe."

"Well, I don't want it! I want an ordinary tray!" I said hotly.

"I know," he said sympathetically. "However, you'll have broth until you recover from your . . . *illness.*"

"You wouldn't dare!" I whispered.

"Try me!" His voice was hard. Then, more quietly, "You need only give me your word, Heather. I shall not ill-treat you. And you must realise I mean it for the best."

"No!"

He shrugged and opened the door. *"Bon appétit,"* he said, and was gone.

I confess I wanted to throw the tray, with its broth, after him. But I knew that if I did I should have nothing to eat. And so I consumed the broth, suppressing my dislike for it. When Meg returned for the tray, I asked about Leslie. "Oh, I believe he has gone out, my lady," she replied, somewhat timidly.

"Very well, that will be all," I said.

As soon as she had departed, I was out of bed. I would search his room at once. And if I found my clothes, I vowed I should soon be gone! Quietly I opened the doors between our rooms and soundlessly entered his. It was arranged much the same as mine, and I quickly moved to the drawers which I knew must hold his nether garments. I was sure this was where my things had been hidden. Why else say I would not dare search where they were hidden? I had scarcely begun my search when I heard a noise. I froze. The footsteps, for that was the sound I heard, came closer. I forced myself to turn. It was, as I knew it would be, Leslie. He regarded me a moment, then said quietly and with amusement, "Well, Heather, I didn't know such things interested you."

I followed his eyes to my hands, where I still held two of his garments. Hastily I thrust them away and turned back to face him. He regarded me as steadily as ever. "Now, Heather, may I have my room to myself? Unless you prefer to watch as I undress?"

I fled. Tears in my eyes, I fled to my room, slamming and bolting the door behind me. There I threw myself on my bed and cried with frustration. No doubt Leslie was well content! When I could cry no more, I paced. And when that palled, I determined to defy him some way. As a beginning, he should not know I cared that I was a prisoner. I would keep myself well amused with books and letters. Only . . . where to begin? How to post my letters? Leslie had surely given orders not to carry them for me. Well, still I could read, and in time discover a way to send my letters. Only . . . there were no books in my chamber. It took a moment for realisation to reach me. *There were no books in my chamber!* Resolutely, I strode to the door. I would go to the library myself and choose some books! I halted. A footman stood outside my door. I drew my dressing gown closer about me as he asked, respectfully, "Yes, my lady?"

"I wish some books . . . from the library."

"A moment, my lady. I will fetch Sir Leslie."

"There is no need. I shall fetch the books myself," I said lightly.

"Please, my lady," he said respectfully but firmly, "I will fetch Sir Leslie."

I retreated to my room, afraid to test the notion that this servant had orders to restrain me forcibly if I attempted to leave my room. A moment later, Leslie entered. "I am very sorry, Heather," he said in a sympathetic tone, one I was beginning to hate, "the doctor feels you should not tire your eyes by reading."

"Or writing?" I demanded.

He bowed. "Or writing."

"What doctor?"

"Doctor Kinwell, of course." His voice grew hard, "You have but to give your word, madam. . . ."

I stared at him with murderous intent. He bowed mockingly and left. And I threw a candlestick at the closing door. Was he mad? I wondered. Much as I had hated him, I had never deemed him capable of such behaviour. I could not doubt the seriousness of his intent, nor his determination to keep me so until I gave my word. I truly wondered if he were sane, this man who was now such a stranger. For the first time, I began to be afraid.

In this manner, broodingly, the afternoon passed. I was not surprised to find that for me, tea consisted of just tea and plain toast. All in form of course. As I sipped my tea I tried to reason out why Leslie should be so determined to keep me. And I could only conclude that he viewed me as a possession he would not give up, no matter how flawed it might be, no matter how he loathed it. Leslie spoke of "appearances" and of Jane and of becoming an outcast. But I could not believe he would care so much for that. Could he be less happy than he was with me? Ah, then I had it. Perhaps he felt my absence would interfere with acquiring a mistress, as my presence would not. Perhaps he had already determined on the woman and waited only until our marriage should be sufficiently old not to arouse censure. But if that were so, why did he not fear I should speak of this outrage? Or did he feel that I should fear to, having given my word to remain in his power? Would I? I began to feel caught in a nightmare I could not wake from. And when Meg came to take away the tea tray, she found me strangely silent.

I did not see Leslie again that day. He had patience enough, it seemed. My evening meal was, of course, another bowl of broth, and I ate it with resignation. I retired early. Surely, tomorrow, I should come about.

Morning came soon, and with it, tea and plain toast to break my fast. I was tired of this nonsense and determined to tell Leslie so when he came. But he did not come that morning. At noon, Meg brought my bowl of broth, and my patience was at an end. "Please inform Sir Leslie that I wish to speak with him," I told her.

Meg bobbed a curtsy and tried to hide a smile. "I am sorry, my lady, but he said to inform you he should not come so long as there were broth in the bowl. That he did not wish to find it on his clothes."

I found it difficult to suppress a smile myself, for he had read my intentions rightly. I sighed. "Very well, Meg. When you return for the tray you may inform Sir Leslie I wish to speak with him."

"Yes, my lady."

I was oddly cheered by this bit of news, for it made Leslie seem familiar again. Surely he was not as mad as he had seemed the day before. I should speak with him and we would reach an understanding. But when he came, his manner was as cold as ever. "I trust you are almost well, madam?" he said.

I waited until Meg had left the room. "Oh, Leslie, stop this nonsense! Can we not discuss the matter calmly?"

"There is nothing to discuss, Heather," he replied quietly. "I will settle for nothing short of your word not to run away again."

"Well, you shall not have it," I said petulantly.

176

He shrugged. "As you wish. It is no trouble to me to have you an invalid."

"Leslie . . ."

"Your word, Heather."

"No!"

"Good day."

He was gone. I stared at the closed door in disbelief. And I threw another candlestick. A moment later, the footman timidly opened the door. "You wish something, my lady?"

"Get out!" I shouted, and he hastily withdrew.

I determined to again search for my clothes. But this time, the door to Leslie's chamber was bolted from his side. I was truly a prisoner now, for I knew the footman still guarded my door. I began to pace, determined to hit upon a scheme for my escape. But none occurred to me that I did not soon dismiss as foolish or impossible. At tea, I sounded Meg as to the possibility of her aid. I was soon stripped of my illusions: her loyalty, and indeed that of all the servants, lay with Leslie. For some reason (what it might be, I could not conceive) the servants had a high regard for him. Without question, they would follow his orders, and it signified nothing if the orders were bizarre. So, I must act alone. But I could think of no plan. Leslie had come to know me well, and taken all precautions, it seemed. Broth arrived at the usual hour. I grew more and more discouraged, trying the door and, each time, finding the footman still outside. And finding, each time I tried it, Leslie's door was bolted. That night, sleep would not come.

I arose, sleepless, at my usual hour. My head ached and I felt close to tears of frustration. Had Leslie appeared, I should have screamed at him and thrown all that I could find. But he did not appear. And would not, Meg informed me, until I felt "better." She brought my broth early that day. When I said it lacked the proper hour, Meg explained, "I know, my lady. But I thought I might bring it early for 'tis a busy day in the kitchen. Sir Leslie has commanded a large noon meal."

And in that moment, I recognised what had disturbed me . . . the smells of the kitchen. I looked at the tray with my broth and suddenly wondered what was the point of my futile resistance? "Take away the broth, Meg," I said quietly. "And please inform Sir Leslie I am feeling *quite well*."

"Yes, my lady."

When she had gone, I privately resolved to give Leslie my word, but not to keep it if he did not change his manner toward me. For he had offered an exchange: my freedom for my word. If he failed to keep his side of the bargain, I should not keep mine. And then he was there. He closed the door and regarded me with his piercing eyes. "Meg said you felt *recovered?*"

"Yes," I said wearily, "I give you my word, I shall not run away again."

He advanced and placed a hand on my shoulder. "You shall not regret it, Heather," he said quietly. Then he grinned. "I'll send Meg with your clothes, for I suspect you would prefer to dine at table."

I did not answer and he left. So. I was bound here, and what the future held I could not guess. When Meg arrived, I dressed quickly, and after checking my bag to be sure the journal still lay there untouched, I went downstairs, arriving before the table had even been set. As we sat down to dine it seemed Leslie gazed at me oddly. But I dismissed the notion impatiently. I was hungry and I ate as one who had not dined for many days. We had started the final course when there was a noise in the hall. Leslie and I rose as one to investigate. And I stood frozen as I watched Peter and Ellen enter with a mass of luggage. I looked at Leslie, and catching my eye, he flushed. Truly I felt ill, for in that moment, I understood. Had I but been firm two hours more, I should have won. Leslie could not have kept me prisoner with Ellen here to aid me. And even Peter, I was certain, should have protested. Slowly I turned and went back to the table. I forced myself to eat to cover my confusion. He had won by such a short margin! Had I but understood him better. . . . But I understood him, it seemed, not at all. Leslie returned to the table, and as we completed the meal, I said, "And what should you have done this afternoon?"

"I don't know," he confessed, understanding well enough what I asked. "But it doesn't matter as I do have your word."

"Yes. You have my word."

Quietly I rose and walked away from the table. I could not yet face Ellen and, instead, sought out a maid (not Meg) to show me the house. If I must stay here, I should at least be mistress of the house. It was a house much as any other in this fashionable district of London, save that it was furnished in a manner already out of favour. And I knew Leslie must have left it as his mother had chosen, so many years before. I had made no changes at the castle, but here I would. Some rooms were well enough: the library, the dining hall, Leslie's bedchamber. But the others . . . As we finished the tour of the house and the maid left me I encountered Leslie. Rather defiantly I told him of my intentions. He sighed and, taking my arm, propelled me into the library. Once there, he pushed me into a seat and faced me. "Heather," he said frankly, "you are angry with me. But we need not be enemies. I shall not stop you if you wish to make changes here. It is your house as well as mine." He hesitated. "I have spoken with Philip. You will no doubt meet him in Town, but I suspect you will find him cool and distant."

"Do you expect surprise or dismay of me?" I asked.

"No. I understand well enough what passed between the two of you. Perhaps better than you do."

"It is of no concern to me what you think," I said coldly. "Nevertheless, in view of your behaviour, I cannot believe you do understand."

"Heather!" His voice was quiet, dangerously so. "It is you who does not understand. Nor will you until you cease to behave as a child." As I started to protest he cut me off. "Yes, a child! It is a child's reaction to run away. Or a coward's. Oh, I know well enough that you are angry with me . . . for having tricked you into giving your word. But it was necessary. And I hold you to your word, Heather. You have behaved as a child long enough. It is time to grow up. You are quite capable of doing so, I know."

I was angry and could not speak. Twice angry, for I could not decide whether his words held truth or not. Worse, I was close to tears. It was at that moment my father arrived. He did not wait for a servant to announce him and he did not bother to knock. He did, however, think to close the library door behind himself. "Why the devil didn't you warn me you were coming to Town so soon? And why have I not heard from you? It took a chance acquaintance to inform me of your presence!" He paused for breath.

Leslie answered quietly. "Frankly, I felt it none of your affair. Heather and I need not answer to you for each action we take, Lord Pellen."

As though he meant to be soothing, my father said, "No, of course not. But I was worried a new problem had appeared."

I felt Leslie's hand on my shoulder, warning me. He answered easily, "Then you need not trouble yourself further. Heather and I have remained in seclusion merely to plan her debut. I took a look in at my clubs, of course, and this evening, Heather and I will go to the theatre. We intend to begin discreetly, you see, as though there were no need to question her acceptance. She is not, after all, a young chit being launched onto the Marriage Mart."

"True, quite true," Lord Pellen answered. "The theatre, you say? Well, I had not planned to attend, but I believe I shall put in a brief appearance."

The two men bowed to each other, perfectly in accord on this matter, and at odds on most others. They exchanged suggestions for the following week, and then my father left. Leslie turned back to me, his earlier bad humour lessened. "Heather, we'd best go upstairs and choose your gown for tonight."

I assented and even took his arm. As we mounted the stairs he explained the sort of dress he wanted: simple yet elegant. Something that would suit a matron, not a maiden, yet which did not bespeak sophistication. Tonight was very important, it seemed. Ellen opened the door at our knock, pausing in the midst of unpacking. Leslie greeted her kindly and explained our problem, whereupon Ellen drew out three or four dresses for his inspection. At last, he settled upon one of silver. It was not white as a schoolgirl's would have been, yet it suggested the air of innocence. It was a dress I had not seen before, and I regarded it almost with awe. "What jewels will she wear?" Ellen asked.

"The emeralds," Leslie said at once.

"*Emeralds?*" Ellen asked in surprise.

"Yes, emeralds," he replied quietly. "There are enough people who know their importance . . . it will mean more to them than anything else could."

I was exasperated. "What *do* they mean? Others seem to know, but I do not."

He took my chin in his hand and regarded me seriously. "Someday soon, I shall explain, Heather. But not just yet."

There was that in his eyes which bade me quietly accept what he said. And it mattered little enough, just then. So I nodded. He released my chin and smiled gently, "It will be a long evening, Heather. Rest if you can."

And he left. I stared after him, at the closed door, for several moments, before I turned back to face Ellen. She stood, hands on hips, eyes flashing. "Now, Ellen . . ." I hastened to say.

But she did not heed me. "My lady! How could you do such a thing? Leaving alone and at such a time? With but three *notes* to say good-bye! And such notes they must have been to set each wailing so! My lady, I know well enough you've not had an easy time of it. But could you have seen Sir Leslie's face when he knew you gone, you'd not have left so lightly! He searched for you both day and night, asking everywhere and refusing to rest. Had the message not come from Mademoiselle Suzette, he were desperate. And we, belowstairs, were worried too, my lady. You be so young. Oh, my lady, if you *must* run away again, take me with you."

"There will be no more running away, Ellen," I said slowly. "I have given my word."

"Thank God, my lady!" she replied. Then, timidly: "Do you hate him so very much, my lady?"

"No, I do not hate him, Ellen," I said wearily. "What gave you cause to think I did?"

"He did, my lady. Sir Leslie. When he found you gone, he asked me why you could not cease to hate him. I said I thought you did not, but he laughed bitterly. Then of course, I found the notes you had left. He was quieter after he read the one for him. But still so unhappy, my lady."

My face blushed crimson with the memory of what I had written, not thinking I should see him again. And also with the image of Leslie asking Ellen why I hated him so. Suddenly I wished I could begin again with this strange man who was my husband. And yet, wearily, I knew it should have been of no use, that Leslie and I would always come to cuffs.

Ellen, watching my face, judged me sufficiently subdued and ceased to scold.

I could not rest and she drew a bath for me. Then it was time to dress my hair and, finally, don my gown. I found it difficult to believe that the young woman in the glass was myself. Downstairs, Leslie awaited me, dressed almost as elegantly as I, in his own way. And for the briefest moment, I read approval in his eyes. But then it was gone, and he led me in to dinner with polite formality. What we talked of then, I cannot recall.

Chapter 16

The theatre. I had been there few times before, as the poor guest of some kind friend's parents. My dresses had always been shabby, and once I had even been taken for a young governess. But that was all past now. To me, it would be a night of triumph. A night for all my old schoolmates to envy me. And I knew they would, for none could guess the unhappiness that lay behind my expensive gown and elegant manner. They would wonder, but they could not know. We arrived in Leslie's town barouche, led by a splendid team of chestnuts. We were treated as persons of some importance, and I discovered that I enjoyed the sensation. Leslie had thoughtfully timed our arrival so that, while we were not late, there were few people in the lobby to stare. *That* came when we reached our box. Many eyes turned to see the new Lady Kinwell, but as the curtain was rising, they had little time to note me. Nervously I awaited the intermission. Leslie had drilled me in the barouche as to whom I must watch for, whom I must nod to. I cannot remember the title of the piece we viewed, only that it was a tragedy. Instead I recall the smell of the lamps and the faintest trace of mustiness in the velvet curtains that hung in our box. I recall a woman's high-pitched laugh and some man's sneeze. And I recall the glint of light on diamonds and opera glasses and the stillness at the dénouement. But I cannot recall the play.

I remember the precise moment when the curtain fell for intermission and it seemed all eyes turned to our box. But that was only a fantasy, of course. Yet many did stare at me, some in frank curiosity, some with animosity. To those classmates I noticed, I smiled. Each in turn, with at most a moment's hesitation, returned the smile. I had never been popular, but I had rarely made enemies. This now stood me in good stead. As though on cue, my father appeared at the door of our box. Would we care to go to his box and pay our respects to Lady Pellen, his mother, and Lady Phyllis, his wife? We would. Leslie gave me his arm and squeezed my hand in reassurance. He seemed to understand how I felt. And I was grateful for his presence.

And then I stood before her. The woman who had hidden my existence from my father and was, in a sense, responsible for my present position. She was a formidable woman, though small in stature. She looked at me with hatred and wonder in her eyes. I forced myself to look away from her and smile as Lord Pellen introduced me to his wife. I liked her immediately. She had no nonsense about her, and a sense of humour that made one almost forget she seemed cold. "So this is your daughter, Robert," she said. "She'll do very well, I think. Welcome to London, Heather. I trust you are enjoying your first public appearance? Simply remember never to look embarrassed or guilty, and the *ton* will accept you."

I thanked her rather awkwardly and Leslie paid her some sort of compliment. Lady Phyllis was amused, for she said to me, "Have you reformed him already? London will be quite disappointed to learn he has acquired such polish."

Hastily my father began, "Mother, my daughter, Heather, and her husband, Sir Leslie Kinwell."

I curtsied slightly and Leslie bowed. She surveyed me carefully and said distastefully, "Quite like her mother, I fear."

Lacking wisdom but not courage, I retorted, "Not quite, my lady. *I* should never have allowed my husband to be taken from me!"

A hand closed hard around my arm and tightened until I smiled as she was smiling. Only then did Leslie loose his grip somewhat. My grandmother spoke languidly. "The same deplorable tendency to hysterics. Nevertheless, child, you shall have to do. Pray recall, in the future, that your father was not taken from your mother and that we have only now discovered you. I think it best if you kiss me."

"I will not!" I answered softly.

Leslie's hand tightened on my arm. "I believe you will, Heather," he also said softly, "since everyone seems to be watching."

Though inwardly rebellious, I did as I was bid, kissing the powdered cheek and submitting to a hug. Then I stepped back. We were both smiling false smiles. "There," she said. "I have done my duty by you. I shall acknowledge you when asked, and of course, at times we will meet. But you must expect nothing more of me."

I smiled sweetly. "And that will be such a change!"

Hastily Leslie made our excuses and we withdrew. "Now *my* family," he said when we were in the corridor.

I hung back a moment. "No . . . Leslie . . . I . . . could we not go home? Or, at the least, return to our box?"

He paused long enough to put an arm about my waist. "Heather, Lady Pellen is an unpleasant woman . . . and always has been. Forget her and be calm. I think you will not find my aunts so formidable."

But they were. As we entered their box and Leslie introduced me I felt them scrutinise me as carefully as my grandmother had. Anne, Jennifer, and Harriet, they were named, in order of age. Harriet wore mourning, but Leslie enquired after the husbands of Jennifer and Anne. Such politeness taken care of, Leslie presented me. I curtsied awkwardly, I fear. As I had heard Leslie speak the names of his uncles by marriage, I had realised I stood before women who were powerful in London society. They were frequent guests at Carlton House and held, morever, the power to ruin a young girl simply by declaring her fast. The silence grew longer until Anne spoke. "Why didn't you warn us, Leslie?"

"There was no time," he said quietly, "nor did I feel it was your affair."

"Father? Mother? Education?"

"Robert, Earl of Pellen. Elizabeth Wade. Mrs. Gilwen's School for Young Ladies." My voice was as crisp as hers had been. I continued, "Married by Mr. Watly. Dressed by Mademoiselle Suzette. Aged eighteen."

Jennifer nodded. "Well, at least she's no milk-and-water chit, Nephew."

"Pretty enough," Harriet added thoughtfully, "and knowing Leslie, needle-witted as well."

The silence fell again and grew until I demanded impatiently, "Well? Am I to be accepted?"

Harriet shrugged. "Oh, *accepted*. There was never any question of that since you wear the Kinwell emeralds. We know our nephew is not a sapskull." She turned to Leslie. "I suppose you want her to receive the proper vouchers? She shall. I've taken a fancy to the child."

Leslie bowed, and as the intermission was drawing to a close, we prepared to withdraw. I almost thought Anne would have spoken again. But she did not. As we hurried to our box I felt Leslie's arm taking mine; he was in excellent humour. And amused. But he would not explain. The women had been formidable, but not, strangely, intimidating. Perhaps it was because I felt a kinship with the three women. They would not have submitted meekly to Mrs. Gilwen's offer either. Nor to marriage against their will.

We barely entered our box in time, as the curtain was rising. My thoughts, however, were on the other members of the audience. Leslie, too, seemed preoccupied. And once or twice his eyes strayed to a nearby box. In the dim light I could only see the profiles of the occupants: two men and two women. Then one of the women turned toward us for a moment, as though returning Leslie's gaze, and nodded. I sat stiffly, then forced myself to look at the stage. The nod had clearly been directed at Leslie. It was nothing to me, of course, if Leslie had a female friend. We were not, after all, married except as a matter of convenience. But I wished he had shown more discretion than to signal her in the theatre. I relaxed only as I realised she was probably simply another relative.

The play finally over, Leslie was the perfect attentive husband. He offered me his arm and helped me with my things and smiled tenderly at me. I matched him, smile for smile, and even, as we turned to leave our box, rested my head against his shoulder for a moment. We were very convincing, for more than one person stopped to congratulate us on our marriage and comment on the true "love match." The glances of the men were admiring, those of the women almost envious. One young matron told me, "Lady Kinwell, you are accounted something of a sorceress. You have married one of London's most elusive bachelors. And, it appears, made him more human. We have missed him in recent years."

It was an auspicious beginning, and in the barouche I laughed easily with Leslie. So much so that he said, "You see? Is it so terrible to be with me?"

The laughter died in my throat. I wanted to say I was sorry

I had run away. And my hand moved to his arm. But I did not speak. My voice should have betrayed more than I wished, and Leslie might have asked so many questions to which I would have had no answer. I could feel his eyes on me, piercing, even in the darkness. And then . . . then he was leaning back, speaking easily about his aunts. Had they been my age, he said, their reputations should not have survived a Season. But they had been young at a time when high spirits were admired. And there was nothing they despised so much as what they termed the growing hypocrisy of respectability. But they had married well: all titled men. And they therefore remained powerful in the *ton*, if a bit eccentric. "What did she mean," I asked, "when she said that because I wore the emeralds, they must accept me?"

He looked away and spoke so softly I could barely hear his voice. "The emeralds have always meant . . . something special . . . not given to all the Lady Kinwells. . . ."

He stopped and I knew I should pry no more from him. I was puzzled and a little frightened by something I could not name. I did not understand. I did not *want* to understand.

We were a silent pair as the barouche drew up to Leslie's town house. Once inside, driven by something I could not explain, I bid a hasty good night to Leslie and fled to my room. Ellen awaited me and I chattered helplessly, as she prepared me for bed. She looked at me oddly, once or twice, but then said sympathetically, "Yes, my lady. I expect it was quite an exciting evening for you. And looking fine as ninepence, you were."

Childishly I cried myself to sleep that night, not knowing what it was I cried for.

So began our social life in London. Invitations arrived, some procured, as promised, by Lady Phyllis and Leslie's aunts, others that came of themselves. I began to pay and receive morning calls, to and from old school friends. How happy they seemed to see me! And I chided that cynical side of me which noted how much friendlier they were now than when I had been poor Heather Wade. How romantic my story was, they said. And all wondered (though they were too well bred to ask) how I had contrived to be courted under the very noses of our schoolmistresses.

There were a few friends, of course, who had shown me

kindness when I'd been at school. These I greeted with true pleasure, and we would laugh and exchange memories of those years. At such times, I was happy. But at other times, I would stare at myself in the mirror and wonder at the ease with which I was being bribed. For that was what it was: my position, my clothes, the trinkets Leslie would upon occasion bring home to amuse me. And when next I saw Leslie, I would stare at him, wondering how he felt. I could remember his words and tone of contempt as he said that the muslin-set at least provided what they were paid for. At such times, I would grow angry and tell myself *he* was the one who insisted upon marriage. *He* had known and accepted then that life would be so. And yet . . . I began to wonder at his patience . . . wonder if he had a mistress. And because I wondered, I began to observe Leslie more closely.

My mind was upon household matters, however, the day Melinda Corvil came to call. Her first action after we had kissed was to scold me. "You *promised* I should be the first you told!" she said. For a moment, I stared at her bewildered, and she continued, "Oh, you must remember! The night before you ran off . . . at table . . . I asked what was wrong and you told me it was a surprise, and that I should know of it first." Here, her eyes began to dance, "It was Sir Leslie's proposal, no doubt. How you made game of us all! With your meek and quiet air we, none of us, thought to suspect you of a secret *tendre*. And yet, when I think now upon the matter, you were often slipping off to be alone. And you did miss history class that day!"

She laughed and I breathed a silent prayer of thanks for my solitary habits. I forced myself to laugh as well. "I recall my promise. But I only said that I would *tell* none of the other girls, first. And I did not. But come, sit down. I am delighted to see you. Tell me what happened the next day, when my absence was discovered."

She laughed again. "Oh, it was beyond everything, Heather! You were not missed until bedtime. And then what a fuss! Mrs. Brenner demanding to know where you had gone, and all of us believing you were in the sickroom! Then, Mrs. Gilwen appeared. I never saw her so angry or so distressed. She demanded an account of Mrs. Brenner, who was quite overset. Then, realising we were all listening, she summoned

Mrs. Brenner to her parlour. You can be sure we talked late that night.''

I smiled at the thought of Mrs. Gilwen's distress. It was well deserved. I had no fear she should betray me. . . . I was too powerful now. Melinda was speaking again. ''. . . Sir Leslie! He is such a figure of mystery. I've heard it said he is nip-farthing and harsh and unpleasant.''

''Not true!'' I protested. ''He is just and honourable and often gentle and patient. And *never* clutch-fisted.''

She looked at me with surprise. ''But his nephew Philip Gainesfield says . . .''

I cut her short. ''Philip is, in many ways, a . . . a sapskull. He expects Leslie to frank him when he is afraid to face his father with his debts. And he dislikes Leslie because Leslie has given him more than one sharp setdown!'' In fairness, I added, ''Though I grant you that Leslie has a temper and has, no doubt, ridden roughshod over Philip. But how do you know Philip so well?'' I asked.

She blushed. ''Well, I've a brother at Oxford . . . and you know the circles we move in are so small. . . .''

In spite of myself, I smiled. Yes, the *haut ton* seemed very small indeed. I only hoped she was not too set on Philip since I suspected he would think her a blue-stocking. Well, no matter, she was pretty enough and would soon find a suitor. ''In any event,'' I added, ''I did not mean to disparage Philip. I think him rather nice. I just could not bear to hear you speak so of Leslie.''

She nodded in understanding. ''Of course, when one is in love . . .''

I blushed guiltily, wondering what she should think if she knew the truth. I turned the talk to that of the Season. I had, of course, missed much of it and she told me the latest *on-dits*. We were chattering so when I heard a footstep and turned to see Leslie enter the room. He bowed over Melinda's hand as she blushed in confusion. Then I gave him my cheek to kiss. ''I am sorry to intrude, Heather,'' he said, ''but I've just this moment received an invitation for tomorrow and the courier waits a response. Lady Willby requests our presence for cards in the evening.''

I wrinkled my nose. ''Lady Willby? Very well, if you wish it, Leslie. But, indeed, I cannot recall who she is, nor understand why the invitation comes so late. . . .''

Melinda began to laugh. I stared at her in amazement, and after a moment, she explained, "You know her very well, Heather! Lisa! Lisa Stanton who left school two years ago. You were always helping her with her history. She finally married this year. How famous . . . you *must* go, Heather. I am sure the invitation comes so late only because she has just discovered who *you* are."

I was easily convinced, for I remembered Lisa with affection. She had been neither handsome nor clever, but always amiable. As soon as Leslie left to inform the messenger of our reply, Melinda rose. "I must be leaving, Heather," she said. "But I am glad to have seen you and shall again. And I am glad to find you happy."

I smiled wryly at her words and murmured the conventional phrases as she prepared to leave. Then she was gone and Leslie returned. "You're managing very well," he said. "Soon there will be no house where you are not welcome." He noted my confusion, for he placed a hand on my shoulder and asked, "What troubles you?"

I shrugged helplessly. "Leslie . . . they would not welcome me if they knew the truth. . . . I . . ."

He gathered me up in his arms. "Calm yourself, Heather. You've no need to feel an outsider. You do belong. Where is your courage?"

It was the right thing to ask of me. I sat erect. "You are quite right, Leslie. I shall not be such a pea-goose again."

He smiled and touched my chin with a finger. Then he drew something from a pocket. It was a lovely painted fan. "Oh, thank you!" I cried, and kissed his cheek.

He smiled at me oddly and suddenly, unaccountably, I was nervous. I sprang up and muttered some excuse and left the room. Behind me, Leslie only smiled more strangely still.

Melinda had been correct. Lady Willby was Lisa. She greeted me eagerly. "So it *is* you! I am so glad, Heather. Good evening, Sir Leslie. Heather, I must introduce you to *everyone*. Some you'll remember from school . . . though as a rule, I avoid my old classmates."

I understood that well enough. Lisa had never been popular, and I wondered how she had found a husband until I remembered that she had been an heiress. One of the very few to attend Mrs. Gilwen's school. *That* had not aided her popularity. I found myself remembering little kindnesses, such as being taken to tea by her. It had been a small thing for her to buy us both sweet buns, but withal, a gesture few others had made. And now? It was perhaps a small thing to take pains to introduce me to each guest, but it was not a kindness I should soon forget. Last, she introduced us to her husband Drake, Lord Willby. As he smiled at us, half mockingly, I began to blush. For his eyes swept over me as though I stood unclothed. Instinctively I glanced at Lisa, who stood unhappily beside him. I dared not look at Leslie. Instead I stared at Lord Willby as coldly and haughtily as I could manage. He continued to smile, but rather more coldly himself. He spoke to Leslie. "Now that I have seen your charming wife, I am even angrier that you did not tell me of her beforehand. I should have liked to dance at your wedding."

Leslie's voice was cool but calm. "Indeed? I am sorry to have disappointed you, then. We preferred a small ceremony, however, as my wife suffers from shyness."

I did my best to look shy. Lord Willby's voice continued silkily, "We have heard of her romantic background. Tell me, how did you meet? No doubt that also is romantic."

Leslie lied without hesitation. "I saw her at the theatre once when she had gone as someone-or-other's guest. I was intrigued and asked a few discreet questions to learn her identity. Not wishing to beard the dragon, Mrs. Gilwen, I contrived to accidentally encounter her outside."

Lord Willby seemed disappointed. When he spoke again, it was in a different tone. "By the by, Leslie, a curious thing has occurred. The domestic agency I once suggested to you closed a month or two ago. Mr. Thornsby was the director."

I held myself rigid. But Leslie seemed not in the least disturbed. "Oh? How curious, as you say. Fortunately such matters are now my wife's concern. Still, I once found their services quite useful."

I felt a cold rage growing in me. How dare Leslie speak so casually of . . . of that man! Yet I could not betray that I knew of what they spoke. I said in a light voice, "Surely, there are any number of excellent domestic agencies in London? Personally, I should distrust a man to supply me female servants. Only a woman understands such matters."

Both men smiled and Leslie squeezed my waist reassuringly. And I knew I had allayed any suspicions Lord Willby might have had. Lisa, silent until now, suggested the card games begin and we found places. The stakes were small, and though I played well, I did not truly care whether I won or lost. My table was congenial and I enjoyed myself.

At midnight, a supper was served and I was again with Lisa. We talked some, but there was a sense of constraint that arose because of her husband. Yet I felt Lisa needed a friend more than she ever had at school. So I invited her to come to tea within the week. She tilted her chin as she replied, "Thank you, Heather, but I cannot. Drake has decreed I leave for our country house tomorrow. You see I . . ." She blushed. "I may be breeding and Drake wishes me to pass the next few months quietly and comfortably, away from London."

I did not know what to say. I was deeply shocked, for I saw that Lisa was not eager to go. And what should her husband be doing in London while she were away? I did not want to guess. Nonetheless I forced myself to say, "Felicitations, my dear Lisa! Well, then, you must come to see me when you return to London. And write to me."

She smiled shyly, and with relief that I did not speak those thoughts we both held. Soon after, Leslie appeared, and making our excuses, we left. In the barouche I found myself releasing my pent-up rage. With a clenched fist, I struck the seat. "Poor Lisa! How can she bear being married to that . . . that court-card?"

At Leslie's look of surprise, I told him about Lisa's condition and her move to the country. He did not speak but his face revealed he felt much as I did. "Oh, Leslie," I said impulsively, "I'm glad you are not like Lord Willby!"

"Are you so sure of me?" he asked.

I looked at him in shock. "You are not . . . you would not . . . no, I don't believe it of you!"

"I thought you considered me utterly depraved?" he said quietly.

"I . . . I . . ."

I fell silent. No, I knew Leslie was not so bad as Lisa's husband. Yet I could not speak freely as I wanted to. In the darkness, I felt Leslie's eyes on me, and then after a few moments he said, "I know it could not have been easy to hear us speak of Mr. Thornsby, but I dared not do otherwise.

I . . . Heather, do you truly regret being forced to marry me?''

"You know that is not what I regret," I whispered, and even in the darkness, I felt him flinch.

"That cannot be undone," he said.

"No, nor yet forgotten," I answered softly.

In silence, then, we rode to the town house. And because I could not bear the look of frustration on his face, I fled at once to my room. But I could not run from my own thoughts. Round and round they went long after Ellen had left me for the night. Yet late as I lay awake, I did not hear Leslie come to his room. I did not doubt that he felt as haunted as I. Never had I felt so tempted to go to him. Yet I could not, should not forgive him.

Could I?

Chapter 17

I woke late the next morning, almost at noon. When I chided Ellen for letting me sleep, she replied, "But my lady, I had not the heart to wake you. You seemed so tired, and with the ball tonight . . ."

"Very well," I said, forcing myself awake.

As I dressed I asked if Leslie had also slept late. "Oh, no, my lady. He rose at his usual hour. In a brown study today, one of the footmen told me. Refused his breakfast and went out without a word to anyone."

"Thank you, Ellen," I said, trying to avoid the question in her eyes.

Was he angry? At me? I could not absolve myself of guilt. And yet, and yet, what was I to do? Not wishing to brood, I informed Ellen I would accompany her to Mademoiselle Suzette's establishment to pick up my new ball gown. "Yes, my lady," she said with some surprise.

I had not set foot in Mademoiselle's establishment since the day Leslie had found me there. Always I had sent Ellen or another servant to fetch or leave orders. I was not altogether sure I wanted to go there now. But I had to get out of the house. Perhaps I secretly hoped to have Mademoiselle give me advice about Leslie. A naive notion, but then, I was a naive young woman.

Dragon (whom I could not think of by any other name) showed us to a fitting room and took Ellen with her to fetch the gown. This required some time for it seemed half of London society would be at this night's ball, and many of the women ordered their dresses from Mademoiselle Suzette. At last Ellen returned. The dress was silver again. It fit me perfectly, of course, and yet I could not help longing for a dress which would make me appear older and more mature. Mademoiselle Suzette entered just in time to hear me voice my thoughts aloud. She cocked her head to one side. "Monsieur . . . Sir Leslie . . . does not wish it." I flushed angrily, and signalling Ellen to leave us, she stepped closer. "You are a little pea-hen. Do you not understand? *Oui, mon enfant*, I could dress you as you wish. And all of London would say, 'Yes, that is the sort of *hussy* to trap Sir Leslie.' You must to look innocent."

My shoulders drooped in resignation. Would we never have done with such worries? Mademoiselle Suzette placed a hand on my arm. "What is wrong, *ma petite?*"

I shrugged and moved away. The memory of her treachery warred with my desire to tell someone how I felt. She must have read much from my face for she said, "*Pauvre enfant!* You still are apart? Do you think him so terrible . . . worse than other men?"

"No!" I said. Then: "You do not understand."

"You are wrong. I understand much. But I believe Sir Leslie to be a good man, also. And I believe that if you persist too long like this, he will lose patience. He is not a man to be long lonely, and he will easily find a woman to please him. And then you will understand what you have lost. *Tiens!* From your face I would say you do not hate him so very much. Perhaps you begin to care? *Enfin*, you must not to let a stupid pride keep you from him. You . . ."-

She broke off as someone knocked at the door. It was Dragon. "Excuse me, Mademoiselle, but you are needed at once. The duchess . . ."

Mademoiselle Suzette nodded. She squeezed her hand on my arm and was gone. A few minutes later, Ellen returned. She was in excellent spirits, having spent the time with the seamstresses, even, she confided, helping with one of the hems. As Ellen fastened up my dress she chattered, repeating the gossip she had heard. Soon the ball gown was packed and we departed. We had not come in Leslie's barouche but by hackney, and I determined we should walk a bit. There were nearby shops displaying various goods: trinkets, hats, gloves, shawls . . . On impulse, I entered a shop and purchased a pair of fine gloves for Leslie. It required most of the money left in my reticule, but I did not care. Feeling rather light-hearted, I hailed a cab and we rode back to the town house.

As I drew off my bonnet and mittens in the foyer I asked after Leslie, eager to give him my present. But he was not at home. I sent Ellen upstairs with careful instructions as to what I should wear with my gown and at what time to draw my bathwater. Then I proceeded to the library, still clutching the gloves.

The library at the town house was not such a comfortable room as the library in the castle. Somehow it seemed too formal. Yet by its very function, it was a refuge to me. I took down a book and began to read. Each time I heard footsteps, I would look up, hoping to see Leslie, and I found myself listening for the sound of the front door. But he did not come. At four, one of the maids brought me a light tea. It grew later and still Leslie did not return. Finally I mounted the stairs to dress. At Leslie's chamber, I paused and knocked. Peter was, as I expected, laying out Leslie's evening clothes. "Yes, my lady?" he asked respectfully. "I am afraid Sir Leslie is not here."

"Yes . . . yes, I know that," I replied self-consciously. "Could you . . . please give this to him when he returns?"

"Yes, my lady."

And then the door was closed. Slowly, I continued to my chamber. Ellen was waiting.

When I descended later, I found Leslie waiting in the drawing room, dressed for the ball. He bowed but did not comment on my gown. Nor did he mention the gloves. And I had not the courage to ask if he had liked them. Before we could speak, the footman announced the arrival of Lord and Lady Pellen. They were to dine with us and ride in our carriage to the ball. Phyllis wore a blue satin gown that set off her blond hair perfectly. My father was dressed in the same careless elegance as Leslie. Phyllis drew me aside as the two men began to talk of business matters. "Well, Heather," she began, "one hears you have made powerful friends in Town. Few young matrons have the ladies Ormsby, Rifton, and Crombie as sponsors."

"Leslie's aunts," I said with a smile. "I met them at the theatre the same evening I met you."

"You seem to have pleased them."

"Who?" Leslie asked, moving to my side.

"Your aunts," I explained.

Lord Pellen chuckled proudly. "Yes, my daughter is contriving quite well. Quite well indeed. I've made arrangements, Heather, by the by, and you will appear at the Queen's drawing-room on the eleventh of next month."

We moved to the dining room, I on father's arm, Phyllis on Leslie's. My father was in excellent humour. "You see? Everything is resolving itself quite nicely. You have the *entrée* virtually everywhere. And pretty things, do you not? And from the look in Sir Leslie's eyes when they rest on you, you can use him as you will."

I blushed and shook my head but dared not answer. We were soon seated and it was with relief that I greeted my father's new list of questions. For they were only a catechism of my recent social activities, and therefore rather impersonal. Leslie listened quietly, adding from time to time a brief comment. Phyllis was also silent, save when we spoke of an event that had led to a mention of my name by one of her friends. I tried, now and again, to surprise Leslie's eyes on me, hoping to catch sight of that which my father said I should find. But all I could read in those dark depths was a quiet mockery.

After what seemed an interminable time, we were rising from the table. The usual sorts of confusion and activity ensued before we left for the ball. And still Leslie had not mentioned the gloves.

The rooms were already crowded when we arrived, though my father warned me it was still early. Lady Pontworth was pleased to be gracious. "Ah, Lady Kinwell. One has heard much about you! You have tamed Sir Leslie Kinwell, it seems. Sir Leslie, your sister Lady Mary and her charming son are already here. Lord and Lady Pellen! How delighted I am to see you. Such a romantic story of your daughter. But then one expects romance of you. May I have the honour to present *my* daughter, Clarissa."

A pale yet pretty girl curtsied to us. She seemed scarcely sixteen, but I knew she must have been my age. My father, of course, kissed her hand. "Charming, Lady Pontworth."

We escaped as new guests took our place. The music was beginning and Leslie, ever courteous to others, led Lady Phyllis into the dance. My father, it seemed, did not care for dancing. "Let us instead find Lady Mary and pay our respects," he suggested.

I nodded. I was not eager for the encounter, but I could not delay it forever, and she had been kind to me. She was sitting with several other women but sprang up as soon as she saw us. We embraced and then my father kissed her hand and took his leave. Mary and I moved to a quiet alcove before we began to talk. "Oh, Heather, my dear!" she began. "I was so worried about you! How have you fared? Does he treat you well? I am sorry for Philip's indiscretion, but he is so young."

I smiled wryly. "Yes, I am well and Leslie is kind enough. We deal much as before. As for Philip, I fear my own foolishness misled him. I am only sorry I could only leave a note for you. You had been so kind to me."

My father returned and we were forced to talk of other matters. "And you?" I asked. "How have you and Philip fared?"

Mary began to chatter, speaking of her journey, her family, and London during the Season. I almost felt back in the castle again, away from the demands of the *ton*. Then someone placed a hand on my shoulder. I looked up to see Philip towering over me, his face an unreadable mask. And just as suddenly, his hand was gone, and he was bowing. "Mother. Aunt Heather. May I have the pleasure of this dance, Aunt Heather?"

I wanted to refuse but could not see how to do so without being rude. Instead I forced myself to smile and reply, "Certainly, Philip."

He held out a hand and I took it, rising as I did so. It was a waltz and I held my breath as Philip's arm went round me. But it was not tighter than was proper. For a moment, we said nothing, giving ourselves over to the dance. "You are very lovely tonight," he began quietly. "No, don't be alarmed. I shan't make a cake of myself *again*. Ever since you left the castle, I've been thinking what I should say to you if we met. When I first read your note and heard you were gone, I was furious. I was afraid Leslie had hurt you and you had run away because of that, and the letter was meant to throw dust in our eyes. I came straightaway to London, sure you would try to contact me here. But you didn't. You went back to Leslie." His voice became tinged with bitterness, "I thought, at first, you had been dragged back and would run away again. And I was ready to help you. Even if you didn't love

198

me. But I began to see you often on the street or at the theatre, alone or with Leslie. And always you were laughing. And it was clear you had a *tendre* for my uncle. Then it came to me. You had used me to make Leslie jealous. It was a pleasant little game for you. But you caught cold, didn't you, and had to run away. Knowing, of course, that my uncle would come after you. Well, you succeeded. Never have I seen a man so cast down as Leslie was that day, or the next when we found you had gone. My mother, of course, insists you are merely young and heedless and didn't know what you were about.''

"Philip, I . . . I . . .''

"You what? *Were* you scheming to make him jealous? Or were you just so stupid?''

The music had stopped and we stood staring at each other. "I didn't know," I whispered. "But it was no scheme.''

He gave me his arm to escort me from the dance floor. "Doing it much too brown," he said at last, wearily. "I only hope you've decided. Leslie isn't the sort to wait forever to have a woman make up her mind. Not even when he loves her." Then, in a completely different tone, "Oh, Lord! We're for it now! Leslie must have seen us dancing. He's coming toward us.''

I looked up. Leslie was indeed approaching, his eyes full of thunder. I stepped forward to meet it. "Leslie!" I said, forcing pleasure into my voice, "look whom I have found.''

He halted and nodded to Philip, too well mannered to let anger show in his voice or face. They exchanged polite words, then Leslie turned to me. "Shall we dance, madam?''

I smiled graciously. As he put his arm around me, his eyes were growing darker. Before he could speak, I said hastily, "Your nephew has been scolding me roundly, sir.''

"Indeed? No doubt with justice, madam.''

"No doubt. He told me I had behaved monstrous bad *toward you*.''

That shook Leslie, as I hoped it would, and he missed a step. His arm also loosened, slightly, and his eyes were more quizzical than angry. "How curious," he said as though it were a matter of no import, "of my nephew to take such an interest in my affairs. However, I wish he would not.''

There seemed nothing to say to that so I was silent. We danced quietly for several moments and I began to feel at ease, for I love to dance. Yet I was intolerably conscious of Leslie's arm around me, and his dark eyes. The anger was gone from them, but yet they were not untroubled. Then finally the music was ended and a man of Leslie's age stood near us. "Leslie, you must introduce me!" he commanded.

"Heather, this is Lord Weltham. Peter, this is my wife," Leslie answered wryly. "I assume you have come to claim a dance?"

"But of course!"

"Very well. Heather, should he be impertinent, rap him smartly with your fan." Leslie tempered this with a smile and then melted into the crush of people.

"My lady?" Lord Weltham was holding out his hand, and I was swept into the dance again. "I have been quite eager to make your acquaintance, Lady Kinwell," my partner said.

"Why?" I asked in surprise.

He chuckled. "Leslie and I have much in common. We were both well on our way to becoming accepted misogynists. Then suddenly he married you. You must understand my consternation. I had considered both of us to be fairly impregnable to the matrimonial assaults of the fair sex. If *he* could capitulate so quickly—(and without warning)—could it not happen to me? Naturally I have been eager to see what sort of sorceress had captured him."

In spite of myself, I laughed. "And? Your conclusions?"

He answered mournfully. "Alas, I feel more in danger than ever. You are not some exotic woman, the sort I could recognise in advance and be warned of. You seem perfectly ordinary. That is to say: lovely, well bred, and no doubt accomplished in the usual way. You sing, draw, perhaps write poems, and are excellent at the needle. You dance and dress well. You are docile, your understanding no more than moderate. . . ."

At this point, having grown stiff with anger, I retorted, "Clearly you deserve the title of misogynist! But you need not fear matrimony, sir. I cannot imagine any woman choosing to marry you! I have never met such a boorish man in my life. I do not look for Spanish coin, and indeed I prefer pound dealings. But neither do I look for slander!"

Lord Weltham merely laughed in a mocking way. "Lord! Leslie has found one with spirit, at any rate. Scarcely a Bath

200

miss. But I protest, what means this anger? I have simply described you as quite unexceptionable.''

I knew I was being roasted and I refused to answer. Lord Weltham continued to stare at me with amusement. At last, with the merest touch of exasperation to his voice, he said, ''Oh, very well. I apologise. Will you correct my ignorance and tell me what sort of woman you truly are?''

''Why? You would simply roast me further. And truly, Lord Weltham, I cannot find it in me to care whether your impression of me is true or false,'' I replied coolly.

At that moment the music drew to a close, and I gratefully slipped out of Lord Weltham's reach. ''Thank you for the dance, my lord.''

Then I turned to disappear into the crush myself. As we were at the edge of the dance floor, this should have been simply accomplished had not Weltham grasped my wrist. ''My lord!'' I exclaimed in a shocked voice.

He looked rather thoughtful. ''Your pardon, Lady Kinwell, but I had a notion you meant to escape me just now. And I wished to talk with you further.''

Others were beginning to notice us. I pretended to go limp and then, with a sudden twist of my wrist, broke free and slipped between two people and disappeared. Behind me I heard Weltham's ''Damme!'' and amused laughter. I knew my behaviour had been rude, but he had somehow roused the ire in me, and I would not allow him his way! Leslie might scold me later as he willed; I was glad I had acted so. I looked about for someone I might know and spied one of my school friends. She was surrounded by several people and I felt I should be free from pursuit if I joined them. Chloë greeted me eagerly, ''Heather! How delightful to see you! My friends, this is *the* Lady Kinwell. Oh, Heather, don't frown at me so. You cannot avoid being such a figure of renown. Not, at any rate, for a few weeks. Not until London is accustomed to the sight of you. After all, not every woman tames a tiger as you have done.''

Everyone laughed, though Chloë's husband gave me a kindly smile, for which I was grateful. A young, rather handsome man detached himself from her side. ''May I have the pleasure of a dance?'' he asked me.

I repressed a desire to giggle. The men all seemed to say the same words and began to seem like puppets. Nevertheless

I like to dance and agreed, adding, "If Chloë does not mind."

"Not at all, my dear, but mind your toes!"

I did laugh, then, at the glare of anger on the young man's face. "Are you such a terrible dancer?" I asked.

He flushed as we were caught up by the music. "No. But Mrs. Soames nabs the rust when attention is paid to anyone but her."

"Oh, Well, may I ask your name, or is that to be a mystery?" I teased.

He flushed again. I judged him to be a bit above twenty, but he was as unpolished as a sixteen-year-old. "I . . . I'm sorry, Lady Kinwell. I'm Reginald Crewes. My father is a baron, but I'm only a younger son."

I said gently, "I was not questioning your *ton,* sir. I simply wondered how I should call you. By the way, I find you an excellent dancer."

This was not quite true, but it seemed to give him a confidence he needed. And as he relaxed, his steps improved as well. Soon we were chatting amiably. I even risked quizzing him that he danced with me and not one of the plentiful number of maidens. I should not have, for he flushed. "What point to it? Most of the good ladies can't quite decide whether I am eligible or not. You see, I am the *fourth* son. They've got to receive me, but there's not many as would encourage me with their daughters. Especially since I want to be a doctor. Outlandish, don't ya know!"

"Why, Mr. Crewes," I said forcefully, "I think it's an excellent notion. As for the mothers who find you ineligible . . . well, I find them ninnyhammers."

He flushed again, this time with pleasure. "Thank you, Lady Kinwell. You're very kind. Quite out of the common way. Don't let yourself be changed."

"Don't let *yourself* be diverted from what you want to do," I countered.

The music stopped, and he requested and I agreed to another dance. As we whirled about I caught sight of Leslie. He was dancing and laughing and his eyes sparkled in a way I had never seen before. Unconsciously I stiffened. Reginald asked anxiously, "Is something wrong, Lady Kinwell?"

I forced myself to relax and smile. "No, nothing."

But I continued to watch Leslie, and suddenly I saw the

woman in profile. Memory flooded in on me. It was the woman from the theatre. By now I knew enough of Leslie's family to know she was no relative. "Mr. Crewes, do you see my husband?" I attempted to sound casual.

"Sir Leslie? Just a moment . . . yes, now I do."

"Who is the woman he is dancing with?"

Reginald whistled softly. "The Duchess of Carston. Quite lovely, of course, but rather notorious. Oh, she's never been involved in an open scandal . . . too careful for that. But they say the duke had to hush up a few. He's much older than she and doesn't *seem* to mind, but that could be pride. She's only twenty-six. Better beware of her. She's been casting out lures to Sir Leslie. Chased him more or less openly last season. Several people were wagering she'd made a conquest, until we heard he'd married you. Oh, but I say! You aren't to worry. After all, he is in love with you."

I felt myself to be pale, but I forced a gay laugh. "Of course I am not worried! My dear Mr. Crewes, I know my husband *very* well."

It was sheer bravado, of course. The longer I watched him dancing with her, the weaker I felt. He had warned me: what I would not provide, he would seek elsewhere. And from the way her delicate fingers stroked his neck as they danced, it was obvious the duchess was willing. I suppose I continued to converse with Reginald, but I cannot recall what was said. I was far more concerned with my own inexplicable feelings. Why was I so distressed? The answer, of course, is obvious, but I would not allow myself to think it. In my naivety, I thought it impossible. No woman could have a *tendre* for a man who had ravished her. And then the music was ending and Mr. Crewes was excusing himself. I looked about helplessly for some small group to join, but my lack of height betrayed me. I could not see past the few people who surrounded me. Abruptly I found my father at my side. "Are you enjoying yourself, my dear?" he asked.

"Yes . . . yes of course, Father," I stammered.

"Good. I've a young man I should like you to meet."

And so it began again: the introduction, dancing, and the return to my father's side. My partners changed frequently, and I spoke much the same words with each. Occasionally I saw Leslie dancing. Always with lovely women. At last, Mr. Crewes claimed me for another dance, and I was grateful to him for rescuing me from a middle-aged, balding earl. I felt a kinship with Reginald, for we were both misfits. He was kind and understanding and offered to escort me to supper. I had accepted and we were moving toward the supper rooms when Leslie intercepted us. "I've come to take you in to dinner, my dear," he said, "if your companion will excuse us?"

Reginald flushed. "Yes, of course, Sir Leslie."

Leslie regarded him quizzically for a moment. "Ah, yes. Mr. Crewes, is it not?" Reginald nodded. "Thank you for taking care of my wife. Come along, Heather."

Helplessly I was swept away, managing only a smile in Reginald's direction. Leslie's grip was tight on my arm, and in his face I could read anger. He did not speak until he had procured us both plates and found a quiet alcove (actually, a window seat). Even then he allowed me to eat a bit first. Finally, his voice dangerously soft, he asked, "Why do you choose to make a cake of yourself?" Utter amazement must have shown on my face, for he said impatiently, "Come, come, Heather. You are not a widgeon. You must have realised that dancing *four* times with the same young man would cause comment. Particularly as he is neither your husband nor a close relative. Had I allowed you the folly of also coming to supper with him, your reputation should have been irreparably damaged. Tomorrow, all the tattle-boxes of London should have been linking your names together talking of an affair!" He paused, and as I did not speak, he said, "I repeat, madam, *why?*"

Feeling close to tears, I countered, "What else was I to do? I know so few people here . . . and *you* had disappeared! Mr. Crewes was very nice and I found him congenial and . . ."

"Yes?" his voice was quiet but dangerous.

"And I did not think!" I cried.

His face relaxed somewhat, and it was only then I realised how stiffly he had been holding himself. When he spoke, his voice was still quiet, but this time it lacked the quality of velvet-covered steel. "Very well, Heather. You must not dance with him again this evening, however. And if he calls, you must not be in. Later, perhaps, you need not be so careful. But for the moment . . ." He shrugged. "Shall we return to the ballroom?"

I nodded. Leslie kept a grip on my elbow as we moved

through the press of people. He stopped, now and again, to speak with someone and introduce me. But his aim, it seemed, was for the dancing. Perhaps the surprise showed on my face, for he smiled and said grimly, "I must dance with you at least as many times as any other gentleman."

His arm closed around me, and I discovered I did not shrink from his touch. I wanted it. We chattered lightly, or rather, I chattered. Leslie said little and regarded me oddly from his height. We danced twice and then moved to talk with some of his friends. From then on, he did not leave me all evening, save to send me to dance with one fellow or another while he danced with the man's wife. And we left the ball early.

In the barouche, Leslie spoke little, his thoughts far away. But I feared I knew whither they went. For as he handed me into my seat, the Duchess of Carston had come running out and laid one hand on Leslie's arm. As he bent to listen to her I noted the duchess well. Never had I seen such soft blond hair coupled with such an exquisite figure. She could almost have been a Dresden figurine. I felt both clumsy and ugly. Then I saw Leslie laugh and nod before springing into the barouche. "Melissa," he said, still smiling at her, "may I present my wife, Heather?"

She arched her eyebrows as I murmured some greeting. And her eyes mocked me as she smiled. "Good evening, Lady Kinwell. No doubt you are a most *unusual* woman. We must speak together, sometime."

I nodded, wanting instead to be vulgar and show her my tongue. Then she backed away and the chestnuts began to move. Leslie's abstraction continued even after we had reached the town house. He sent me up to bed, saying he would follow shortly. In my chamber, I answered Ellen's questions of the ball absently and was relieved when she left me for the night. I lay in bed, attempting to resolve my feelings. I could not deny I was jealous of the Duchess of Carston. Mademoiselle Suzette's words rang in my head. "He is not a man to be lonely, and he will easily find a woman to please him."

In the next room, I could hear Leslie preparing for bed. And I knew, then, that I did love him. God help me, it no longer seemed to matter what he had done. And I began to fear I should lose him. I lay in bed, considering what I might do. Then, trembling at my audacity, I rose and threw off my nightdress. Instead I chose one of sheer lawn: the one I was to have worn on my wedding night. I moved quietly to the connecting doors, a candle in my still-trembling hand. All was quiet in Leslie's room. I prayed he were already asleep that I might slip into his bed and then waken him. I could not have traversed the distance under his piercing gaze. Swallowing, I silently unbolted my door and stepped through to his. I turned the handle. *And found the door bolted from the other side*. I could not believe this and tried, quietly but frantically, to open the door. It would not open, and I could no longer doubt he had bolted it as I had mine. In disbelief and hurt pride, I retreated to my room and bolted my own door. Sitting on my bed, head swimming, I tried to understand. Only one thought was clear: he did not want me! *He did not want me*. And I began to cry.

Chapter 18

I did not sleep that night, but considered carefully my position. By the hour Ellen brought my morning tea, I had made my decisions. I wore, again, my usual nightdress and the fine one of lawn was back in its place. I was determined no one would know of my attempt or of my newfound feelings for Leslie, feelings I had finally come to accept. I loved Leslie. In the cold light of dawn, I could face that fact. But I had come too late to such a point. For Leslie had clearly embarked on a course that did not include me save in the most formal sense. I had too much pride to try to move him from it. No, again I deceived myself. No pride could have stopped me had I only been able to see how to reach him. But I could not expose myself to his contempt. I should continue as before unless, or until, I had cause to believe he had altered *his* feelings. Ellen's calm voice drew me from my reverie. "My lady, are you well? You seem tired and a bit pale."

I smiled, wanly at first, then more firmly. "I am fine, Ellen. I shall wear my favourite green muslin this morning."

"Yes, my lady."

I was soon dressed and could no longer postpone my descent to table. Leslie was already seated but looked up quickly as I entered the room. For a moment he merely regarded me quizzically, then he spoke. "Peter informs me, Heather, that it was you who left a pair of gloves with him. Intended for me."

I spoke coolly, afraid that I should betray my emotions. "Why, so I did, Leslie. They caught my fancy and I thought you might like them."

He continued to eye me carefully, and to cover my confusion, I bent over my plate. "Indeed?" he said evenly, "well I do. You needn't have troubled yourself, however."

I blushed, feeling unwell at the odd note of irritation in his voice. Again, I took refuge in coolness. " 'Twas no trouble, I assure you."

He watched me a moment longer, then stood, tossing his napkin to the table. When he spoke, the edge to his voice was sharper. "I see. Well, if you intend to pursue such habits—that is to say, purchasing all that catches your fancy—I suppose I must replenish your purse. No doubt it has grown light of late."

He made a soft sound of contempt and turned, clearly intending to leave the room. I rose saying, "Leslie! Wait . . . I . . ."

But my voice was too soft and he would not or could not hear me. I sank back into my seat, knowing I was so far from the love I wanted between Leslie and myself. I ate mechanically, without noting what I was served. It was Sunday and I knew, save for family, I should be safe from callers and I determined to seek refuge in the library, where I had so often found it before.

The room was empty, and I curled up into a chair. My book was one I had begun days before. But today the words seemed to dance on the page and would not be still. My frustration grew, aided by the lack of sleep I was now beginning to feel. Then a footman came to announce a caller. "Who is it, William?" I asked, helpless to eliminate the petulance from my voice.

"Lady Anne," was the ominous reply.

With resignation, I rose and followed William to the morning room. There stood Lady Anne, the most formidable of Leslie's aunts. "Good day, my lady," I said.

She stepped forward to greet me. "Nonsense, child! There is no need for such formality between us. You are to call me Anne. And how are you enjoying your first taste of society?"

I smiled as we both seated ourselves. "Very much. Everyone has been kind and there are so many invitations it is difficult to choose between them."

"Kind?" she exclaimed tartly. "Beware of kindness, Heather. In women it usually hides a pair of sharp claws! They are kind only until they've some fault to charge against you. Then beware!"

I suppressed a smile and asked as gravely as I could, "Are the men also like that?"

She gave me a sharp look. "No, of course not. But there are other dangers. Now, I presume you are to be presented?"

"Yes."

"Good. Very proper." Again the sharp glance. "Though I hope you are not *too* proper. I find such women unutterably boring!"

I laughed. "You need not fear on that score! Leslie's sister Mary has more than once chided me for . . ."

I broke off, seeing a glint in Lady Anne's eye. Her voice was dangerously soft, as Leslie's could be at times. "And how have you displeased Lady Mary?"

I chose the least dangerous response I could think of. "I delivered a baby."

"By yourself?"

"No, no," I said hastily. "There was a midwife also. The mother was one of Leslie's tenants. Her husband was off to market and she was alone. So I sent Leslie for the midwife and stayed myself."

Ann's laughter rang out loudly for several moments. Then, wiping her eyes, she said, "Yes, I can see that should have distressed Mary. I like you, child. But I trust you are more discreet in Town?"

"Oh, yes," I said wryly. "I am discreet when it is necessary to be so."

She nodded approvingly. "Good. Now tell me about the ball."

"The ball?" I asked.

"The ball!" she retorted impatiently. "At my age, it isn't considered fitting to attend unless one is sponsoring a granddaughter or something. But *I* have not yet lost my taste for such things. Who were the musicians? Who was there? What did Lady Pontworth's daughter look like? Whom did you dance with?"

I answered her questions as best I could. It was painful, for I could not erase from my mind the picture of Leslie with the duchess. When I thought we had finally done with the matter of the ball, Lady Anne asked, "Was the Duchess of Carston there?"

I jumped. As I answered, my voice sounded strained even to my ears, "Yes, she was."

"Still setting her cap for Leslie?" she demanded. I blushed and she took that as an answer, for she muttered, "My nephew is a gudgeon!"

I raised my chin and said coldly, "He found her attentions rather wearying, I think."

Anne nodded slowly. "Yes, that's the tone to take. With Leslie as well."

"Would you care for some tea?" I asked, still speaking coolly.

"No, child. I must be leaving." As we both stood she tilted her head. "I shall see you again."

I rang for William to escort her out, then sank back into a chair. Everyone seemed to know about the duchess. Not feeling well, I retreated to my room, informing Ellen I would take my meals there. She thought it odd, of course, and asked anxiously over my health until I bluntly dismissed her. I tried to read, but with no greater success than in the library. Nor could I sleep. Leslie came to my room that afternoon. "Heather?" he said as he entered. "Are you ill?"

"I . . . a little," I confessed.

His dark eyes roamed over my face until I felt he must read my thoughts. "My aunt was here this morning, the servants tell me," he said frowning. "Did *she* disturb you?"

"No." Then more firmly: "No, of course not. We dealt famously with each other."

His eyebrows were raised. "Indeed? I never found her an easy woman."

"Ah, but you are not female," I parried.

Leslie frowned again, pacing back and forth. He, too, seemed aware of the change in how we answered one another. But neither would he speak of it. Then, remembering, he paused. "I saw your father at White's, this morning. He begs you will call upon Lady Phyllis tomorrow. The two of you are to begin preparations for your presentation. If you are still ill, I shall have a note sent round, explaining you cannot go."

"Oh, I shall be well enough," I said quickly.

Leslie regarded me. "Indeed? You seem very sure."

I flushed at the sound of sharp suspicion in his voice. I could almost read his thoughts, considering and discarding possibilities. When he spoke, it was caustically. "You are neither pale nor unduly flushed, madam, save at passing moments. Ellen informs me your appetite is undiminished.

You inform me you know you will be well tomorrow. I must conclude your illness is a convenient means of avoiding someone. And there can be only one person you mean to avoid, since you need only ask the servants to inform callers you are not at home. That person must be myself. Very well, madam, I shall not inflict my presence on you. You may safely roam the house and take your meals at table. I shall be out all day."

And night? I wondered. Close to tears, I tried to speak but could not. In his presence, I was helpless. His face dark with anger, Leslie strode from the room, the door slamming behind him. A few moments later I heard him shouting for his phaeton. And then he was gone, careless of the pace he set his horses. And I? I softly cried.

He kept his word and did not return until midnight. I know, for I sat with my needlework waiting for the sound of his voice in the room next to mine. Ellen vainly tried to convince me to take myself to bed before then. But I would not and dismissed her, saying I would tend to myself that night. Though the evening was warm, I shivered often. Sleep was elusive and came in fits. And my pillow was wet when I woke the next day.

Leslie rose as I entered the dining room. "I am happy to see you in better health," he said bitterly. "If it is to continue, I had best absent myself, hadn't I."

This time I found voice. "No, Leslie . . . please stay!"

He hesitated, then seated himself, regarding me warily. Suddenly he smiled wryly. "Ah, yes, I have it. Your purse is sadly flat and you need to ask for funds." He drew a pouch from his pocket. "Very well, here is—"

"I don't want your horrid money!" I cried out, and promptly burst into tears.

Leslie slowly set down the pouch. He walked over and tilted up my chin. "Heather?" he asked, quietly, "What's wrong?"

His voice was almost tender, and at its sound, the tears came more freely. He handed me his handkerchief as I searched in vain for mine. At that moment, William entered the room. I hid my face as he spoke. "My lady, a gentleman wishes to see you. A Mr. Reginald Crewes. He begs you will forgive the earliness of his visit."

Leslie stood very still, his face dark with anger. "Now I understand, madam! Well, I will be reasonable in all other demands. But not that!"

And then he was gone, leaving William staring at me, openmouthed. I strove to speak calmly. "Please tell Mr. Crewes I am not at home, William. And you may inform him that should he call again, no matter when, I shall not be at home."

William was again in control of himself, though I fancied I saw relief in his face. "Very well, my lady."

And I was left to myself, unable to eat, but afraid to leave the privacy of the room until I should be calmer. Soon I slipped upstairs and sent Ellen for cold water. I bathed my face with it but would not answer her anxious queries. Soon she stopped asking. Silently she helped me change dresses, for mine was wet with tears. Unable to bear the house any longer, I pulled on my gloves and hat and called for the barouche to take me to my father's town house.

Fortunately Lady Phyllis was also an early riser and she greeted me warmly. "How I shall enjoy myself!" she said. "I confess I have always thought it would be great fun to bring out a daughter. Now at the least, I shall have be able to present one!" In spite of myself, I smiled. "That's better," she said frankly. "Never look as though you have been crying . . . even if you have. Always smile. Now, to business. Is your carriage outside? Good, I feared you might have sent it home, and Robert is using ours. We are off, at once, to Mademoiselle Suzette to arrange for your gown. The earlier we arrive, the longer we shall be able to have her for ourselves. Come along, dear."

Feeling rather as though I were embarking on an adventure, I followed Lady Phyllis to the barouche. As we moved from the house she nodded approvingly. "The carriage is well sprung. I wish ours were as good. Well, never mind. How did you enjoy the ball?"

By now the pain was only a dull ache. "Oh, 'twas quite exciting," I replied.

She looked at me shrewdly. "I ought to warn you, Heather, it will be an *on-dit* if you dance with any man more than with Leslie."

"Mr. Crewes?"

"Mr. Crewes," she confirmed. "Oh, you need not fear. In this case, your attentiveness to Leslie after was well marked. By all except, perhaps, Mr. Crewes. And therein lies the danger. He may feel you have encouraged his attentions and try to call and further his position with you."

I sighed. "He . . . he called this morning. I have given orders that I am not at home—ever—should he call."

Phyllis nodded. "Excellent. Oh, do not frown so, Heather. 'Tis no great matter, I assure you. Ah, we are here. Smile!"

I obeyed her, though I had little heart for it. The coachman was instructed to call at three and we swept into the shop. I doubted we should need so many hours, but Lady Phyllis proved to be correct. We would have fifteen or twenty minutes with Mademoiselle Suzette, and then she would be called away for twice again as long. At some point, a nuncheon was brought and we ate with hearty appetites. Between times, however, Lady Phyllis set herself to lecture me on the delicate matter of court etiquette.

I also tried to somehow talk with her about Leslie. And about marriage. But she misunderstood my veiled questions and spoke instead about herself and my father. There was amusement in her voice as she said, "Robert? Oh, of course he loves me. But he doesn't know it. He thinks us a quiet, rational couple ruled by reason and not emotions. And I? I have loved him passionately. Ever since I was a young girl. But I was wise enough never to let him know it. It would have frightened him. Therefore I have let him believe I felt only a comradely affection. And above all, I have never allowed him to see my jealousy, even when I felt I should die of it. And in time he came to love me, even if he doesn't know it."

I was silent, wondering if this were the course I, too, must take. I considered Lady Phyllis's understanding to be superior and yet, our cases were not the same. For there had never been a question of Lady Phillis fulfilling her wifely duty. Was it an unpleasant task I was well saved from, as Mary would have me believe? Lady Phyllis did not seem to feel it such a burden. And I? I wanted Leslie's arms around me, holding me close. But more? I did not know.

And then it was over. All the fitting and choosing done with. And it was a little after three. Our barouche was waiting, and we stopped first at my father's town house. As she stepped out of the carriage Phyllis exacted a promise to visit her again soon. "I know," she said, "that there is not so very much more to be done to prepare you, but Robert will feel reassured if he sees you often at our home. And I confess, I enjoy your company."

"I will come," I assured her.

Then I was alone in the barouche and the horses swept away from the curb. I was no closer to an answer to my problems: indeed, I was more confused. And yet, Lady Phyllis's calm could not but affect me. I was now less afraid of disgracing myself with tears when next I saw Leslie. But he was not home when I returned. Quietly I stripped off my gloves and removed my bonnet as I climbed to my chamber. Ellen was waiting and I told her I would rest before tea. But peace was as elusive as ever.

We met over the evening meal, Leslie and I. He was cool and distant, as though I were a stranger. I was not well enough to care, though I had not dared anger Leslie by refusing to dine at table. Yet I could not hide the occasional spasm of pain that caught me unaware. After one of these, I looked at Leslie to find him staring at me. "You have spilt your wine," he said quietly. "Is something wrong?"

I blushed. I could not explain, even if he were my husband. I shook my head, but was betrayed by another spasm. Leslie's hand gripped my wrist. His voice was soft but harsh. "I have asked a question, madam. I expect an answer. Come . . . the truth, this time. What is wrong?"

I tried to smile and would again have denied it, but his hand closed tighter. "Oh, very well. 'Tis just the . . . the time . . . of . . . month. I . . . am late and . . . there is more trouble than usual."

His hand released my wrist. He signalled for a footman to refill my glass. "Drink it!" he ordered. "It will help."

I obeyed and indeed did feel a little easier. I even managed a creditable smile. He nodded. "Good. But why the devil did you come down to table if you felt unwell?"

I replied hesitantly. "I feared you would misunderstand and grow angry."

Our voices were low, but still Leslie dismissed the servants before he replied. Then it was with a mixture of chagrin and exasperation that he said, "Heather . . . I never meant to frighten you. Had you told me the cause of your indisposition, I should have understood."

I blushed and bent my head. " 'Tis . . . 'tis not a thing that comes easy to tell."

"But I am your husband!" His voice was a protest.

I murmured, "Even so, a well-bred woman finds it difficult to speak of such things."

Too late I saw how he would take my words. He pushed back his chair and, after a moment, stood, tossing down his napkin. "I see, madam. And, of course, I have had so little experience with *well-bred* women that I could not know it. I understand you well enough. And I grant you, madam, the women I am accustomed to speak more *honestly* than do ladies."

Then, with a mock bow, he was gone. Once more I had driven him from me. I, too, fled the room.

The next few days continued in much the same manner. I would pay calls or others would call on me. Between times, I would read or bend over my needlework. Leslie appeared only at meals, and not always then. He had taken to dismissing the servants as soon as they had served, that we might speak more freely. Such conversations were usually half mocking, half angry. As the days passed I grew more and more unhappy. I could not understand the depth of Leslie's anger at me. Annoyance, yes, that was to be expected. But not this constant, half-suppressed fury. I was sure he spent his evenings with other women. Though not the Duchess of Carston. Several friends took care to mention that her Grace had left for the duke's estate shortly after the ball.

It was one such evening, as I sat stitching at one of his shirts, that Leslie came into the drawing room. He had not been home for the evening meal. It was a cold, stormy night and I had ordered a fire. I was sewing by its light. At first, I kept my head bent over my work, afraid of what he might say. He walked slowly to the fireplace and stood there looking down at me, until I had to lift my eyes to meet his. He was smiling gently, and in spite of myself, I smiled in return. His voice was soft as he said, "A lovely domestic portrait. What are you working at?"

"A shirt." I smiled, lifting it for him to see.

A shadow crossed his face, then he said, jestingly, "I wonder whose it is? Ought I to be jealous?"

I laughed uneasily, puzzled by his words. "Why, yours, of course."

"Of course." He hesitated. "Are you happy here?"

I bent my head as though it were a difficult stitch I must place. "Happy enough."

Leslie seemed uncomfortable. Guilt? I wondered. Frustration that the duchess had been gone this week? He frowned. "If there is anything you need . . ."

"There is not," I replied shortly.

For several moments we did not speak. Then, unable to keep my tongue between my teeth, I said, "They say the Duchess of Carston has deserted you for the countryside."

Leslie gave a snort of disgust. "If I have ever seen a spoiled woman, it is she! Lovely enough, but with such a soul I cannot imagine any man wanting her."

I bent my head still lower to hide my smile and the relief I felt. I knew there must still be women, but perhaps only passing fancies. And in time . . . Leslie was speaking again, ". . . Crewes?"

"Oh," I said indifferently, "I have told him he is not to call."

"Yet you meet him often enough elsewhere!" Leslie's voice was cold.

"I would not be rude to the man," I protested.

"Oh? And is that why you have taken tea with him in private? I suppose you call it accident he frequents the same houses you do?"

I stared at Leslie, my mouth gaping wide. As always at such times, I was helpless to defend myself. He turned and strode to the door. Pausing, he said, "Really, madam! You take me for a nodcock! I pray you will have a care to show more discretion in the future."

Anger grew. In my mind, I reviewed all the times I had encountered Reginald. Reluctantly I admitted they were too many for coincidence. Grimly I vowed that when next I saw him, I should make him understand his attentions were not welcome! I would not forgive him for giving Leslie cause for suspicion and anger. With this resolve, I put away my work and ascended to bed.

Chapter 19

We were dining together, next morning, when the note came. William handed it to Leslie without a word, then left the room. With a slight frown, Leslie opened the note, glanced at the signature, and sat up sharply. As I watched his eyes, I could tell he read with a growing sense of urgency. When done, he hastily rose, letting the note fall to the table beside his plate. He muttered something to me and left the room. For some moments, I stared at the paper, knowing I should not touch it, but unable to let it be. Finally, I picked it up and read the words written in a delicate hand.

My Dearest Leslie,
  I know you must remember me in Anger. But I beg of you that for the Sake of What You Once Felt, you will speak with me now.
                                                                            Jane

I read it twice, unable to believe what I read. She could not be here! Not now. Perhaps a different Jane? No, recalling Leslie's face I knew it was not. Trembling slightly, I stood and walked to the drawing room, trying to calm myself. The door stood open. Leslie's back was to me and *he was kissing her*. She was tall and slender, with a blond beauty that could rival the Duchess of Carston's. As I watched, Leslie released her but kept hold of her hands as they smiled at one another. I stood, still as stone, wanting to cry. Jane saw me first and said something to Leslie. He turned quickly, crossed to my side, and drew me into the room. "My wife, Heather," Leslie murmured. "Heather, this is Mrs. Keith."

"Hello," she said prettily.

I smiled mechanically. "Good day . . . Jane, is it not? Mrs. Jane Keith?"

She and Leslie looked at one another. Then Jane nodded awkwardly. Leslie was frowning. We stared at one another in silence for several moments. It was clear that they wished to be alone. From some reserve of strength, I summoned my dignity. I smiled at Jane. "I pray you will excuse me, as I have household matters to attend to. I shall order tea for you, however, as it seems a cold morning. Is there anything else you would like?"

"No, no thank you," she said with some confusion.

I nodded and turned to go, pausing only to kiss Leslie on the cheek, tears stinging my eyes. I did not doubt he was startled and displeased that I should do such a thing before Jane. But I could not stop myself. It would be the last kiss I should ever have of him.

Somehow I found my way to my room. It was deserted, as Ellen was in the kitchen with the other maids. I began to pull clothes from the wardrobe, sorting which I should need and which were unimportant. And I dragged out, once again, my poor bag. But I also intended to take a trunk. This time I should be leaving by the front door. At some point, Ellen entered and stood staring. "My lady!" she gasped.

"Fetch me a trunk," I ordered.

"Yes, my lady. Are you taking a trip?"

"Stubble it, Ellen! Just do as I say and fetch a trunk!" I retorted, fighting tears.

She turned and was gone. Time passed. A great amount of it, and still she did not return. I was about to ring angrily for her when I heard footsteps. I turned and saw Leslie standing in the door. His mouth was set and his eyes were hard as he stepped forward, closing and bolting the door behind him. "I suppose," his voice slashed at me, "you have an explanation, madam?"

I backed away, though he did not move. "I . . . I am leaving!" I stammered.

His lips twisted. "You have forgotten, madam, you gave your word you would not." I flushed, for there was no answer I could give. His voice was soft now. "Well? Have you no explanation to give? Why you must go? Or *where* you will go?"

"I don't know!"

"No? I believe I do!" In three steps he was beside me, grabbing my wrist and pulling me round to face him. "You are running away with him, aren't you? You've planned this all ahead."

"Who?" I demanded.

Leslie's other hand bit into my shoulder as he shook me impatiently. "Reginald Crewes! Why must you pretend to misunderstand!"

His gaze was dark with rage. But now I felt my own anger growing. "How dare you! Crewes means nothing to me . . . do you hear? Nothing! Let us speak plainly, sir. You think to cover your own infidelity with accusations. Well it won't serve. If you must know, I am leaving because of Jane!"

"Jane?" His astonishment was unfeigned.

His hold slackened and I tore free. I went to the wardrobe and began dragging more dresses from it. His voice was harsh, demanding. "What the devil do you mean?"

I turned to face him defiantly, my arms full of clothes. "I saw you kiss her. And I saw how you both looked at each other. I am not such a wet-goose that I cannot see you still love her!"

As I flung these words at him Leslie's face grew angry again. "And if I said, madam, that she came to see me *because* of my marriage? *Because* she felt she could now explain why she left me in the church? *Because* she felt that having found someone else I could now forgive her? Perhaps even understand?"

"Liar! She came to intrigue you!" I retorted. But his eyes frightened me and I said hastily, "Perhaps not. But you . . . you still love her. And I cannot stay, wondering when you will slip out to meet her. Or some other woman."

I was crying again. Leslie's voice, when it came, was thoughtful. "And why should you care?" I turned away, still crying, but he came and shook me by the shoulders, his voice harsh as he demanded, "Why should you care? You knew very well this was to be a marriage of convenience!"

My head hurt as he shook me and I could no longer be quiet. "Because I love you!" I spat out. In amazement, Leslie stopped shaking me and I continued, "I didn't want to! Indeed, I tried to hate you. But, God help me, I love you! And I cannot bear to be your wife in a marriage of *conve-*

nience, wondering always where you are or whom you are with. I'd rather be alone. So I'm leaving!"

Without words, he took the gowns from me and threw them on a chair. I stared at him, uncertainly. Then suddenly his arms were around me, drawing me close to him. And his face was buried in my hair. After a moment, he spoke, gently, "Forgive me, Heather. I love you. There are no other women and there will be none. I swear it."

In astonishment, I lifted my face to meet his eyes. They were grave as he bent closer and kissed me. It was a tentative kiss, but I met it joyfully and the second one was sure. At last he stopped to speak. "All these weeks, Heather, I've loved you and been consumed with jealousy. First of Philip and later every man you smiled at. Above all, Reginald Crewes! Do you remember the day I gave you the Kinwell emeralds? That was the day I knew. The Kinwell heirs have often married for money or policy, rarely for love. Only if the Kinwell man came to love the woman would she be given the emeralds. There were wives who never wore them. But I could not tell you then what they meant."

I shivered and held him tighter. He smiled down at me, and even in my ignorance, I knew his desire matched mine. Trembling at my audacity, I said softly, "I . . . I know it is midmorning, Leslie, but . . . but we . . . I . . . love me?"

I looked at him, then at the bed. He threw back his head and roared with happiness. And then I was being swept off my feet and carried to the waiting couch.

About the Author

April Lynn Kihlstrom was born in Buffalo, New York, and graduated from Cornell University with an M.S. in Operations Research. She, her husband, and their two children enjoy traveling and have lived in Paris, Honolulu, Georgia, and New Jersey. When not writing, April Lynn Kihlstrom enjoys needlework and devotes her time to handicapped children.